The Crown for Castlewood Manor

My American Almost-Royal Cousin Series

Veronica Cline Barton

ISBN: 1984195824
ISBN 13: 9781984195821
Library of Congress Control Number: 2017918877
CreateSpace Independent Publishing Platform
North Charleston, South Carolina

1

Beaches of Malibu, August

eep breath—...The musty smell of sand and sea pulsed in my lungs as I inhaled and walked down the steps of my Malibu beach cottage. Cold, soothing sand wrapped around my bare feet as I stepped down onto the beach. A brilliant full moon sat on the horizon of the Pacific Ocean, spilling its soft light over the waves. It was cold this August night, just after midnight, with the sea wind blowing. Chills rippled down my skin. The loose gauze nightgown I was wearing offered me little protection against the cold night air. My long hair flew around me like a lion's mane, as I looked straight up to the giant moon. "Oww-Uuhhhhhhh!" I howled, screaming really, wanting the moon to take the pain away. I collapsed on the cold, damp sand, hot tears flowing down my face. My world, my plans—all seemed to have evaporated in an instant. What was I going to do now?

Earlier this week I had invited my friend Greta to join me for dinner at CeeMee, the chic restaurant in Malibu on Pacific Coast Highway where the hip goes to see and be seen. This aspect really didn't interest me. My mother, Jillian, was an actress, so I had grown up in the celebrity limelight. I was pretty immune to the celebrity lure. I had seen too many people pretend to be something they weren't or become so self-obsessed that nothing or no one else mattered. Greta and I had just completed our doctoral programs at the University of California. It was time to celebrate, just us girls.

"My treat," I'd told her when we settled on a date and time.

"Thanks, Gemma. I can't wait. Can you believe we're finally through?" Greta asked.

"Unbelievable, isn't it? Time to let our hair down, girl-friend, with some very fine glasses of Mon Cheri champagne. See you soon. Hugs," I said as we rang off. The years of heads-down studying and doing research had seemed never ending, and all at once, it was officially over. I had loved working toward my degree. It was time now to decide what my next steps would be, and I just didn't know.

Earlier this evening, I'd driven my sleek black little sports car into the valet parking lane at CeeMee. It was a stunning evening, with the air crisp and the sunset beautiful over the Pacific. I had left the cabrio top of my convertible down as I drove to the restaurant, the wind whipping my long blond hair. I straightened my tresses and smoothed out the camel sheath dress I was wearing as I exited the car. I loved this dress. It hugged my body and looked killer with my matching Rockstud flats.

"Reservation for Phillips," I said as I entered the lobby.

"Gemma," Greta called, waving to me from the bar. "Be right there," she said as she gulped her last swallow of martini and headed over to me.

The maître d' led us over to a coveted window table where we could watch the remnants of the sun setting down into the ocean. "Isn't this beautiful?" Greta said as she looked around the restaurant, hoping to see movie stars.

"Yes, it is," I said as I saw the last bit of sun disappear below the horizon. I turned and smiled at Greta, who was grinning widely. She was so pretty and smart and had been one of my closest friends these past few years. I ordered the promised bottle of Mon Cheri, and the waiter soon handed us the glasses of the bubbly liquid.

"Here's to us, Greta—or should I say, Dr. Hastings?" I laughed.

"Yes, definitely, Dr. Phillips," she said as we giggled and clinked glasses. "So what's next for you, Gemma?" Greta asked as we drank our first sips. "Have you decided if you're going to a university? And more importantly, what about you and Michael?"

I drew a deep breath before answering. "Well, unlike you, Dr. Hastings, I haven't decided yet. It's kind of complicated with Michael right now. I have had inquiries from Mass and Conn, but I just can't see myself being a professor there—not now anyway."

"Gemma, you are the only person I know who thumbs her nose at the most prestigious universities in Massachusetts and Connecticut. You could always come to Denver with me, you know. There's still an open associate professorship, I hear." Greta had just accepted a position at the University of Colorado and was moving there in two weeks.

"I could see myself in Denver, but I don't think Michael would come there. I think he sees Beverly Hills as his permanent address."

The fact was, I didn't know what Michael wanted to do now that I had graduated. My boyfriend, Michael West, still had another year to complete his medical residency at Beverly Hospital, where he was specializing in plastic surgery. Our two-year relationship had stalled suddenly and dramatically after I received my doctorate. We had started out passionate enough, traveling and following our love of the outdoors, hiking and climbing the California coastline. Michael had golden hair and a toned, tan body. Our friends called us the "Muses of Malibu," teasing us for our quintessential California beach looks. Michael loved the glitz and glamour of Southern California—the cars, the mansions, the promise of big money. Sometimes I thought he enjoyed being with my actress mother and her friends more than me. PhDs can't compete with actresses and actors, especially for a plastic surgeon in Beverly Hills.

"I haven't talked with him for over a week and a half, much less seen him." I stared into my champagne glass.

"What? Where is he?"

"I don't know. I've left messages, but—"

I was cut off by Greta's angry yell. "Michael!"

"What? Huh?" I stammered as I turned around to see what Greta was staring and yelling at.

"Oh," I said dully as I saw my boyfriend, Dr. Michael West, laying a long and heavy kiss on a black-haired beauty, her leg wrapping suggestively around his leg. He hadn't heard Greta's yell.

"Shh," I hissed at Greta, as she was getting ready to yell his name again. I quickly pulled out some large bills to cover our drinks and placed them on the table, not even waiting for our bill.

"Come on, Greta; let's get out of here," I said as I darted to find a way out without going past Michael and his dark-haired kissing babe. Just as I stood, ready to run, I was stopped in my tracks by a force stronger than my wanting to escape.

Don't let him treat you this way, I thought, drawing up all the bravado I could muster. I straightened my dress to full hug position and fluffed my hair. I walked right over to him and drew up to my full five feet ten to tower over him.

"New patient, Dr. West? Looks like she could use more work. Get a room, you...you...you plastic quack," I hissed, glaring at him, daring him to say anything to me.

He looked up in shock, his mouth open. His black-haired babe stood looking at me with her pumped-up lips shaped in a hideous, catlike, surgically enhanced grin. That was until she felt the icy wetness of Michael's tilted martini dripping down the front of her dress. Her pumped-up lips began to deflate rapidly as she saw the stain grow and grow.

"You ruined my dress, idiot!" she yelled, hitting his arm and making Michael's already tilted drink douse her completely. The drenched babe threw her mojito at Michael's head, hitting it with a thud as she stomped off to try to dry herself off, to the laughter of everyone at CeeMee. I hissed one more time in his direction and went out the entry, leaving a humiliated gigolo doctor in my wake.

I hugged Greta good-bye as I waited for the valet to bring my convertible around. I had called a limousine to take Greta back to her apartment in Westwood. "Sorry about this, Greta," I apologized, trying to slow down my racing heart.

"Hey, you're better off without that jerk. Did you see that girl's face when he spilled the martini on her?" She laughed.

"Now please, seriously consider Denver," she pleaded. "We can room together until you find a place. Skiing will be great this winter. Think about the great slopes and parties."

"I'll see, Greta. I'm not sure I'd be a very good snow bunny right now. Thanks, friend," I said, giving her another hug.

I smiled as I got into my car and waved to Greta one last time. I headed north on PCH to my beach cottage. My smile soon faded, and tears began to flow down my cheeks, becoming cold daggers stabbing my face as they hit the wind. My phone started vibrating on my seat. It was Michael. I reached over and turned it off. I wasn't going to talk with anyone tonight—especially not Michael.

So hours later, here I was, rocking back and forth in the cold sand, crying and howling in the bright light of the full moon. I hugged my knees close to me and finally sniffed out the last tear. My tear ducts had dried out. I stood with my body bathed in the moonlight and took off my gauze gown, standing naked, arms outstretched to the moon. Channeling all my inner angst, I howled again, this time with the strength of a newfound freedom, spiritually alive, standing like this, the wind wrapping my naked body. Until I heard the voice of my neighbor Mrs. Hines yelling over to me.

"Gemma? Gemma, is that you? Are you all right?" she asked, leaning over her deck railing, straining to see me. I crashed down from my spiritual realm and ran to grab my gown that was now blowing down the beach. Catching it, I quickly turned and ran up the stairs to my beach cottage, buck naked and freezing.

"Umm, I'm all right, Nancy. Good night!" I yelled back, totally embarrassed, wondering how much she had seen. I closed the deck doors and headed upstairs to my bathroom. I turned on the shower jets, waiting for the hot water to start steaming.

I stepped under the hot mist and let the streams cleanse me of the night's drama. I was feeling the impact of the stress and strain and could stand no more. I toweled off as best I could and flopped into bed, pulling the soft down covers over my now worn-out body.

"Help me," I prayed. The full moon's light beamed down on my bed through the bedroom window, covering me in soft light, and I was soon fast asleep.

Rrriiinnnggg!

My doorbell was ringing loudly and repeatedly. I raised my head from under the covers and looked up at the clock. It was nine o'clock in the morning. "Who is it?" I yelled as I wrapped a terry robe around my still-naked body. I straightened my hair and clipped it back as I skipped down the stairs. The ringing of the doorbell had now been replaced with hammering knocks.

"Ma-ma," I huffed as I opened the door, seeing my mother. I quickly kissed her cheek as she barged in. "What are you doing here?" I asked, graciously accepting the grande mocha she handed to me. She plopped her Puccini bag down on the kitchen island countertop and took a seat on a stool. She looked at me with her "I'm your ma-ma" eyes. I decided I needed some fresh air for this encounter and opened the sliding-glass doors, taking the seat next to her.

"Greta called me last night. She couldn't get through to you and thought you might have come to my house. She told me what happened, Gemma. You shouldn't turn off your phone, dear," she said as she gently pinched my chin.

"I'll call her later today," I said. "I didn't feel like talking with anyone last night, Ma-ma."

"Nancy thought you were talking to the moon." She laughed.

Really, did everyone have to call Ma-ma? I am twenty-seven years old. I grimaced to myself.

"Come on; go get dressed," she said. "Let's take a walk on the beach and get some fresh air. I have something to tell you."

She shooed me upstairs to change. I washed my face and put on leggings and a crop top. I ran back down and smiled at my mother, who was now standing on the deck, looking out at the ocean. She stood in the sunlight, the wind blowing her palazzo pants out like a small parachute. Her shoulder-length blond hair was wrapped with one of her signature silk scarves, keeping her hair in place even in the blowing wind. She reminded me of the regal starlets of the thirties and forties, and I loved her very much. She had worked hard to give me a wonderful, adventurous, stable life, unlike many of her actor peers. I called her *Mama* because she felt *Mom* and *Mommy* were too informal, and *Mother* too formal. I think it was her training as an actress. Things had to be just right for her role as *Ma-ma*.

I joined her on the deck, grabbing her hand and walking down the stairs to the sand. We went to the water's edge, our feet getting splashed with the cold Pacific water, and headed south. The ocean was to our right, and lines of Malibu beach houses to the left gave us some protection from the bright morning sun. Ma-ma decided to get straight to the point.

"He's not right for you, Gemma. You know that. A Beverly Hills plastic surgeon is just not PhD husband material. You'll never be a trophy wife. It's not your destiny, my girl."

"We had great times, Ma-ma. I thought he was proud of me getting my doctorate. Lately though, I knew he was pulling away. I just didn't want to acknowledge it. I didn't press him to get married or anything. I just didn't expect him to be cheating on me. That I cannot stand."

"And you should never stand for nor stay with a cheater! Gemma, I'm sure he was proud. But I'm sure he also liked the fact that you have a sizable trust fund and a wonderfully fabulous actress Ma-ma." She laughed. "Don't get me wrong. I thought Michael was charming—superficial but charming. There are lots of Michaels here, darling, more than you can count—believe me. They don't think a second about cheating."

We continued our walk down the beach, arm in arm in silence. I was taking my ma-ma's words to heart, and deep down I knew she was right. That didn't make the sting of being dumped any easier. I was going to have to heal for a while.

"Evan called me last night, Gemma. He called me when he couldn't reach you. He was excited to talk with you. He has a project he wants to discuss. I think you should listen to what he has to say."

"Ma-ma, did everyone we know call you last night?" I laughed.

"Must have been the full moon. I did have quite a few calls actually."

"What kind of project could Evan possibly want to discuss with me?"

"Gemma, your cousin is a British marquess, practically royalty. That may not mean much to an American, but it's kind of a big deal over there. If he has a project, call him." She laughed, bending and splashing some seawater at me.

I should introduce you to my family since it is a bit different from the everyday American lineage. My name is Gemma Alexandra Lancaster Phillips, and I'm a twenty-seven-year-old California girl, born and bred. As you know by now, I was newly awarded my PhD degree, which was largely based upon my family's heritage.

My American Lancaster family had been one of the first industrial giants who made huge fortunes as the railways pushed west across the United States. My great-great-grandfather was Patrick Lancaster, who had the brilliant idea that the railways were going to need iron and labor and lots of it. His company became the major supplier of these items and the associated services across the western United States as he built his business with the major millionaire industrialists of the nineteenth century.

I emphasize *American Lancaster family* because Patrick's great-great-grandfather, John Lancaster, had left his ancestral home in England to come over to the American colonies, as they were known then, just before the Revolutionary War. John was the second son of the Marquess of Kentshire, James Lancaster, who lived on the family estate, Cherrywood Hall. Male preference primogeniture was the rule of the day. First sons inherited. Second sons on down did not. Women inherited nothing unless they had no brothers or no male heirs. John migrated to the American colonies, and that is how my family became the American Lancaster branch of the family. There was more than one British-versus-American conflict in my family heritage.

Patrick had two daughters, Phillipa (Pippa), my great-great-aunt, and Lillian, my great-gran-mama. Pippa went to England in 1912, loaded with a generous multimillion-dollar dowry Patrick had bestowed upon her. She came over to marry her distant Lancaster family cousin, Charles Edward Lancaster, who was the fourth Marquess of Kentshire. Pippa was somewhat of a renegade for her time. She didn't want to just be an American socialite in the hills of San Francisco or New York. She had bigger aspirations, and it included becoming a British, almost royal, living half a world away.

Her marriage to Charles reunited the American and British Lancaster families, a huge event, given we had been separated by years of wars, family ill feelings, and miles and miles of sea and land. Pippa was bringing a badly needed fortune to the marquess and the Cherrywood estate. Taxation and industrialization impacted the economy catastrophically, causing the collapse of many of the old British aristocratic establishments. Thanks to Pippa and her American money, Cherrywood Hall and the peerage were saved, and my cousin Evan was now the eighth Marquess of Kentshire. Now, I know you are saying that Evan is a cousin many times removed, and you are correct. However, the British Lancasters had survived and renewed their fortunes, thanks to Pippa. The connection between the British and American families was strong, and we had made a family commitment to keep it that way.

Lillian and her descendants made history as well. My great-gran-mama Lillian became one of the first female medical doctors of her time, as did her daughter, Meredith. Lillian was endowed with a multimillion-dollar trust just as Pippa had been, but she chose to have her career and live in more modest abodes in the Knob Hill area of San Francisco, moving later to Montecito and Malibu in Southern California. Lillian's family trust had grown over the years and has generously supported her descendants in a comfortable style of life, which is how I happen to have a rather large trust fund.

My ma-ma, Jillian, scandalously broke with the medical profession tradition and went out on her own to become a successful film and television actress. She married my father, David Phillips, who had pursued his doctoral degree in history at the University of California while surfing the shores of Malibu. They divorced when I was two, history and acting not mixing in their case. My father has been a traveling academic, taking positions at universities around the world, so I haven't spent much time with him except for summers and vacations.

I did decide to follow my father's academic route, however, and that is how I ended up pursuing my PhD at the University of California. I wanted to make my own mark, not just be a Malibu trust-fund baby. I have an enormous appreciation for my family's feats, especially those of Pippa. Her reunification of the Lancaster family and inheritance became the subject of my dissertation: "Twentieth-Century Reunification of British and American Aristocratic Families with the Influx of American Heiress Inheritances." Pippa and Lillian both believed that a family united is invincible. They both dedicated their lives to making each of their family structures complete and whole. So in a nutshell, that's me and my family, British and American.

Ma-ma and I finished up our walk on the beach and headed back to my cottage, enjoying the warmth of the sun on our faces. We walked up the stairs to the cottage and went inside. Ma-ma grabbed her bag off the counter.

"Need to run, dear. I have an audition—a final audition," she said, kissing my cheek. I walked her outside, where she got into her cherry-red convertible. "Don't give Michael another thought, and call Evan now."

"I will," I said, waving good-bye. She smiled as she drove off, scarf blowing in the wind.

I went back inside and checked the time to make sure it was a reasonable hour in the United Kingdom. I rang Evan's mobile number.

"Hallo, Evan Lancaster here," he answered.

"Evan, it's me, Gemma. Is this a good time to talk?"

"Gemma, I'm so glad to hear from you. I've been trying to reach you."

"I know. Ma-ma just left. She told me you had called. She insisted I have to talk with you."

"Gemma, I have a huge project, and I need your help."

"That's what I've heard. What's up?"

"I have a unique opportunity for Cherrywood Hall and its future. It's huge, Gemma, and could mean millions of pounds for Cherrywood and the surrounding village and county."

"Well, that's impressive. What on earth is going on?" I asked, totally interested now.

"Some of what I'm about to tell you is highly confidential. Cherrywood Hall is being considered as the estate to be used for a major new period series, *Castlewood Manor*, which is to begin production next year. It's right up your alley, Gemma. It's about the wealthy American women who came to Britain in the late nineteenth and early twentieth centuries to marry into aristocratic families. The American matron of *Castlewood Manor* is not only absorbed with getting her daughters married into aristocratic families, but she also happens to be the unlikely best friend of the queen, who is trying to do the same with her daughters. So think of a show with lots of American dollars, competing, meddling mothers, both American and royal, and deep, dark manor-house secrets. It's a bit scandalous really." He laughed.

"You're kidding. Haven't you Brits had your fill of these *Upton Park* and royal anything productions?"

"Gemma, now you're kidding. Don't you know how popular and profitable these types of series are? Syndication and digital rights, merchandising—it's huge. A worldwide business, Gemma," he said. "You live right in the heart of the film industry, for Pete's sake. You should know this."

It was for that very reason I was hesitant. I had just earned my PhD. I hadn't dreamed at all of being involved in a series production in the film industry. This just wasn't in my cards. I did love my cousin, though, and he was family—

"What do you want me to do, Evan? I don't know anything about television series or productions."

"Don't worry about that, Gemma. You'll soon learn more than you ever thought on the subject, I promise. I need you to come over here as soon as possible. Cherrywood Hall has not been selected yet. We are in final competition with three other very formidable estates. I need your brains, Gemma, and of course I want to spend time with my favorite cousin," he teased.

"Your only cousin," I deadpanned. "How long do you need me to stay? I haven't decided what my next steps are, but I was thinking it would be at a university, not a period series competition."

"Exactly why you should come over, Gemma—expand your world before you decide. You never know. I need you here through New Year's Eve. The final selection of the estate to be used as Castlewood Manor will be announced that night. Think about it, Gemma," he pleaded. "Let me know what you decide. Soon, please."

"I will, Evan. Thank you, and love you. Tell Aunt Margaret hello," I said as I hung up the phone.

"Four months," I said to myself, walking over to the glass doors overlooking the beach. I looked out at the waves splashing back and forth. "Go, go, go," their rhythmic splashes whispered. This was insane. I had just received my PhD. I was going to teach or something. Or something...this was my dilemma, and probably why I had not pursued Mass and Conn more actively. I didn't know where my heart was right now with respect to a career. The situation with Michael had certainly not helped on a personal front either.

Is this what you felt, Auntie Pippa, I thought, that you needed to get away to a new world, a new life? It's only four months, Gemma. Evan needs you. There is no downside to this. I decided to go. It would be fun to be with Evan again for an extended time. I loved a challenge too. Michael was done, and I needed something new to revitalize my spirit. Mass, Conn, and Denver would have to wait until I decided what I wanted to do with my career.

I called Evan later that evening to let him know I was coming. I was becoming more and more excited as I pulled out two large Francois trunks from my attic and started to pack for my four-month journey. I am rather obsessed with designer and vintage outfits and gowns. And boots—I love my boots. I could fill two trunks, no problem.

"I'm going to need more luggage." I laughed.

I was leaving Malibu in a week, becoming the second American cousin in my family to go to Cherrywood Hall to seek a new life. Sometimes history needs to be repeated.

2

Journey to Cherrywood Hall, Courtesy Atlantic Air and Balmore Motors, Early September

"Here is your seat, Miss Phillips—excuse me, Dr. Phillips," the flight attendant said. Evan had graciously booked me on an Atlantic Air flight in their fabulous first-class compartment, and I'm sure he told them to make sure to address me as *Dr. Phillips*. I had my own wonderful pod to settle into for the eleven-hour flight, and for this I was very grateful. We were soon up in the air for the trip that went almost halfway around the world.

I had reclined my pod seat and propped my knees up to comfortably read the estate selection guidelines from Rosehill Productions that Evan had sent to me. He also included recent pictures of Cherrywood Hall that had been taken for the competition. I smiled when I went through the pictures first. Cherrywood Hall was a magnificent, palatial structure sitting high on the cliffs overlooking the North Sea. Not too many miles across were the beaches of Belgium and France. The four turrets on each corner of the hall gave it a regal appearance—one it had had for hundreds of years.

I read through the opening pages that detailed the importance of having the *right* estate for their production of the *Castlewood Manor* series and smiled. "Imagine not having Kingston Castle as the setting for *Upton Park*," it read, "or *Honor and Arrogance*'s Chippington Manor. The estate selected will become a critical part of the series associated with the mind-set of the viewer. International recognition is expected, and the estate should expect dramatic increases in visitor opportunities and publicity from all types of media."

I thought about it and had to agree. Kingston Castle and Chippington Manor as portrayed in *Upton Park* and *Honor and Arrogance* made the setting for everything written and watched for the viewing fans, myself included. I had never been to either estate, but I had to admit I felt as if I had. Engrained in my mind, along with the characters I loved, were my favorite rooms. I had been hooked.

In summary, the key criteria the production company would scrutinize over the coming months read as follows:

1. Setting of the estates and proximity to the production studio: Distance alone was not necessarily a hard criterion. The producers were more focused on being able to re-create the estate rooms to be used for filming at Rosehill Productions and having the flexibility to shoot scenes in the main house of the estate and its auxiliary buildings.

2. Support of the townships and counties to be impacted by the Castlewood Manor production.

3. Estate liaison: Each estate was expected to have dedicated people to coordinate any activities filmed or held at the estate with the production crew.

4. Advertising and marketing support with the estate would be needed as trailers and publicity photos were taken and events held.

The rest of the criteria were mostly business contractual items and insurance requirements. I was sure Evan would leave these items to be carefully scrutinized and managed by his solicitor team for the Cherrywood Hall estate.

One item in particular piqued my curiosity.

5. Each of the final four estates is to be challenged to host a major event that typifies the grandiose events most often held (or imagined to be held) at a grand English manor house. The events include the following:

> Formal afternoon tea
> Garden tour and village fete
> Breakfast and hunt
> Formal dinner gala

The selection team would assign each event to an estate, depending on each estate's best attributes. All four events were to be held starting in mid-October and going through the end of November.

Evan hasn't told me what event Cherrywood Hall will host, I mused. All these events are going to require a lot of time and planning. How are we going to pull this off?

I looked at the pictures again and thought of my great-great-aunt Pippa. How proud she would be—Cherrywood Manor in the running for a televised series to be seen around the world.

I'm going to need your inspiration for this, Pippa.

Dinner was soon served, and I put all the papers and pictures away in my bag. I didn't eat that much. I don't like to fill up when I'm flying. I did drink a glass of champagne as I settled down into my reclined pod and pulled the blanket up to my chin. I thought about actually living at Cherrywood Hall the next few months and how different it was going to be from Malibu. I wanted to make Evan and Pippa proud, though I had no idea what I would be doing exactly.

Patience, Gemma. One day at a time.

With that thought, I soon fell asleep against the roar of the engines, now carrying me over the Arctic Circle, heading to the shores of the United Kingdom.

Bur-rump. The loud sound boomed as our giant Atlantic jet landed on the runway at Heathrow. I had awakened about an hour earlier to freshen up and drink a much-needed cup of coffee.

Better get used to having tea now, Gemma, I thought.

We taxied for what seemed like hours before we finally arrived at our gate. My departure and entry through customs was expedited, thanks to my Global Entry pass and more likely some diplomatic strings Evan probably called into play. I collected my Francois luggage and had a valet follow with the luggage cart to wheel them out to the airport lobby. I had already sent my two wardrobe trunks that carried my beloved boots and dresses ahead to Cherrywood Hall. I had two large cases and my roll-on bag with me today, so it wasn't too much to handle, I rationalized, for a four-month stay.

Gee, I should have let Evan know how many bags I'd have with me, I thought, a little panicked. I hoped he hadn't brought one of his British sports cars. We'd be in trouble. I made my way through the swing doors out into the lobby at Heathrow.

"Gemma," Evan yelled as he waved his arms at me, "over here!" I smiled when I saw him. He ran over to me and grabbed me up in a big bear hug. "I'm so glad to see you. Let me look at you. Wow, Gemma, you are all grown up," he said as he twirled me around to look at me.

It had been almost two years since we had last seen each other in person. Today I had wanted Evan to see me as a grown-up woman and not as the university student I was the last time we were together. I stood tall and straightened my black leather jacket and scarf. With my jeans tucked into my boots and long blond hair down, I looked every inch the young, sophisticated, chic California muse.

"You definitely will be an asset to Cherrywood Hall." He laughed. "Beauty and brains. The other estates have no chance!"

"I don't know, Evan. I've never done anything like this."

"I have full confidence in you, Dr. Phillips. If you can get your PhD, I am sure you can take on this project. Our family is counting on our most educated member to see us through."

We walked out to the parking structure, and to my delight, Evan had brought his convertible Balmore. It was a lush royal blue, with a buttery tan leather interior that was rich and comfy. I ran my hand over the leather and ingrained wood as Evan and the valet loaded the luggage into the boot. Evan tipped the valet generously, and we started off for the sixty-five-mile journey to Cherrywood Hall. The estate was located southeast of London on the shoreline of the North Sea, just adjacent to the northern edge of the Dover Strait.

I looked over at my cousin, who was immersed in taking the Balmore through the heavy airport and London traffic. He had filled out into a very handsome man. He was now six feet two. His sandy blond hair had darkened into a rich sun-kissed brown, giving his tanned face and buzz-trimmed whiskers a very sexy look. He was wearing a gray tweed jacket, blue button-down oxford shirt, and weathered blue jeans that gave him a very chic British gentrified look. "What are you looking at?" he asked.

"You. You've turned out well yourself," I said smiling. "Do you realize how long it's been since we spent months together, Evan?"

"Yes, I do. Fifteen years," he answered, looking a little sad. "Mother and I came to stay with you and Aunt Jillian just after Father died." Evan's father, Mark, the seventh Marquess of Kentshire, died suddenly of a massive heart attack while walking to a business meeting in London. His death was totally unexpected and had devastated both Evan and his mother. The tabloid coverage went on for several weeks, as Mark was a very popular businessman and benefactor to public causes. The queen and many of her family attended the funeral, making the event ripe for tabloid publicity. Ma-ma and I attended the funeral, of course, and she had insisted Aunt Margaret and Evan come to California to stay with us.

"Ma-ma really outdid herself during your visit." I laughed. "I don't think we ever entertained as much as we did those five months you stayed with us. How many movie stars do you think you met?"

"Well, I know Mother was totally awestruck at meeting Mickey Gibbs and Howard Thomas. Personally, my favorite was Denton Wing. I mean, what teenager wouldn't love meeting Muscle Man of the Universe in person?"

"As I recall, you were pretty smitten with Chrissie Tanner and her starlet entourage. I was in love with you myself that summer and fall, you know." I smiled. "I loved your British accent."

"Well, since you were only twelve at the time, I don't think I broke your heart. If I remember correctly, you impaled me and made me a blood brother!"

"I didn't impale you. It was only a prick. I had to draw blood so that we could put our fingers together and mix it. You're the one who said we needed to be together since we were both the only children left in our families. I was just making sure we would be together forever."

"Well, I guess it worked, although I still have the scar. You're stuck with me now, cousin. Does Aunt Jillian still have the house in Terra Woods?"

"She does, but it's being rented out right now. She just bought a huge estate on the cliffs in Malibu. It used to belong to one of the *Spoiled Spouses* reality series stars, actually. I have no idea what she's going to do with all that space, but it is a lovely property. The ocean views are really stunning."

"Is she dating anyone these days?"

"Not really. She has escorts for her events, but they're more for the photo opportunities. I'd like for her to meet someone significant, but she doesn't seem focused on relationships right now. She's been very busy with auditions recently, but she won't tell me what the project is. What about your mother? Has Aunt Margaret dated anyone?"

"No, she is quite comfortable being alone. I don't think she has ever gotten over my father's death. She keeps busy in London and seems happy with her charities and her friendship with the queen, but I'm sure at times she wishes for more. I try to spend as much time with her as I can, but it's difficult with the estate and my travels."

"Well, it sounds like we have another challenge then: getting our mothers hitched!" I laughed.

"Gemma, I like to win my challenges, and I'm not so sure our mothers are going to cooperate. Better to play only where we can win." He laughed.

Evan pushed the purring Balmore faster, as we made our way out of the London traffic and onto the maze of Britain's famous A and M highways that would take us to Cherrywood Hall. Evan had put the convertible top down. I loved smelling the fresh air in my face, even though it was a bit cool. I took out a silk scarf Ma-ma had given me from her collection right before I left. I smiled as I tied it around my blowing hair, thinking of her.

"So tell me what you have been doing the past few weeks, Evan. I can't wait to hear. I did get a chance to read the competition guidelines on the flight over."

"Well, I've been driving quite a bit between Cherrywood Hall and London." He laughed. "The Rosehill Production executives seem to want to meet every other day. I'm sure they're anxious. They have spent a lot of money in their quest to find the perfect estate for the *Castlewood Manor* series. I've heard they started out looking at over seventy estates, beginning months ago. It's a major honor to have made it this far." Evan smiled.

"I can't wait for you to meet Kyle too. We're business partners now, you know, in addition to him being the estate manager at Cherrywood. You should see the winery and vineyard, Gemma. He's done a brilliant job of getting that started. We'll be opening in a few weeks. We'll have our own label and a very elite offering of sparkling wines. It turns out the ground chemical makeup for sparkling wines is competitive with the Champagne area in

France. There's a very good chance we can give the French a run for their euro." He grinned.

I could tell he was proud of this latest venture with Kyle. Cherrywood Hall provided a lot of agricultural produce to the local community as well as herds of cattle, sheep, and deer. The addition of the winery and vineyard would add a whole new dimension to their offerings.

"Kyle and you grew up together, didn't you? I can't believe I've never met him all these years. You're lucky to have someone so close to you to depend on."

"You did meet him once, at Father's funeral, although you may not remember. He was quite distraught. Kyle is like a brother to me. I don't know what I would do if he weren't managing Cherrywood Hall and the businesses. I certainly wouldn't be able to have my time in South Africa. He's a great friend. I know you'll like him very much. By the way, I heard about Michael, Gemma. Aunt Jillian told me the night I called her looking for you. Are you all right?"

"I've had good days and bad days. He's tried to call me a zillion times, but I just keep deleting his voicemails. I heard through a mutual friend that he thought I was out of town. I guess he figured it was OK to cheat on your girlfriend if she was gone. Unbelievable. I'm done dealing with him. Your invitation came at a most opportune time, cousin. I needed a big change." My eyes welled up a bit, and I wiped them, pretending I had something in my eye.

"What about you, Evan? Any loves in your life?" I asked, wanting to take the focus off my love life. His face scrunched up for a bit, worry lines crossing his brow.

"I have been seeing someone," he said quietly. "She's not convinced I should be dating her."

"Are you kidding? You're a British marquess, rich, smart, good looking...is that not enough for her?"

"That sort of stuff doesn't impress her. I'm afraid she may be looking for someone who doesn't have all the British aristocratic baggage. She lives in South Africa, which makes growing a relationship very difficult. But I'm going to keep trying." Evan shrugged and didn't say anything more. I took his cue to change the subject.

"The selection guidelines were really quite interesting," I said. "I have to admit I never thought about the settings of a movie or television production having such a profound effect on the viewer, but it's true. Kingston Castle will always be known as *Upton Park*, and Chippington Manor known as the manor house in *Honor and Arrogance*. Are you ready for Cherrywood Hall to be known as *Castlewood Manor*? And which of the grand British events has Cherrywood Hall been assigned? I'm dying to know!" I laughed.

"Wow, you are full of questions, aren't you? If Cherrywood Hall is selected as the estate, it would be a great thing," he said in all seriousness. "The benefits aren't only for the estate, but also the surrounding village and county. Maidenford village in particular will receive a great economic boost and employment opportunities if we are selected. It will mean a lot to the local community."

"If you're selected, Cherrywood Hall is going to have international attention. Are you and Kyle ready for the estate to be mobbed by tourists and featured in every tabloid?"

"Kyle has drawn up plans for new business ventures we might take up on the estate and the infrastructure and security measures needed if we are selected. He's thought of having a bed and breakfast and tearoom as one option, giving visitors a chance to stay on the estate, as well as a wedding venue, including a glassed-in pavilion to provide shelter in case of rain or privacy requirements in case of celebrity. It could be quite brilliant really. His sketches of the new building venues are stunning. There will be lots of options to consider. But first we have to win."

"I can't wait to see them. This is very exciting. So tell me, what event have we been selected to host?" I asked again, giving Evan a slight nudge on his arm.

"You are impatient, aren't you? I just learned myself this morning. It looks like Cherrywood Hall will be hosting the formal dinner gala. Are you ready to be hostess? It's going to be on a very grand scale—royal even," he teased.

"Well, as long as you and Kyle are working with me, I'm sure we can pull it off. I suppose we won't be barbecuing hamburgers in the backyard?" I said, teasing.

"No, I think you'll find a formal dinner gala a little bit more involved, although the barbecue in the backyard would probably be more fun." He laughed.

"How does Cherrywood Hall stack up against the other estates, Evan? I'm sure they're beautiful."

"They are all splendid estates, and each of us has some unique things to offer to the series production. Ainsley Abbey and Cherrywood Hall are located on the coastline with sweeping views of the sea. Longthorpe Manor and Shipley House are located farther inland but with gorgeous valley and forest areas surrounding the estates. Everyone will bring their A game to the competition, I'm sure."

Evan shifted down a gear as we exited the highway. "We'll be in Maidenford in just a bit. It's a lovely village on the seashore. I've spent many a night there." He smiled. "It's a good place with fun people. I know you'll love it."

The spires of the church and the skyline of the village came into view as we went over the hill and down toward the sea. Evan slowed as we entered the village proper. "Look at the cobblestone streets," I said, looking from one picturesque building to another. It was a quintessential English village. I saw the Howling Pig Pub sign and let out a huge laugh. "I love it. You definitely need to take me to the Pig for a pint."

Quaint shops and restaurants lined each side of the street. In the center of the village was a beautiful park lined with statues and flowing fountains. Evan waved several times as we made our way through the village to the road leading to Cherrywood Hall.

"You're quite popular," I teased.

"I do know quite a few of the villagers. Family job, you know." He laughed.

"Yes, milord," I teased, looking at my cousin. I found it hard to believe he was really the eighth Marquess of Kentshire. I had a new appreciation for his role and responsibilities. The whole subject of aristocracy and order of birth might not mean as much to Americans, but here in Britain I was sure it had made its influence into the genetic pool of the people.

We made our way through to the outskirts of the village past the harbor and were soon on a winding road that hugged the seashore cliffs. It reminded me of the drive up to Carmel on the PCH through Big Sur. The Balmore took the gentle turns gracefully, and I could tell Evan loved this part of the journey. Who wouldn't, I thought, looking out over the dark blue sea and majestic white cliffs.

We arrived at the massive wrought-iron gates leading to Cherrywood Hall. Evan pushed some codes at the entry switch, and the gates started to slowly crank open. He drove in low gear down the winding drive, so I could take in the views. I was awestruck as we went over stone bridges that had been in place for hundreds of years. The trees were glowing in beautiful golds and oranges showing the onset of fall. The hillsides were sprawling, beautiful, green pastures with some last remaining remnants of lavender giving a purple glow against the green. I saw several granite and marble follies along the hillside, adding a regal elegance to the landscape.

Evan stopped when we got to the largest folly, sitting majestically on top of the hill. It was a templelike stone structure with beautiful columns and a domed ceiling. His cell phone rang, and he excused himself to take the call. He tensed up as he listened, apparently not liking what was being said.

I looked back up at the grand folly and saw another beautiful sight emerge from behind the building. A man on a handsome black horse, standing at least seventeen hands tall, was riding to the top of the hill, looking around at the grounds. He was as striking as the grand landscape, his head full of wavy black hair sweeping his tanned, chiseled face. His muscles strained against his hugging turtleneck sweater. I was instantly drawn to his handsome good looks, but more than that, he exuded a sense of pride and strength. Evan ended his call and waved up to him. He started the Balmore as we continued driving down the road to Cherrywood.

"That's Kyle, Gemma. You'll meet him once more tonight. Be nice to him. He needs his spirits lifted up a bit. He just ended his relationship with his girlfriend. See, you two have something in common already."

I turned my head back and saw that Kyle was still watching us. He smiled when he saw me turn around. I smiled back, feeling a rush of warmth spread through me.

I remember him now, I thought, thinking back to the day of my Uncle Mark's funeral. He was tall even then, hanging his head down in sorrow with his long hair covering his face. We shook hands as we were introduced, and just for a minute, he had smiled at me.

Evan hit a speed bump on the road a little too fast, which brought me back to the present.

"Anything urgent on the call? You looked concerned."

"Well, I'm afraid it wasn't good news. Shocking, actually. It was the production company on the phone. The owners of Ainsley Abbey were killed this morning. Their car apparently missed a turn, and they flew off a cliff as they were heading home. Lord and Lady Hemsworth were killed instantly."

"Oh, Evan, how horrible. What's going to happen? Are they going to stop the competition?"

"They are going to call me later this afternoon with more details. I don't know what they will decide. This has obviously created a major obstacle in their plans. Let's keep this between us for now until we learn more details. It's such a tragedy. Lord and Lady Hemsworth were lovely people."

We continued the drive up to the hall in silence. Evan was obviously shaken. I shivered, thinking about the tragic accident and the potential implications for us. I hoped they didn't suffer. What was going to happen now?

3

Welcome to Magnificent Cherrywood Hall

Evan continued driving up the estate road until he got to the top of the hill. He slowed the Balmore down once more as Cherrywood Hall loomed majestically in front of us. It was a massive building set in red bricks and gray limestone, standing three stories high, with great, round turrets on each corner. A circular driveway took us to the front entry. In the center courtyard were perfectly groomed topiary gardens, trimmed to perfection and adding just the right elegance to the regal house.

"Evan, I can't believe how beautiful and grand Cherrywood Hall is after all these years. The gardens are exquisite. I can't believe you live here alone. Everything is so...well, big," I said, at an unexpected loss for words.

"Thanks, Gemma. I'm...*we're* very proud of it. It takes a lot of effort and planning to take care of things on this scale. Kyle has put together an excellent maintenance regimen and staff to keep things in this condition throughout the estate. I think this is one of our greatest strengths in the competition."

I was surprised to see staff lined up outside to greet us, and to my surprise, I saw Aunt Margaret standing waiting for us too. Evan pulled to a stop and went over to open my door. He handed the keys to the footman as I got out of the car.

"Gemma, welcome," Aunt Margaret said as she walked to me to give me a hug and to air-kiss my two cheeks.

"Hello, Aunt Margaret," I said warmly, returning her hug and kisses. "It's so good to see you. It's been too long. Evan didn't tell me you were here," I said as I playfully punched his arm.

"Well, I just came down from the Belgravia house yesterday. I couldn't wait to see you, so I just invited myself." She laughed.

Aunt Margaret lived in a stunning white-marbled house in the wealthy area of London called Belgravia. The house had been in the Lancaster family for generations. Aunt Margaret moved there shortly after her husband's death. She found living at Cherrywood Hall had too many painful memories, and it was Evan's house now. She kept busy with her charities and limited her social events to those hosted by the queen, or ones Evan escorted her to. Ma-ma and I had stayed with her a few times when we were in London. I loved her house there.

"You are always welcome here, Mother," Evan said lovingly.

"I know, dear. I won't stay long. Don't worry. I know you all have lots of things to do with the competition." She smiled.

Evan guided me over to meet the main staff of the house. "Gemma, this is Bridges, our head butler," Evan said.

"Good day, Miss...er, Dr. Phillips. Welcome to Cherrywood," he said, bowing his head just a bit.

"Please, call me Gemma." I laughed and extended my hand to shake his. He seemed a little taken aback but put out his hand to shake mine. I looked back at Evan, who was smirking a bit. I think I had committed my first American faux pas.

"Gemma, this is Mrs. Smythe, our head housekeeper," Evan continued.

"Pleased to meet you, miss," she said with a little curtsy.

"Finally, this is Chef Karl," Evan said. "I think you will find his art of cuisine quite amazing."

Chef Karl smiled in appreciation. "Nice to meet you, Miss Gemma," he said, hoping he had found the right way to address me. "Please let me know if you have any special dietary requirements. I'll be glad to accommodate you." He smiled.

"Thank you, Chef. I can't wait to try your creations. I love to eat." I smiled.

Evan took his mother's arm and mine and led us through the double-door entrance. We stopped as I gazed at the huge hallway that ran through the center of the house, opening at the other end to a grand stone terrace overlooking the sea. The floors were black and white marble tiles laid on the diagonal. The patterned floor mixed well with the rich burgundy walls on either side. An imposing stone fireplace tall enough for me to stand in was centered in the hall to my left. Opposite was a winding stone staircase that led to the second- and third-floor sitting rooms and bedrooms.

"Oh wow," I said in a very non-PhD manner. "I had forgotten how stunning this is." I moved from the entrance down to the fireplace and then across to the stairs. The library and sitting rooms were located on either side of the staircase. Dark tapestry carpets covered their floors, with rich cherry bookcases and moldings enveloping the walls. Evan and Aunt Margaret were pleased to see me gush over their beautiful home.

"This hallway alone could hold over three hundred people. I can just imagine the events you've had here, and the history."

"Cherrywood Hall is part of your heritage too, Gemma. You Americans have played a big part in our continuance." Aunt Margaret smiled. "You certainly financed it anyway. The hall wouldn't be in the family most likely if Pippa hadn't come. Americans will always have a special place here."

I looked over at her and smiled back. My gaze went up the wall over the fireplace, where I saw a large, full-length portrait of a woman dressed in a cobalt-blue velvet dress, standing tall with her hands against the back of a gold gilded chair.

"Meet Pippa, Gemma," Evan said as he followed my gaze to her portrait. I had never seen this one. The painting showed the young Pippa beaming. "She had just given birth to her first son, the fifth marquess," Evan explained.

"She's so pretty. She bounced back quickly." I laughed. "Look at her waistline. It's so tiny!"

Pippa's smile in the portrait seemed to welcome me to my new surroundings. We walked past the dining room and small sitting room next to the fireplace.

"I'll give you a proper tour of these rooms tonight at dinner, Gemma," Evan said. "Let's go out to the terrace."

We made our way down the great hall and out the French doors leading outside. "It's magnificent," I said as we walked along the hand-carved marble baluster and railings, overlooking the deep, blue-gray North Sea waters.

For just a minute, I thought of my view of the Pacific from my cozy little beach cottage. It could not compare with the majesty of this setting. Every view at Cherrywood Hall was on a totally different scale from what I was used to in Malibu.

"Can you see the continent from here?" I asked.

"On clear days, yes, with a telescope. Aunt Pippa wanted to be able to see it whenever possible. She loved to travel there, and of course she visited Paris whenever she could," Evan explained.

"Pippa is responsible for most of what you see here currently at Cherrywood Hall. She brought not only her fortune when she arrived but also her design expertise. The first-floor rooms and grand hallway were all redesigned by her. She expanded the grand hallway to open out to the terrace, which was a completely new design from the ground up. Look down here." Aunt Margaret pointed.

Beneath the terrace was a large sea path that appeared to go along the cliffside. I could see several benches placed on the path for sitting and taking in the sea view. "It's gorgeous. I'd love to climb those cliffs. How far does the path go?"

"Just about two miles," Evan answered. "It's great for walking or riding. I'm not so sure about climbing, though. I don't believe anyone has done that—except perhaps for Kyle. Come over to this side, Gemma. I want to show you what Kyle found as he was building the winery."

I walked over to the other side of the terrace with Evan, where I saw tented structures covering what looked to be a tunnel-digging operation.

"What is that?"

"When Kyle was digging the foundation for the new winery, he came across some crumbling tunnels that seemed to lead from the hall to the field where the winery is now. He's having them dug out slowly to try to preserve as much of the original tunnel structure as possible. We have no idea where they connect to the hall."

"How exciting to think, after all these years, you have a new feature of the estate to discover."

"Old houses always have lots of secrets," Evan kidded. "We may never know all the secrets of Cherrywood Hall."

We stood outside a few minutes more, enjoying the precious last rays of sunshine we had before the marine layer started to roll in.

"Evan, have Mrs. Smythe take Gemma up to her room. You've got to be exhausted, dear," Aunt Margaret said as she turned and touched my cheek. "Let's let her freshen up. We can talk more at dinner. Gemma, we're dressing formally tonight in honor of your first dinner at Cherrywood Hall. Let me know if you need anything, dear," she said as she headed back to the sitting room to continue her never-ending needlework projects. I smiled as she walked away. I was glad she had taken time to come to Cherrywood Hall to welcome me. It meant a lot.

Evan summoned Mrs. Smythe, who promptly came to walk me upstairs to my room. "See you tonight, cousin." Evan smiled and gently kissed my cheek. "I'm glad you're here. Drinks and dinner will be served at eight o'clock."

Mrs. Smythe guided me up the winding staircase. We passed bedroom after bedroom as we made our way down the hallway to the one that was to be mine. Mrs. Smythe uttered names such as the Anchor Room and the Hunt Room and pointed at them respectively. I tried to pay attention, but I had to admit the jet lag was catching up with me. Mrs. Smythe noticed my fatigue, and we walked a little faster down the hall to my room. If my bearings were correct, my room was located right above the terrace overlooking the sea. Mrs. Smythe opened the double doors at the end of the hall, and I walked in.

"This was Lady Pippa's room," Mrs. Smythe said with pride. "Lord Evan thought you would like it."

I sucked in my breath as I looked at the silk cobalt-blue coverings on the wall and the ornate gold moldings that enveloped them. French doors were on the opposite walls, opening to a little balcony overlooking the sea. A small side table and chair were placed next to the doors to sit and have a cup of tea or write.

I turned and looked at a massive four-poster bed placed in the center of the inner wall, draped in blue satin. It overlooked a small, carved marble fireplace with velvet sitting chairs and love seat placed in front. I looked up and saw another portrait of Pippa. This one was an older Pippa, sitting in a beautiful gold chair. She wore a flowing blue chiffon evening dress and a stunning diamond and sapphire set consisting of a necklace, drop earrings, and tiara.

"That's the Lancaster tiara she's wearing, Miss Gemma," Mrs. Smythe told me. "It was her favorite." She smiled.

"I can see she was partial to the color blue." I laughed.

"Yes, miss, blue was definitely her favorite. Just about all her favorite things in the house are done in blue, like the sea."

She led me over to two large wardrobes in the corner. "I've taken the liberty of unpacking your trunks you sent last week," she said. "Evening gowns are here." She pointed. "Your coats and jackets are on this side. I had Mr. Bridges move another case next to the wardrobe to put your shoes and boots in. I have to say you must love your shoes." She grinned.

"It is a weakness," I said, laughing. "You can never have too many boots is my motto. I must be more like Pippa than I realized. She loved blue, and I love boots." I grinned.

"Let me show you your bath and changing room," Mrs. Smythe said as she led me through the doorway next to my bed.

I entered one of the most beautiful bathrooms I had ever seen. White marble was inlaid with iridescent turquoise miniature tiles that curved and swirled along the floors and walls seamlessly. A claw-foot tub flanked one wall that held a small inset fireplace. Its firelight gave a warm and glowing sparkle to the room. A glassed-in shower with brass fittings sat in another corner, set off by a magnificent mural of Neptune and his muses in its center. A discreet water-closet room housed the toilet. A full-length vanity was on the opposite wall, also cloaked in marble and brass. Mirrors flanked the entire wall behind the vanity, and the sparkle from the crystal chandelier and brass sconces on either side of the mirror gave the room even more opulence.

"This is beautiful, Mrs. Smythe. These sconces are so unique. Are they mermaids? I've never seen anything like them," I said, reaching up to touch them.

"Thank you, miss. Lady Pippa called them Neptune's daughters. She even named them Pippa and Lillian, after herself and her sister, I've been told. She loved this room. Called it her private palace." She smiled. "I'll draw your bath. You go ahead and change out of those clothes," she said as she handed me a soft terry robe. "Just leave them on your bed, miss. I will take care of them."

"Oh really, that's OK," I started to say until I saw her commanding look. "Of course, Mrs. Smythe," I said as I smiled and obeyed her instructions.

I wasn't used to having a full-time maid who came to dress me. I think I can get used to it, I thought.

I undressed and went back to the bathroom where Mrs. Smythe had drawn a nice, hot bath scented with fresh lavender.

I stepped into the hot water and sank in to cover my whole body. The tub was long and comfortable for my tall frame, and the warmth of the water seeped the jet lag right out of my bones.

I leaned back and looked at the flames dancing in the wall fireplace. I shut my eyes and drifted in and out of thoughts.

Well, here I am, right in Pippa's palace. And I have Pippa and Lillian looking right at me. I smiled, looking up at the two gold sconces. I wish I had known you. Were you ever afraid? Did you miss America? I'm sure you missed your sister.

I thought again of the grand rooms and the beautiful grounds I had just seen.

I didn't know you were so architecturally inclined, Auntie Pippa. I'm quite impressed.

And then my mind went to the vision of Kyle. He looked so handsome sitting on that magnificent horse. My body tingled as I thought about him.

I hope he is as nice as he is handsome.

I thought once again of our first meeting and his shy smile that sad day, long ago.

I soaked for a little over an hour, melting away the hours of jet lag and fatigue from my body. I put on the terry robe Mrs. Smythe had provided and went to lie on the four-poster bed for a short nap. I snuggled under the comforter and looked up once again at the portrait of Pippa over the fireplace.

"You've helped me so much, Aunt Pippa," I said to her painting. "I've got a PhD thanks to you. You were so brave, leaving your home, coming across the world, assuming such a different life. I want to get to know you more."

I was just about to drift off when I decided to wear the blue Marie Couture gown I had sent over. It was cobalt blue with jeweled shoulders and neckline. Blue in honor of you, Pippa, I thought as I drifted off into a deep sleep.

I woke as I heard Mrs. Smythe stoke the fire in the fireplace across from my bed. "What time is it?" I asked, slightly panicking that I had overslept and missed dinner.

"It's just before seven o'clock, miss, time to get dressed for dinner. I wanted to help you tonight, given that it's your first night here and all."

We walked into the bath, and I sat at the vanity. "How are you wearing your hair tonight?" she asked.

"I've decided to wear the blue gown tonight, Mrs. Smythe, the one with the high jeweled neckline. I think I should wear it up," I answered. Mrs. Smythe brushed my long blond hair until it shined. We helped each other twist and pin my locks up into a messy bun with flyaway tendrils, a look that was so popular these days.

I was grateful for her help; I was still lagging a bit from the trip. I put on my makeup as Mrs. Smythe got my blue gown out from the wardrobe. She had placed a dress form in the corner of the room, so she could inspect and stage my outfits. I walked out and looked at the lovely dress that now hung on the form.

"It's beautiful, miss," Mrs. Smythe said.

"Thank you. It's one of my favorites too. I thought I'd honor Pippa with the blue." I smiled. We slipped the dress off the form and over my head and managed to get the jewel neckline fastened without too much fuss.

I took out the jewelry case I had forwarded last week. My great-gran-mama Lillian had left us some beautiful blue sapphire jewels she'd collected. "Sisters must like blue." I smiled. I chose sapphire and emerald drop earrings to highlight the soft tendrils that framed my face.

I went to the full-length mirror to see how I looked. "I'm not used to dressing so formally for dinner." I smiled. "Most of the time in Malibu, I'm wearing jeans or shorts."

"You'll represent us well in the competition." Mrs. Smythe smiled. "You resemble Lady Pippa, you know."

"We're American Lancasters," I answered back, smiling. "So what does the staff think of this competition, Mrs. Smythe? Are you all prepared?"

"Well, those of us who live in Maidenford are all pretty much supporting it. It would mean a great deal to the community. And the village girls are all dreaming of being film stars." She laughed. "They're thinking the directors will hire them on the spot. A bit wishful, perhaps, but it's good to see the young people inspired."

"What about Bridges and Chef Karl? What do they think?"

"Well, Mr. Bridges lives here on the estate, miss. I'm not so sure he approves of letting loads of people on the estate. But he is loyal to Lord Evan and Mr. Kyle, so I'm sure he'll support whatever needs to be done. Now Chef Karl—he's a natural. He came here from a boutique hotel in London where he was head chef. He's used to cooking and entertaining large, prestigious groups. He'll do fine. I'm not sure how the ghosts are going to feel about it, though."

"The ghosts?"

"Why yes, miss, Cherrywood Hall has lots of them. I'm sure they'll introduce themselves to you." She smiled. "Didn't Lord Evan tell you?"

"Mrs. Smythe, you are teasing me."

"No, miss, I'm not. You just wait and see. Lady Pippa always liked to entertain in her day. I'm sure she'll love having the competition here."

I couldn't really tell if Mrs. Smythe was teasing me or if she was serious. I'd heard of older castles being haunted, but really... I made a mental note to keep my eye out for any Cherrywood Hall ghosts.

Wish me luck, I thought to Pippa, just in case she was listening or watching. I made my way down the grand staircase to the dining room, feeling just like a princess.

"Bring it on, English. Time to learn more about this competition," I whispered. *If* the competition was still going to be held. "At least I'll get to finally meet Kyle again." I smiled. I hoped he would be partial to Americans.

4

Dinner and Business

I made my way down the grand hall and was amazed at the grandeur of the decor. The hall had been lit with tapered candles hugging the sconces on the walls. I heard laughter coming from the small sitting room adjacent to the dining room. Cocktails were being served here before dinner. Aunt Margaret was sitting on a settee next to the fire sipping a sherry.

"Oh, Gemma," she said as she looked me over, "you look lovely, dear."

"Thank you, Aunt Margaret. I thought I'd wear blue in honor of Aunt Pippa for my first night here," I said as I bent to kiss her cheek. "We Americans need to stick together." I laughed.

"Well, she certainly would have approved of that ensemble. You have a resemblance to her."

"You must be Gemma," Kyle said, reaching out to shake my hand as he walked over toward me.

I turned and saw my dream man from the hill. He was even more gorgeous up close. "Yes, hello. You must be Kyle." I smiled, putting my hand in his.

"Gemma, yes, please meet Kyle Williams, again," Evan said, walking over to us from the bar area and turning to Kyle. "This enchanting young woman, Kyle, is my now grown cousin Gemma, our Dr. Phillips from America," he continued, as he gazed down at Kyle's hand still holding mine. "Would you like a glass of champagne, Gemma? You'll have to let her go, old man."

"Yes, please."

Kyle smiled and slowly dropped my hand as Evan handed me a glass of champagne in a sparkling crystal flute.

"Please, sit." Evan gestured. I took a seat next to Aunt Margaret. Kyle and Evan elected to stay standing near the fireplace, the fire dancing across their cut crystal whiskey glasses. They both looked extremely handsome in their white tie tuxedos, tailored perfectly to their bodies. Kyle was a bit taller than Evan, standing at maybe six feet three or six feet four, I guessed. His black locks hung almost to his chin, giving him a ruggedly handsome, British aristocratic look.

"Were you able to rest up, Gemma?" Evan asked.

"Yes, I did; thank you. The room is lovely, Evan, and Mrs. Smythe is a treasure. I can't believe you put me in Pippa's room. I love it."

"We thought you'd like it, dear," Aunt Margaret said. "Lady Pippa called it the Blue Room in her day, but we have always called it the American Room," she said, laughing at her family reference. "She started the change of many things at Cherrywood Hall. We Lancaster ladies and our guests can thank her for installing the first en suite bedrooms and baths. Personally, I'm glad she brought the comforts of American living here. Cherrywood Hall has almost become habitable." She smiled.

"Pippa's room is more than habitable, Aunt Margaret. I've never seen a more luxurious room, except maybe at Versailles." I laughed.

A gong sounded, sending its vibrations down the grand hallway and into the ground floor rooms. We finished our cocktails and headed into the dining room. The room had ivory brocade walls surrounded by gold moldings and family paintings that seemed to shimmer in the light. Turquoise-blue Persian carpets anchored the floor, and Irish-cut crystal chandeliers and sconces lit the ceilings and walls. The carved cherry table and chairs lent a sophisticated elegance to the room. A massive floor-to-ceiling marble fireplace was at the end of the long room. We were seated at the end of the table next to it, with a softly lit fire to keep the chill out. As I sat down, I looked down the length of the table. With extensions, I guessed it could be expanded to seat over one hundred guests—more if the tables were configured in a U shape.

Wine was poured, and Evan stood to make a toast. "Gemma, thank you for coming over to help us win this competition. Your historical and American expertise, and beauty, will certainly help our cause." He laughed. "No other team is going to bring the wealth of knowledge that you do. I absolutely need your knowledge and technical expertise for archiving and visually presenting all of Cherrywood Hall's assets electronically. Someday they will be able to be viewed by anyone from around the world. You are now the proud manager of this effort." He smiled.

He turned to Kyle. "Kyle, thank you for your business and moral support. You are my true friend," he said. "In all seriousness, this competition has enormous potential for Cherrywood

Hall and the community. Your help and participation for the estate means a great deal to many people."

"Here's to Gemma, Kyle, and you, son," Aunt Margaret said. "May you all have success. I am sure all the Lancasters, both the British and American lines, will be cheering for you." She smiled. We clinked glasses and drank our first sip.

"Ooh, this is lovely, so rich and bubbly," I said.

Kyle smiled. "You're drinking our sparkling white from the Cherrywood winery, Gemma. This is from our first series of offerings. It will be sold commercially in the next two weeks."

"I'm sure it will be a resounding success." Evan smiled. "You wouldn't believe the amount of time and effort Kyle has put into this new business venture. It's incredible really, to think it's finally come to fruition."

"Well done, Kyle," Aunt Margaret chimed in. "You should see the conservatory, Gemma. It's a stunning room that Kyle redesigned. It was just finished a few months ago. His architecture training has been very beneficial to Cherrywood Hall." Aunt Margaret beamed.

"Thank you, Lady Margaret. Oxfordshire training was a success." He smiled. "I concentrated on historical architecture and minored in engineering. I have a great respect for these old estates. I wanted to see what I could do to make sure they survive another couple of hundred years."

"Evan showed me the tunnel excavation you have underway. That must be an exciting find."

"It was quite a surprise. When we were digging the foundation to the winery, the construction crew came upon the crumbling tunnels. I had some archeology experts from the London Museum come out to analyze what we had found. They think the tunnels were built in the seventeen hundreds, so people could escape from the hall if they were attacked. The problem is that the excavation is very slow. I'm trying to keep much of the original infrastructure in place, reinforcing it as we go. I have no idea where we will end up in the hall." He laughed.

"Kyle refurbished all the Cherrywood auxiliary buildings and stables as well, Gemma," Evan added. "The winery was his original design—absolutely stunning. He won't say it, but he's been nominated for an award for outstanding new design by the British Architecture Society. If he wins, he could be knighted by the queen."

"I can't wait to see it," I said. "You must take me around, 'Sir' Kyle."

"It's already planned," he said. "I think Evan wants to show you around the house rooms tomorrow. I'll take you around the grounds on Wednesday. Do you ride?"

"Yes, I do. It's been a while, though, unfortunately. While I was working on my dissertation, I didn't get to ride as much as I used to."

"I'll have the horses ready then, at least for part of the tour."

"I can't wait. The grounds looked so beautiful driving in."

"I have some news from the production company," Evan said. "As you know, tragedy struck this afternoon. With the death of Lord and Lady Hemsworth, Ainsley Abbey has been withdrawn from the competition. They had been selected to host the garden tour and fete. The company has decided to combine the garden tour event with the formal tea. Shipley House will be hosting this event. Longthorpe Manor will be hosting the breakfast and hunt. And that means Cherrywood Hall will be hosting the formal dinner gala," he finished, winking at me.

"It's so sad to hear of their deaths," Aunt Margaret said. "They were a fine couple and did so much for their community. They will be sorely missed."

"They were our strongest competitor from an estate perspective," Kyle added. "I admired all the modernization Lord Hemsworth did on their estate. He was using technology and green techniques to support Ainsley Abbey well into the twenty-first century."

"Rosehill Productions is making a major donation to their community and charities in honor of their participation. So that means we are now in a final-three competition—an even tighter race," Evan said.

"So how do you feel about Cherrywood Hall being selected to host the formal dinner gala?" I asked, looking at Evan, Aunt Margaret, and Kyle.

"I think it's the best event for us really," Evan said. "The house is designed for large, formal events. We had the American president and several dignitaries here for a dinner gala event during World War II."

"With the royals and prime minister," Aunt Margaret added. "Sitting here on the cliffs overlooking the sea gives us a pretty impressive evening venue. The ladies always love coming to Cherrywood Hall. Pippa and Queen Regent Eugenie were close friends. She often came here to visit and brought the children when they were young."

"Well, we can still support having any royals visit. It's set up for the security measures needed for visiting VIPs, from here or around the world. These days that is a very important criterion unfortunately," Kyle added.

Dinner was served. Chef Karl had prepared our delicious meal from locally sourced produce and meats from Cherrywood and the surrounding community. His yellow tomato soup with basil puree was the perfect starter for our fall dinner, followed by crisp fried shrimps with a mild garlic aioli sauce. A prime rib roast garnished with roasted root vegetables followed next. We finished with platters of fresh fruit and cheese selections.

"Let's go into the sitting room," Evan said as we finished our last bites. "Mother has some juicy tidbits to tell us about our remaining competition."

"Evan, really," Aunt Margaret admonished.

We sat in chairs that had been set in a semicircle around the fireplace. I was pleased when Kyle took the seat next to me. Evan served us glasses of port.

"Come on, Mother, tell us what you know about the Paunchleys and Hamptons. It could give us some great insights on what to expect from them in the next few weeks," Evan said.

"Your father and I often socialized with Lord and Lady Paunchley," she began. "They were a few years older than us but were a lovely couple. We had many late evenings together either here at Cherrywood Hall or at Longthorpe Manor. Your father and Lord Paunchley both had a great sense of duty and often collaborated on projects for the estates. Hunting was a passion of theirs too. They loved their hunts and horses." She smiled.

"Lady Paunchley and I were pregnant with you and their daughter, Jane, at the same time, so we became good friends as well. Jane was a blessing to them. They hadn't expected to have any children, so it was quite a surprise when Lady Paunchley became pregnant.

"You were born first, Evan." Aunt Margaret smiled. "Jane was born two months later. We used to laugh about you two marrying—the perfect match. Lady Paunchley and I often took you and Jane out in your prams for walks along the sea path and had picnics holding our babies," she said. "But then something happened. To this day, I don't know all the details. Sad, really.

"When you were nine months old, the Paunchleys just quit coming around, avoiding us and everyone else socially. Your father and I were very hurt, as they had become good friends. He tried talking with Lord Paunchley as I did with Lady Paunchley, but they had changed and became very distant—not only to us but to each other. All their joy over having Jane seemed to dissipate."

Evan poured Kyle and me another glass of port. Aunt Margaret switched to a cup of tea.

"What do you think happened?" I asked. Aunt Margaret looked at the crackling fire a few moments before she answered.

"There were rumors," she continued quietly. "We heard there had been an affair between Lady Paunchley and Lord Hampton. Apparently, Lord Paunchley found out about it a few months after Jane was born. It was terrible really. I didn't like Lord Hampton to begin with. I found him to be rather pompous and rude. And then she died," Lady Margaret said, her voice wandering off.

"Lady Paunchley died? How? Why?" I asked, rather shocked.

"She hanged herself," Aunt Margaret said sadly. "Apparently she was extremely upset that her affair with Lord Hampton had been found out. And well, I hate to repeat it, but it was rumored that perhaps Jane wasn't Lord Paunchley's daughter. Lady Paunchley couldn't handle the shame. Lord Paunchley became distraught and even more reclusive after her death. When I think about how happy they had been when Jane was born..." She trailed off. "Lord Paunchley blamed and never forgave Lord Hampton for his wife's death. It's strange that they will be placed together again after all these years. I don't think it's a good thing."

"I never knew," Evan said. "Jane and I met at some of the parties and events held over the years. She's never mentioned her mother that I recall. Kyle, you obviously knew her better than me. Did you know any of this? Oh, sorry, old man. I forgot. You don't have to answer if you don't want."

Kyle smiled and answered cautiously, as a gentleman should. "It's all right. Jane and I met at a polo match. Her boyfriend and I played on the same team. We went out for a time when she broke up with him. Jane isn't really the type to hash over anything in the past or dwell on family matters, in my opinion. She has two loves: horses and Jane." Kyle smiled. "She can be difficult at times. She doesn't have a lot of patience. It will be interesting to see how she performs with the Longthorpe Manor hunt event. She likes to go in for the kill usually, literally and figuratively, pulling all stops. Not quite my style." He looked at me.

"Well, her loss, old man," Evan said. "I think it important that we remember Jane's alliance with some of the royals too—particularly the horsey set. She may try to bring in some of their influence. I wouldn't put it past her. Mother, we may need you to call Queen Annelyce, to put in a good word for us."

Aunt Margaret raised her eyebrows at Evan, signaling that was not going to happen. "I feel somewhat sorry for Jane. Lord Paunchley doted on her and spoiled her growing up to make up for the rumors and innuendos around her poor mother's death. He took down all the paintings of Lady Paunchley in the house. I rather doubt Jane knew much about her mother at all," Aunt Margaret said sadly. "A girl needs to know her mother."

"What about the Hamptons, Mother?" Evan asked.

"The tragedy continued. A few years after Lady Paunchley's death, Lady Hampton and her two daughters were killed in a fire at Shipley House. Lord Hampton had been smoking in the drawing room next to their bedrooms...and drinking heavily. The servants managed to get him out in time and also their son, Francis, who was just about your age at the time, Evan," Aunt Margaret finished.

"Well, I know that Francis and his father are not close," Kyle said. "I went to architectural school with Francis's partner, Christopher, at Oxfordshire. Francis would often come and stay with him, and we would go to have drinks at the pub. I don't think Francis ever forgave him for his mother and sisters' deaths. And I don't think Lord Hampton approved of Francis's relationship with Christopher."

"No, no, he wouldn't," Aunt Margaret said. "He was rude and crude and thought himself the lord stud of the county," she said with disdain. "After his wife and daughters' deaths, he sent Francis away to boarding school. I don't remember seeing them together much, and when they were, things were definitely strained."

"So why is Lord Hampton letting Francis be in the competition?" I asked. "Given their history, it doesn't seem like he would all of a sudden welcome Francis back and let him volunteer the estate for this."

"I'm not sure, Gemma," Evan said. "At the earlier production meetings, Lord Hampton didn't even attend. It was just Francis and Christopher. I just assumed Lord Hampton had given him full authority to proceed. Christopher did seem to have some prior relationships with the Rosehill Production executives and judges on the selection committee, but to what extent I'm not sure."

"Perhaps Francis is blackmailing his father," Kyle said. "Stranger things have happened. I wouldn't put it past Francis either."

VERONICA CLINE BARTON

"I will let you all figure that out," Aunt Margaret said as she rose to leave us. Evan and Kyle stood to help her up and take her teacup. "I'm going to call it a night now, dears." She smiled warmly. "I will be leaving early in the morning to go back to London. Queen Annelyce is hosting a tea and garden tour on Saturday for one of the charities she sponsors. I will be attending this event. One never disappoints the queen." She leaned over and kissed my cheeks. "Take good care of Gemma now, Kyle and Evan. Evan, be sure and show Gemma the jewel room tomorrow during your tour, and the closets." She smiled. "I think you will enjoy those rooms."

"They're on the list, Mother." Evan smiled.

We said our good-nights, and Evan walked his mother up to her room. Kyle and I were left alone in the sitting room.

"Well, I have to say your English estates have more in common with Malibu than I thought." I laughed, thinking about the scandalous affairs that were commonplace back home. "I thought I was getting into a stuffy old competition. Little did I know..."

"Love and lust do strange things," Kyle said. His deep green eyes were now studying me. I tried to stop myself from blushing. Right now I had a growing warmth for Kyle, and I believed the feeling was mutual.

"How long did you date Jane, if you don't mind me asking? I just ended a relationship too. I can empathize."

"We saw each other for a little less than a year, off and on. Jane is a free spirit of sorts. She may disappear for a month and then show up at your front door, as if she had never been gone. She expected to pick up things just as they were before she left. That was a bit hard to get used to."

"Are you going to be OK seeing her in the competition? I couldn't imagine seeing my ex, much less attending events with him."

52

"It could be awkward I admit. Jane's a strong woman. I doubt she will be fazed by seeing me." He laughed.

"Well, let's toast," I said, holding my glass to his. "To love and lust, past, present, and future."

"Love and lust. I look forward to it, Gemma," Kyle whispered. All I could think of was running my fingers through his thick hair. I wouldn't leave you for a month, I thought.

Evan came back into the room. "Well, that was interesting, wasn't it?" he asked as he poured himself another port. "Perhaps the production company should consider another series based upon the Hamptons and Paunchleys." He laughed. "All kidding aside, we have our work cut out for us. Jane and Francis will be in this to win. There's a lot at stake for all of us."

We stayed in the sitting room for another half hour pondering the tasks in front of us. At midnight, Evan and I walked Kyle to the front entrance. Kyle bent down to kiss my cheek. "Pleased meeting you, Gemma, again," he whispered, once again staring at me with his deep green eyes. "Good night," he said to both of us.

Evan walked me to my room. "Good night, Gemma," he said, kissing my cheeks. "Breakfast is served in the dining room, so sleep tight and join us when you can. We'll go on the tour of the house right after."

I went into my room and did a twirl in my beautiful gown, thinking of the evening. I walked over to the fireplace and looked up at Pippa's painting. "I think I am going to like it here, Aunt Pippa. Let's see what the Americans can bring to this British competition. We did win the war, you know."

I undressed and slipped into the warmth of the covers on my four-poster bed. I could hear the wind howling and the waves crashing against the hillside. I fell asleep quickly, enveloped in the stately walls of Cherrywood Hall.

5

Rooms and History

I ended up tossing and turning a lot my first night at Cherrywood Hall, dreaming about the automobile death of the Hemsworths, Lady Paunchley hanging herself, and the terrible fire that killed Lady Hampton and her daughters. So much sadness and heartbreak. How would the family feuds of the Paunchleys and Hamptons play out in the competition?

I dreamed Evan and I were running through the vast halls of the house, trying to figure out where we were, panicked. The Pippa and Lillian sconces pointed at us, vying for our attention. The dreams swept me round and round until I finally woke up. I was still exhausted, but I decided to get up and dress rather than risk facing the crazy dreams again.

The sun was just rising. I went to the French doors that overlooked the sea and looked out. Cold fog had rolled in, giving the air a brisk chill. I decided to wear a black turtleneck and tan jeggings tucked into my black leather boots to keep the chill off. I slipped on the gold charm bracelet that was handed down to me from Great-Gran-mama Lillian. I fingered the surfboard and diploma charms Evan had given me, the surfboard for when he stayed with us in Malibu and the diploma given for my graduation. I was excited to see Cherrywood's rooms today with Evan. I couldn't imagine what we'd see in all one hundred fifty rooms. My curiosity was piqued. And I had to admit the thought of seeing Kyle again gave me added incentive to get downstairs.

It was just seven o'clock when I started down the grand staircase. I thought I would go to the dining room to see if I could get a cup of coffee. I didn't think anyone else would be up yet. To my surprise, Evan, Aunt Margaret, and Kyle were already seated at the dining table, tucking into a true English country breakfast of bacon, eggs, grilled tomatoes, sautéed mushrooms, baked beans, and kidneys. As I walked into the room, Evan and Kyle stood to greet me.

"Gemma, what a surprise to see you this early," Evan said.

"Good morning, dear." Aunt Margaret smiled as I bent down to kiss her cheek. Kyle nodded and stood looking at me with a slight grin, fully enjoying the view of my figure-hugging outfit.

"Did you sleep well, dear?" Aunt Margaret asked.

"Well, yes," I said, deciding not to tell them of the hectic dreams. "I think I'm still adjusting to the time difference, but a strong cup of coffee should help with that. Breakfast looks yummy."

"Please, help yourself. You need to build up your strength. We have lots of rooms to cover." Evan laughed. "Bridges, can you get Dr. Philips a cup of coffee, please? We're just having tea, Gemma. I forgot how you Yanks have an addiction to caffeine of the java variety." I gave Evan an embarrassed shush, loaded my plate, and sat down.

"Kyle was just saying he's going up to Oxford today to make final arrangements for the launch of our Cherrywood wine," Aunt Margaret said, sipping her tea daintily.

"Yes, we're almost there," Kyle said in between bites. "Our distributors are lined up, and we have several restaurants that will be showcasing the sparkling whites in the next few weeks. I'll be back tonight. I don't want to miss our tour of the grounds tomorrow." He grinned, looking intently at me. "Evan tells me you were interested in climbing the cliffs. I can show you where I launch from. We'll plan an afternoon of climbing once you're settled in."

My heart flipped a beat. "Good. I can't wait."

"Gemma, I've told Evan to be sure and take you to the jewel room and the closets. Make sure he does." Aunt Margaret smiled.

"I remember you saying that last night, Aunt Margaret. I can kind of figure out what the jewel room is, but what closets do you want me to see?" I asked.

Evan, Aunt Margaret, and Kyle chuckled at my question. "The closets are a set of rooms that hold many of the gowns and dresses the ladies of Cherrywood Hall have worn over the years. Many of them are designer originals from the early nineteen hundreds. Some were owned by your Aunt Pippa, dear," Aunt Margaret said. "Each generation of Lancasters has tried to preserve their favorites, and we have accumulated quite a few garments over the years. And the shoes, of course."

"A few? Mother, there are four huge rooms that comprise the Lancaster ladies' closets." Evan laughed.

"Those are only the ones we know about, Evan. One of the Cherrywood mysteries is what happened to the earlier crowns and gowns from the seventeen and eighteen hundreds. We've looked and looked but have never found them."

"They were likely sold, Mother, to help pay for the estate expenses over the years, don't you think? There were some lean years in previous generations, you know. Running Cherrywood Hall has always been expensive."

"It could be, dear, but there's no documentation of any sales prior to the nineteen hundreds, which is very strange. There should have been bills of sale or notes if anything like that was done. I think they are still here somewhere at Cherrywood. Perhaps in a secret room? Lord knows there are still rooms to be found here, just like the tunnels. We've only scratched the surface." She smiled.

"Secret rooms? You really don't know how many rooms are in Cherrywood?" I asked.

"It's more difficult than it seems, Gemma," Kyle said. "Many of these older homes were added on to throughout the years, and unfortunately many of the additions had no drawings or notes to document them. Security has always been a concern, but back then they didn't have alarms and monitoring systems. The best way to hide your valuables was to have secret rooms with unique access points. The problem is if they are not documented for future generations, the contents and rooms may be lost."

"Well, it sounds like I have my work cut out for me for the data archive and presentation video effort, especially if we have secret rooms to find and film. I had just assumed you knew every nook and cranny here. Maybe the tunnel will lead us to them." I grinned. "I'll see if I can get the Cherrywood ghosts to give us any clues."

"Well, that may be needed," Aunt Margaret said, not batting an eye. "I should have thought of that." I noticed Evan and

Kyle didn't bat an eye over the ghost comment either. I shivered, thinking that perhaps the ghosts of Cherrywood Hall weren't just imagined after all.

We finished our breakfast and went out to the grand hall-way. Aunt Margaret was preparing to leave to go back to London. "I'm glad I got to see you before I left, dear. Keep these men in line." She winked. "Please be careful, all of you. The excitement of the competition is all well and good but keep your eyes and ears open. You have two competitors with a dark history between them." Evan walked his mother to the car to say good-bye and to wave her on her way.

I went back to the dining room to get another cup of cof-fee that Bridges had graciously brought in. Kyle was also in the room, just finishing a call on his cell phone. "I'm glad I got to see you this morning as well, Gemma." He smiled. "Don't get too worn out today. I need you to have some strength left over for tomorrow," he said, winking at me.

"I'll be ready." I couldn't believe how drawn I was to Kyle so soon. He was easy to be around, though, and made you want to be close to him. He radiated a warmth and friendliness that was hard to resist. Better slow down girl, I thought. You just broke up with Michael.

I walked Kyle to the front door, where Evan was just coming in. "Get lots of orders for us today, old man." Evan grinned.

"That's the plan. We're going to do well. Have a good day, you two. Hope you find some hidden treasures. Say hello to the ghosts for me if you see them." Kyle smiled as he left.

Evan clapped his hands. "Right. Let's get started with the tour then, Gemma. I seriously doubt we'll be able to get to all the rooms today, but we'll see as much as we can. Let's go into the li-brary first. I have some of the Cherrywood floor drawings I want you to see so that you have an idea of where we're going today," he said, leading me to the room. "Kyle has had these all digitized, but I thought you'd like seeing some of the original drawings."

Several rolls of drawings lay on the large mahogany chart table in the middle of the library. Evan rolled out a larger one, which showed the first-floor rooms. "You've seen most of these rooms," he said, anchoring the corners, so we could get a good view. Chart one showed the grand hallway. The dining room and small sitting room were on the left.

A large room paralleled the dining room, one I had not seen. "What is this room, Evan?" I pointed.

"That's the conservatory, the one designed by Aunt Pippa and redesigned by Kyle. If you don't mind, I'd like to skip that for today. Kyle and I have a surprise for you tomorrow evening." He smiled.

"Really? That's sweet of both of you. Now I'm really curious, though."

On the right side of the house were the library, which we were in, and a large reception drawing room that stood next to the entrance. The grand staircase separated these two rooms.

"What are these?" I asked, pointing to what looked like hallways that went along the length of the rooms. I hadn't seen any hallway doors in the first-floor rooms.

"Ah," Evan said, "these are the hallways the servants use to clear the tables and move between the various rooms. It's a bit of an embarrassment, but servants originally were meant to be almost invisible." He walked over to a large panel on the wall of the library and pushed one corner. Sure enough, a large door opened, and we went through to see the servant hall.

"Are these all throughout the house?" I asked.

"They are primarily on the first floor, since this is where most of the formal entertaining is done in the house. The hallways go around the perimeter and have staircases leading down to the kitchen and servants' hall, and upstairs leading to the bedrooms and chambers on the second floor, and the bedrooms, nurseries, closet storage areas, and servants' rooms on the third floor. As Mother said, though, there are likely secret rooms or cubbies on every floor. We just haven't found them yet."

Evan rolled out the second chart that showed the bedroom and bath chambers on the second floor. I was amazed to see that there were over thirty bedrooms on the floor, with twenty-five bathrooms, five of which were shared between bedrooms.

"Evan, this is like a hotel!" I gushed. The larger bedrooms—Evan's, Aunt Margaret's, and the one I was in, which was formerly Pippa's—were facing the sea. There were two other large rooms on the end next to Aunt Margaret's room, these five being the largest suites that occupied the entire width of the house. I noticed that Evan's room was the largest, centered in between my room and Aunt Margaret's. It was the largest, befitting of the marquess status. Around the perimeter were the other bedrooms and baths. There was an inner perimeter of smaller rooms and baths connected by hallways.

"It is rather intimidating," Evan said. "We've done a lot of entertaining here at Cherrywood Hall throughout the years. You have to keep in mind that most dinners and parties lasted well into the evening, if not the next morning. Most guests stayed over, so we had to make sure they were accommodated in a stylish manner—a rather expensive manner, in fact. Guests had, and have, very high expectations when they stay at an estate house, even if we are in 'the country,'" he added. "The two rooms next to Mother's have held visiting kings and queens from all over."

On the chart showing the third-floor rooms, the house was basically divided into two areas. Along the walls facing the sea and grounds were fifteen more bedrooms, nurseries, and bath chambers. The remaining areas showed the four rooms labeled "closet" and tiny rooms that were the servants' bedrooms and baths. Finally, Evan pulled out the fourth chart, which showed the layout of the rooms in the basement. Cherrywood Hall had an extensive kitchen that included a large pantry area, cold rooms, prep stations, and cook areas.

"Chef Karl can give you the detailed tour of this area, Gemma. It's quite impressive. We have four English stoves and ovens he uses for the large parties and events. Freezers and the cold rooms are here." He pointed. A large wine cellar was in one corner. "Kyle has designed a private wine cellar in the winery for the house to use as well. We want to be able to store our finer Cherrywood vintages for years to come. Someday our grandchildren will be opening the bottles we put in storage today," Evan said, giving me a squeeze.

"What are these rooms?" I asked, pointing at the rooms not labeled.

"Those are the storage areas for the china, crystal, and silverware we use here. There are many sets that have been collected throughout the years by the marquesses." He smiled. "Bridges can give you a detailed tour. He knows much more about that area than I do." Evan laughed. The servants' main room took up a large section. Evan explained that this was where they took their meals and relaxed.

On the remaining corner was a large room that appeared to be a vault. "This," Evan explained, "is the jewel room Mother mentioned this morning. It houses all the jewelry, rings, tiaras, and crowns worn over the years by the ladies and gents of

Cherrywood Hall. It had a major overhaul by Kyle two years ago to add up-to-date security features. The items in there are worth several millions of pounds. Some are irreplaceable and priceless. Kyle also wanted the vault fireproofed. We couldn't imagine having any of the items destroyed."

Evan and I decided to go to the second floor to check out the bedrooms and chambers. We started with Evan's room, which was next to mine. He opened the double doors that led into a room with dark cherry-red walls and red Persian carpets on the floor. His room was twice the size of mine. It had a huge four-poster bed and bath chamber on one side. On the side looking out to the sea was a large sitting area with leather chairs and couches framing the two French doors and carved marble fireplace. Paintings of previous marquesses of Cherrywood decorated the walls, including a recent painting of Evan. I went up and down the room, savoring its detail.

"This is stunning, Evan," I said as I ran my hand over the rich leather of the sofa. The French doors led out to his balcony that also overlooked the sea. A telescope stood at one end.

"I like to watch the stars here, weather permitting." Evan smiled. "I'll come and get you one night if you want to join me. We have a rather clever way to get to each other's rooms." He went over to his bedside table and pressed a hidden button. A panel along his bed opened and led right into my room, next to my bed.

"How did you do that?"

Evan laughed and showed me the hidden buttons at his bedside. "Since you were not in your room, the panel opened when I pressed this; lights came on showing the button had been pushed." He pointed. "There is a delay built in, so if you did not wish the panel to open, you could press the corresponding button at your bedside table. You see, the lords and ladies of Cherrywood wanted to keep any assignations discreet between rooms." He blushed. "And of course, one would have the right to turn down a request if one did not wish to be disturbed. However, two pushes of the button open the panel automatically. Sometimes one doesn't care if the other doesn't wish to be disturbed." He laughed.

"Well, I think your hidden panel buttons are quite civilized." I smiled.

We continued our tour of the bedrooms. Aunt Margaret's room was covered in a rose chintz wallpaper with intricately carved cherry furniture. Her room was the reverse floor plan of mine. I still smelled whiffs of the perfume she'd worn this morning. The last two rooms facing the sea were the royal rooms, as Evan had explained.

"This is the Anchor Room, which usually was where the king or queen stayed—or the most senior royal." He smiled. "They could, of course, elect to have their spouse in this room or put them next door." He laughed. The adjoining room, the Crown Room, was also opulent in design and decor. Royals were used to a certain standard, and these rooms did not disappoint.

We spent the next hour poking our heads into the other bedrooms. "No guest is going to be disappointed staying in these rooms, Evan," I said. "The details and fabrics for each room are magnificent. I can't imagine the planning and effort that went into each room's design."

"Thanks, Gemma. Many of the marquesses contributed to the designs. Everyone had their own sense of style," Evan said with pride, "although main credit today must go to Bridges and the staff. They do a wonderful job making sure every room stays in top shape."

Evan and I took a quick lunch break down in the dining room to rest and refresh ourselves. Chef Karl had prepared a wonderful arugula salad with pears and walnuts, and a halibut filet with crab and sauce *au beurre*. We finished with biscuits and a cup of tea, ready to resume our tour.

"Really, Evan, I could so get used to having a private chef. I feel like I'm eating out every day. It's wonderful."

"Enjoy it. Chef Karl is a treasure; that's for sure. If you're ready, let's head downstairs. I want to take you to the jewel room." We took the stone stairway leading down and went along the hall to the vault. An elaborate keyboard hung on the wall next to the vault door. Evan entered codes in and placed his hand on a small window, which swept his handprint for verification.

"It's like Fort Knox," I said, referring to the army location that supposedly housed the US gold bullion reserves.

"Well, not quite that scale, but almost." Evan smiled. The vault door clicked, and he opened the massive steel door. Lights went on in the room automatically as we entered. I gasped as we walked in. It sparkled like the showroom of a glamorous jewelry store.

Row after row of glass cases stood in the room. As we walked around each row, I saw that it was organized by jewelry type. Magnificent rings made up one row, separated by stone type: emeralds, rubies, diamonds, sapphires, and semiprecious gems. The next rows had a similar setup for earrings, bracelets, broaches, and necklaces. The case around the perimeter of the room housed the tiaras and crowns worn by generations of Lancaster ladies.

"Evan, these are so beautiful," I said as we went around each case. I could see why Kyle had insisted on the extra security measures. I had never seen so many large and exquisite stones and one-of-a-kind pieces.

"I want you to wear any of the pieces you desire, Gemma," Evan said. "We are going to a number of events the next few months. You are going to have to represent us well." He smiled.

"Oh, Evan," I gushed, "I can't wait to wear these. This is definitely a woman's dream."

"Look at this." Evan beckoned me over to a large case housing the tiaras. In the center was an elaborate one comprised of teardrop diamonds and blue sapphires. I had never seen anything so beautiful. "This was the Lancaster tiara commissioned by Aunt Pippa," he explained. "It alone is worth over three million pounds."

"I know this. She's wearing the tiara and matching jewels in the painting in my room. They're stunning."

Evan and I spent the next hour looking at the jewelry. He opened cases to let me try on the gorgeous gems. "I feel like a princess." I smiled. Not many girls were privy to their own private showroom, just like the famous ones in New York and Paris.

We decided to take tea up on the terrace overlooking the sea. Bridges had set the table with gorgeous tiered plates offering sandwiches, savory pies, scones, and pastries. My appetite perked up at the sight of these goodies.

"Good thing we're walking so much," I said as I popped a cucumber-and-cress sandwich in my mouth. "Everything is so delicious. Trying on jewels gives a girl an appetite." We sat on the terrace and ate until we were stuffed. The day's walk and my lack of sleep the night before were starting to take hold.

"Why don't we call it a day," Evan said kindly, seeing my weariness set in. "Get a good rest tonight. You have a big day with Kyle tomorrow. We can go into the other rooms in the next few days. I'll have Mrs. Smythe bring you up a tray later in case you're hungry."

We went back into the library before I headed up to my room. Evan gave me some more of the booklets describing the content of the closet rooms that I was yet to see. He also handed me some handwritten diaries.

"These were Pippa's," he said. "I haven't had a chance to look at them, so you will have to fill me in."

I gave him a kiss and went upstairs to my room.

I lay down on the bed and opened one of Pippa's diaries. "Starting construction of the terrace today," it began. I tried concentrating as she described the digging and excavating, but the jet lag and exercise from today's tour soon had me slumbering deeply. I dreamed of the beautiful rooms I had seen and the gorgeous gems.

Mrs. Smythe did bring me a tray of sandwiches and tea a few hours later. I ate a few bites but decided just to change and go back to sleep. I wanted to be fully rested for my tour of the grounds with Kyle. That night I didn't toss and turn thinking of the sad events. Instead I dreamed of what it would be like to be cradled in Kyle's arms and kissed.

6

The Grounds of Cherrywood Hall

I woke up the next morning fully rested and blushing at some of the dreams I had conjured that focused on Kyle. My ex, Michael, was fast becoming a distant memory for me, and for that I was very glad. I looked out my French doors and saw that it was going to be a gloomy day. I decided to dress warmly, wearing blue jeans, a tan turtleneck, and a quilted navy vest. I put on my black leather riding boots and headed down to the dining room for breakfast. I was giddy at the thought of riding again. It had been far too long since my last ride.

Kyle and Evan were at the buffet table loading their plates with another wonderful English breakfast. They turned to greet me as I walked in. I planted a kiss on Evan's cheek and smiled over at Kyle to wish them good morning and then grabbed a plate of my own.

"Well, it looks like you've recovered, Gemma. Glad to see it." Evan smiled.

"Evan told me you and he explored quite a few rooms yesterday, Gemma. What do you think?" Kyle asked as we took our filled plates over to the dining table and sat down to eat.

"I truly am amazed, Kyle," I said. "The second floor could be a hotel on its own. I've never seen such grand rooms, and so many in the same house. And the jewel room—I don't even know what to say. It's like a private New York or Paris showroom right in your basement!" I gushed. "We didn't even get to the closets. Evan wouldn't take me into the conservatory. He said that you both wanted to surprise me tonight."

"We'll finish seeing the rest of the rooms in the next few days," Evan said. "Today you will be in Kyle's capable hands. I have to run into the village for a meeting with the local administrators to go over some more details on the competition. And tonight...Well, all I can say is that you will be amazed." He laughed. "Everything is under control, thanks to the capable hands of Bridges and Chef Karl." We finished our breakfast, and Evan left to go into the village.

"Can you find your way to the stables?" Kyle asked. "I thought we'd start our tour of the grounds on horseback and then head over to the winery. I've arranged for us to have lunch there. We can take the Rover after lunch to see the rest of the grounds."

"Sounds great, Kyle. I'll meet you at the stables in a half hour."

I ran upstairs to change my vest and wear instead a quilted field jacket, gloves, and a black oiled hat since it had started to drizzle. Duly protected, I left to walk to the stables.

Cherrywood's stables were located to the left of the main house, approximately a half-mile walk along a gravel road. The air was still crisp and cool, and the clouds grayed the skies and sprinkled cold drops intermittently. Cherrywood Hall's magnificence showed through the gloom, however, and I marveled at the brilliant greens of the grass and oranges and golds on the oak and maple trees lining the road. I turned the corner and saw Kyle outside the stable with two beautiful horses that had been saddled. I recognized the huge black stallion I had seen him riding when I first came to Cherrywood.

"Hello." I waved and met Kyle down by the horses.

"I've picked Lady Kins for you to ride today, Gemma." He smiled. "I think you'll find she's an excellent mount and won't give you too much trouble."

"She looks beautiful," I said as I rubbed Lady Kin's nose and scratched her head. "Introduce me to your steed," I said. "He's magnificent."

"This is Sir Lad, and he's been with me over fifteen years. I played polo with him originally, but he injured his leg. I kept him for riding, though. He's a superb horse," he said, rubbing Sir Lad affectionately. We mounted the horses and began our ride.

"I thought we'd go along the sea path to give you a cliffside view of Cherrywood. The path runs over two miles and will give us a chance to see the coastline. It was built over a hundred years ago. In fact, your Aunt Pippa is responsible for much of its design. I've had to do some engineering repairs. There was some slippage a few years back due to a rockslide, but it's stable now. Don't worry." He smiled.

The pathway views were truly spectacular, even with the gloomy cloud cover. The North Sea was raging today, with white tops cresting the waves. I stopped and turned to look back at Cherrywood Hall. The estate was sitting on the hilltop, majestically reigning over its land.

About a mile down the path, before we turned to ride along the forest, Kyle dismounted. "Come look over here," he said, walking down toward the cliff edge. I dismounted Lady Kins and walked over to the edge. Kyle held my left arm while pointing out the climbing ledges he preferred. "It's steep, and you have to watch for slipping ledges, but I've staked my way down to the shoreline, about two hundred feet. I'll take you down once you settle in. It's a tough climb, but the shore below is striking with the waves—and very private." He smiled, winking at me.

The wind was blowing so hard; it was difficult for me to stand. I ended up holding on to Kyle as he showed me the edge. I looked up to his face and smiled. "I can't wait, but can we go down when the wind isn't quite so strong! I feel like I'm going to blow away."

Kyle helped me turn around, and we went back to the horses and mounted to get on with our ride. We continued down the path as it wound and curved along the forest and soon were on the main road leading out on to the fields of the estate. Kyle took us up the hill to the main temple folly where I had first seen him. It was a beautiful structure made of limestone with marble columns. We slid off the horses to stand on the folly terrace, which overlooked the rolling terrain of the estate.

"Over to the right is the winery and vineyard." Kyle pointed. "Straight ahead is the pasture for the cattle, sheep, and deer herds we raise. Everything is raised organically. We're trying to follow the lead of Prince Hadley and Princess Alyce and the wonderful organic practices they started at Evergreen."

"Where is the main farming done?" I asked. "Chef Karl told me he tries to source everything from Cherrywood's fields or local farms."

"We'll go over to the farm area after lunch. It will be easier to drive over in the Rover. We have over five thousand acres of farmland in production these days, providing grains and corn for us and our animals. What we don't use here, we sell locally to the smaller farms outside the estate. You'll find we have a wonderful sense of community. It's the main reason I love it here so much." He smiled.

Kyle gave me a boost as we remounted our horses and headed over to the winery. "How long have you been at Cherrywood, Kyle?"

"I was born here. My father was the estate agent when Kyle's father, Lord Mark, was alive. My mother was an artist and jewelry designer. I'll show you her paintings of Cherrywood sometime. She was really quite good," he said, with a note of sadness. "They both came from aristocratic backgrounds, but they chose to leave that life behind and utilize their talents doing things they loved."

"Are your parents still in the area?"

"No, they were killed in an automobile accident ten years ago. I had just started classes at Oxfordshire. They were coming up to visit and take me to dinner. I was a mess for quite some time, but Evan and Lady Margaret were there for me. I don't know what I would have done without them."

"I'm sorry. It must have been awful. How did you end up back at Cherrywood Hall?"

"It was in my blood. Evan and I had grown up together. We rode, hunted, and fished here. I grew up with the buildings and have walked every inch of the estate many times. When I finished my architectural degree, he asked if I wanted to come back to Cherrywood Hall to run the estate. He was traveling back and forth to his ranch in South Africa and needed someone here to run things. It was a perfect arrangement for me at the time. I had decided not to go into an architecture firm. I'm not the office type." He smiled.

"I wanted to do my own designs anyway. My parents had left me quite well off with their own inheritance and insurance plans, so I had the financial luxury of setting my own course. Here at Cherrywood Hall, I was able to deploy several designs to fix and redesign areas of the estate that were failing as well as implement my own new designs. When I saw the opportunity for the vineyard and winery operations, I proposed a plan to Evan. That's when he and I became business partners."

"I'd love to see some of your drawings and designs. Evan's told me you've drawn up plans for a Cherrywood Hall bed and breakfast, tearoom, and wedding pavilion. You're very ambitious."

"You bet. It's a date." He smiled. "I'd love to see the ventures materialize. Now all we have to do is win the competition."

We arrived at the winery building and dismounted. It was a modern structure with cherry and mahogany paneling juxtaposed with steel and metal columns and railings. Its modern design strangely complemented the ancient grounds. A groomsman took our horses back to the stables.

Kyle led me up the modern staircase to a deck that overlooked the vineyards. The winery operations were on the ground-level floor. The second and third floors were the main gallery, with Kyle's office on the third floor. As far as the eyes could see were perfect rows of grapes staked to the hillsides. In the front of the gallery level were huge floor-to-ceiling doors that could be opened to the deck that ran down the length of the building.

The gallery included rustic concrete floors and stacked stone walls, giving the impression of being in a massive wine cellar. Leather couches and chairs were arranged around the floor-to-ceiling stone fireplace. Bar tables were spread around the floor to allow for standing tastings. A rough-hewn cherry table, made of a lacquered slab, was against the main wall with bench seating. The room could easily host one hundred or so guests at a time, even more if the doors to the deck were opened.

"It's our plan to have weekly tastings and events at the estate, potentially using this building and the gardens to host town and corporate events. Evan and I want to involve the local community and businesses as much as possible. It's important that Cherrywood Hall stays a part of their heritage, not just another decrepit estate. We have too many of them in England these days. If you look down this way, this would be where the glass wedding pavilion would be built," he said, pointing to the right to an open field next to the grapes.

We had lunch in Kyle's office, which was on the third floor. It too had floor-to-ceiling windows that had an even more magnificent view of the vineyard. In addition to his desk, there stood a cherry slab drawing table, beautiful in its rustic detail.

"I stay here a lot at nights. It's a good place to draw and think." He smiled.

Chef Karl had delivered a picnic lunch for us to share. Kyle's office had a stone fireplace that had been lit to ward off the chilly air outside. We sat in the leather chairs flanking it and dove into wonderful roast-beef sandwiches with crusty rolls and creamed horseradish. Kyle served us a glass of the Cherrywood sparkling white to drink with our sandwiches. The fire felt good after our long ride. It was still cloudy outside, and a chilly fog was beginning to roll in from the sea. We cut into a wedge of Parmesan and drank our wine.

"How did you come to Cherrywood?" Kyle asked. "Evan told me he was going to ask you here a while ago. He also told me that you had just finished your doctoral program. Why didn't you go on to a professorship?"

I looked into the fire for a while before answering. "Mass and Conn both made inquiries to me for a professorship, which in theory should be perfect. And my best friend wants me to join her in a program at the University of Colorado. I haven't pursued things very aggressively. To be honest, I just didn't feel I fit in those programs. Not now anyway. I don't know if I want to teach or do research. I was involved with someone too, as you now know, someone I thought might want to join me in whatever came. He obviously had other plans."

"I'm sorry it didn't work out for you. For what it's worth, I think the guy must be an idiot." He smiled.

"Thanks, Kyle. Actually, it was a good thing," I said, standing and looking out the window at the vineyard. "If I had been with Michael, I would never have come to Cherrywood Hall. This estate competition is certainly a unique challenge that I was not expecting. I've heard, and believe, that sometimes you have to take a totally different path than expected to get where you're supposed to be."

Kyle came over to where I was standing and took my hand. "I'm glad your path led you here, Gemma," he said, taking my hand and kissing it. His strong gaze made me forget where I was. The drop of a log in the fireplace broke our intense moment. I turned away quickly and gulped the last of my wine.

"We should be heading out for the rest of the tour," I said, a little out of breath.

Kyle laughed and led me downstairs to the winery operations. Large computerized vats ran along the length of the building. Test areas were along one wall where the oenologists sampled
and tested the batches. A huge warehouse was attached at the end
where the wine was barreled and aged until ready for bottling.
The musty smell of oak and wine filled the warehouse.

"The wine is bottled and distributed out of Oxford," Kyle
explained. "I've been traveling there quite a bit the past year,
but I believe things are finally firmed up. We'll be shipping on
time—a huge accomplishment."

We got in the Rover SUV and started the drive over to the
agricultural fields. We stopped along the road to watch the herds
of cattle, sheep, and deer grazing slowly on the hillside.

"How many animals do you have here?" I asked.

"Last count was over one thousand. We have sustainable
herds for our meat and dairy needs, and they're one hundred
percent organically raised too. Chef Karl insists." Kyle smiled.
He continued the drive until we crested a large hill. We hopped
out of the Rover to get a better look at the fields. Rows of corn
and hay stretched as far as the eye could see.

"Is this all Cherrywood property?"

"Everything that you can see." Kyle pointed. "We have the
locals come and farm this for us. We share part of the profits
with them, in addition to their wages."

We continued down the road, which circled back to where
the stables were located. Next to them stood two other barns
and eight houses. One in particular stood out. It was uniquely
nestled against the forest, almost like a tree house. Its wood and
stone exterior had a large glass room that seemed to float behind
it.

"How beautiful," I said.

"That's mine," Kyle said as he slowed the Rover. "I'll have you over some night to see it. Right now we'd better head back. Evan would not forgive me if I had you miss our dinner this evening." Kyle drove up to the entrance of Cherrywood Hall. He came over to open my door. "I hope you enjoyed your tour today, Gemma."

"It was fantastic, Kyle. Thank you. I can see why you love it here so much."

"I'll let you go then. Until tonight." He smiled.

I had a huge grin on my face as I climbed the grand staircase to go up to my room.

At eight o'clock, I went down the stairs to meet Kyle and Evan for dinner. Tonight I decided to wear a white silk collared shirt with a royal-blue, maxi-length skirt. A leather belt cinched my waist. I styled my hair in a long braid that ran down my back. I finished my look with a pearl choker and pearl drop earrings. Evan and Kyle were waiting for me in the dining room, looking very handsome themselves in their black-tie tuxes.

"OK, you two, where is my surprise?" I teased. To my delight two large sections of draperies started to draw back automatically to reveal the conservatory, which stood behind the sets of French doors that ran down the length of the dining room. Evan and Kyle guided me through one set of doors into the magical-looking glass room.

The conservatory was the full length of the dining room and spanned out as far. Marble floors snaked around the trees and plants. Statues and carvings that were hundreds of years old stood all around the gardens. The central feature of the room was a towering, thirty-foot-high waterfall that roared into a catch pool at its base. Fairy lights and strategically placed spotlights gave a wonderful ambiance to the room.

"I've never seen anything like this," I gushed as we walked around the pathways.

"Kyle designed the waterfall. He found some drawings that Pippa had commissioned years before. She had wanted a waterfall in the room but sadly was never able to get it done before she died," Evan explained.

"Well, I'm sure she would have loved this." I smiled, looking at both of them. "It's stunning."

"Lady Pippa originally wanted a diving platform from the top of the falls." Kyle laughed. "I couldn't quite accommodate that, given the footprint of the room. But I think she would like this compromise."

At the center of the court, facing the waterfall was our dinner table, sparkling with candles and crystal. A sidebar stood next to the table, with bottles of Mon Cheri champagne and crystal flutes waiting for us. Kyle popped open a bottle and poured us a glass.

"To Pippa," Kyle toasted.

"And to you." I smiled. We sat down at our table for dinner. Chef Karl had once again prepared a delicious meal for us to share. Sweet potato soup with onion garnee, followed by lobster salad, started our dinner. Medallions of venison served with a grape jelly came next. Dessert was a crème brûlée garnished with fresh raspberries.

We moved over to the side of the waterfall, where big wicker chairs had been placed overlooking the falls. Evan handed us a snifter of brandy as we sat and watched the streaming water. As I looked at the falls, I thought I saw some lights flickering behind.

"Is there another room behind the falls?" I asked.

"I was wondering if you would notice." Kyle laughed. "It's actually a grotto behind the falls. And if you are really clever, you can trigger the secret doors to open and lead into the swimming room. We decided to build a lap pool to use year-round. It's not as dramatic as Lady Pippa's diving platform, but it does have its own charm. Would you like to see it?"

Kyle led us over to what looked to be a set of boulders stacked up against the falls. He reached over and pressed a hidden switch. The "boulders" started to slide away and opened to the swimming room. As we walked through the doorway, I gasped. The room was covered floor to ceiling in miniature blue iridescent tiles, making the walls, walkways, and pool all seem to flow together. A full-length glass ceiling gave swimmers a view of the sky that was gorgeous both in daytime and night. Blue pool lights made the room sparkle as the light hit the iridescent tiles.

"This is incredible," I gushed as I walked around the pool perimeter. "It's more stunning than the indoor pool at Pinehurst Castle."

"I'm glad you like it," Evan said. "Another miracle of design Kyle has given us. Use the pool anytime. It's always heated."

"Let me know when you take a swim." Kyle smiled. "I'll join you."

"I will," I said, walking by, whispering in his ear.

We walked back, and Evan refilled our brandy glasses. "I'd like to take you to Maidenford tomorrow afternoon, Gemma, after we tour the closet rooms. I want to introduce you to some of the people in the village I've been coordinating with for the competition. We can walk around the park and see the church grounds as well.

"I've also scheduled lunch at the Howling Pig. I'm having Charles Linford join us. He's the chap who's been helping Kyle and me with the estate website design, and more recently, helping Kyle with the winery section. I'd like you to work with him for the house archive and video projects, if you agree. We have tons of written documents and charts that need to be digitized and stored. I thought you could give him some academic and creative guidance."

"I'd be glad to, Evan. Besides digitizing the paper documents and filming the room inventories for the archives, what else would you like to see done?"

"I'd love for people who visit the website to see and experience Cherrywood Hall and the people who have lived here. I'm not sure how that would be done." He laughed. "There is so much beauty and grandeur here in the house and around the estate. I'd love for people to experience it somehow—to make our history come alive."

"Charles is filming the rooms of the winery for a virtual tour people can access from the website," Kyle said. "That way they can see the venue and decide if they want to reserve it for events. I've also ordered a drone for the property. We can attach a camera to it to give a bird's-eye view of the grounds if you'd like. You'd have a three-hundred-sixty-degree view of the estate."

"That's an awesome idea," I said. "There's so much here to work with; I'm sure we can craft something together." I'd have to figure out a way to combine the indoor film archive project with the outside grounds filming to bring their concepts to life. Some of the work I did for my dissertation involved incorporating video and animations to give readers a visual view of the subject matter and people discussed, including some family footage of the Lancasters and prints and paintings with voiceovers. I was sure we could do some unique things for Cherrywood Hall, given what I had to work with.

We spent the rest of the evening talking about the escapades Evan and Kyle had gotten into as children growing up here at

Cherrywood. We laughed and kidded as the brandy kicked in. As we finished the last sips, we stood and took one more walk around the conservatory.

"Thank you, gentlemen," I said. "I've had a wonderful day and evening." I smiled.

Evan and I walked Kyle to the door to say good night.

As Kyle left, he came over to kiss my cheek. "Let me know when you want to take that swim, Gemma," he whispered in my ear.

I smiled back at him and blushed and panicked a bit as he turned and left. Oh gosh, please let me have brought my bathing suit!

7

The Village of Maidenford

"Gemma, come on up. I want to show you the closet rooms this morning before we go to the village," Evan yelled from the grand staircase.

"Be right there," I said as I finished up my breakfast. I couldn't wait to see these rooms and the promised collections Aunt Margaret had described. I ran up to the second floor to join Evan. He took me round to a corner door that shielded a winding staircase leading directly to the largest of the rooms known as the closets on the third floor.

Evan opened the door at the top of the staircase and led me in. I was amazed to see rack after rack of dresses dating back at least a century. Most were stored in clear plastic garment bags to preserve them. They were separated by designer and by period. It was like walking through the City Museum's designer clothing exhibit in New York. Lucille's, Tres Soeurs, Poisoine, House of Fashion—all were displayed on one side of the room. On the other side were more contemporary designs from Dia, Gigi, and Yvette, one of my personal favorites. I marveled at the details of the dresses and gowns—a true, unexpected treasure trove.

"Evan, this is amazing. Do you know what you have here? This room alone has some priceless garments. How many rooms of clothing do you have?"

"Well, there are four rooms on this floor. Mother had some of the nondesigner items packed and stored up in the attic. This is definitely one of the areas we need to capture in the archive for inventory purposes, and I think they would be great to have in the film overview. And, if we can find the secret room or rooms where the older ancestral collections might be, that would score major points with Mother. She truly seems upset that they've disappeared. I really have my doubts that they still exist, at least not here."

We made our way into the adjacent room that held nothing but furs and coats that had been worn by the Lancaster ladies for generations: mink, fox, lynx, furs that I would never buy today, but marvelous garments from the past. I was drawn to one rack that held luxurious velvet coats and cloaks, many embellished with exquisite embroidery and gems.

"These are one-of-a-kind items, Evan, and extremely valuable. I think we need to talk with Kyle. These need to be preserved professionally and protected. The plastic garment bags alone are not adequate. Look at this coat." I pointed. "The sapphires and emeralds here are real. Some are even the size of the jewels held in the vault."

"You're right, Gemma. I've never paid these a moment's notice," he said, examining the garments. "We're going to need a larger vault."

We continued into the third closet room, where I thought I had died and gone to heaven. "Oh, I love it," I squealed, seeing rows and rows of custom-made shoes and boots. This room was divided into men, women, and children sections. I immediately gravitated to the rows of ladies' boots, my particular weakness. Riding boots, lace-up boots, ankle boots—I was in my element.

"I'll be back," I whispered to the shoes, hoping against hope that I wore the same size as my Lancaster ancestors.

In the last room were accessories. Hats, gloves, scarves, purses, umbrellas—I was amazed at the extensive collection of items, most of which were handmade, one-of-a-kind creations. Silks of every color beamed up from the collections. Feathers, lacework, beading, leatherwork, and needlepoint wove about in every conceivable pattern.

"Evan, this is incredible. I don't even know where to begin with all this. We're definitely going to have to have Kyle look at this and come up with a design plan to better store and display these treasures. Are you open for some new construction to house these? Some of these items are priceless. You may have millions of pounds' worth of items here."

"I'm amazed, Gemma. Mother has always referred to these rooms as the closets. I just thought there were a bunch of old clothes here. Pretty things, I knew, but I had no idea they were priceless. Mother is going to be speechless."

"I can tell you right now that many of these are museum quality. I researched many of the designers of the period during my dissertation. You would not believe how the influx of Americans over to Britain influenced the clothing designers of the time. It's miraculous that these are still here. This could be invaluable to the competition too. I'm sure the *Castlewood Manor* wardrobe team would love to see these items. We've got to highlight this find somehow. I'm sure the production and costume designers on the show would be fighting to have access here."

"I'll let you run with this, Gemma. Talk with Kyle and see what he recommends. I'll support whatever you both decide." Evan smiled. "I'm out of my element in this area; that is for sure. See, you've already made a major contribution, as I knew you would."

We ended the tour of the closet rooms and went to freshen up and get ready to drive to the village. I couldn't wait to go back and walk around the cobblestone streets to see the buildings and businesses we drove by the other day.

The village of Maidenford was two miles outside the main gates of Cherrywood Hall. It was built around a small harbor along the cliffside shore in the sixteen-hundreds and supported a thriving fishing and tourist business during the summer season. The houses along the shore and harbor were painted bright colors to compensate for the often-gray skyline and dark blue of the sea. Within the harbor were restaurants, pubs, and shops, in addition to the fishery processing businesses. In the summertime, bands played along the harbor walkways, giving the villagers and visitors a festive place to gather during the warm summer evenings. Kyle was working with the village officials and business owners to extend some areas for the Cherrywood wine-tasting experiences. He put together a generous advertising budget for the wines and wanted to have them accessible to the public in as many venues as possible.

The village proper was built up along the hillsides, giving many of the villagers a beautiful view of the sea and harbor from their homes. In the village center was a large park edged by neatly trimmed shrubs and hedges. The Ladies' Guild kept the flowers blooming for much of the year in the park beds and worked with the village council to ensure the flower funds were put to good use. Carved marble statues were located around the perimeter of the park. Highlighting the center of the park was a large multi-tier fountain spraying out into a dark-bottomed reflective pool. At night, fairy lights lit and twinkled all around the park, giving it a magical look.

Cobblestone streets ran throughout the village. The church and cemetery were located along one side of the central park. Markets, a bank, and several clothing shops made up the businesses across from the church. The village hall, barrister office, and newspaper office were located next to the Howling Pig Pub, where Evan was taking me to lunch today.

Evan drove his classic, green British convertible today, a beautiful two-seater with rich tan leather interior. As we drove out on the estate road, I saw construction crews working in a large field bordering the estate perimeter.

"What's that going to be?" I asked.

"Kyle's building a polo field to be used locally by the villagers and for training and playing grounds for our surrounding clubs. We will have a barn area, viewing pavilion, and a sit-down concession dining area. We've invited some of the local eateries and pubs to service the crowds during the matches, and of course we will be featuring our Cherrywood wines. Polo is big business here in Britain—around the world actually. Now all we have to add is a cricket field, and we'll be all set." He laughed.

"What a wonderful idea. I love how you and Kyle include the local village and township in your endeavors. You're very public minded."

"It's important, Gemma, not only for the locals but also for the future of Cherrywood Hall. You can drive all through the

UK and Ireland and see what happens to the old estates that try to stand alone. Most all fail and fall into abandoned ruin."

"I know you've met with the village council and county administrators to walk them through the competition. Have the villagers been told publicly about what you're doing? What do they think?" I asked.

"We held a public forum in the village hall the week before you arrived. The production executives put together a video overviewing the story line of *Castlewood Manor.* They briefed the audience on the rules of the competition for the final estates and took questions. For the most part, the villagers were very supportive," Evan explained.

"You'll meet Mayor Brown today during our visit. He's a big supporter and is doing whatever he can to assist us. He sees the potential economic benefits for the village as a great windfall if it happens. And I must warn you about the vicar. He's a fine man but is very star struck with all this. I think he fancies himself as an actor. No doubt he will be in line for local parts if we're selected." He laughed.

As we drove into the village, Evan first went down to the harbor area. There was not a lot of traffic on the docks and piers, other than the fisheries. "We're in a lull right now," Evan explained. "It's transition time between summer and fall. Schools have started, and the new tourists coming to see and experience a tranquil village with autumn leaves have not yet started to arrive. Give it another week, though, and you'll be amazed at the tourist traffic we have here."

"If Cherrywood is selected for the production, is the village prepared to invest in new infrastructure or businesses that might be needed to support the influx of new tourists and workers?" I asked.

"Kyle has been very involved with the businesses, village council, and county to examine exactly what changes or growth would be needed. He's drawn some expansion plans for some of the businesses that are expected to grow during production, like the pubs and restaurants and the hotels. You won't find large business chains here in Maidenford, Gemma. Most of our businesses are small or family owned. Kyle's been doing a lot of pro bono work to make sure these businesses are included and feel supported should we win. He's really a great business visionary and cares about the people as much as I do." He smiled.

Evan drove us up the hills and wound through some of the village streets. We had to slow down for several people riding their horses in the street. Stone houses with quaint little gardens lined either side.

"It reminds me of what I envision the villages look like in all the British murder mysteries I love. See, it really is true how important a set location is," I said. "I hope Maidenford doesn't have the frequent murders some of these fictional towns have. It gets pretty gory at times."

"I guess it does rather. I never thought of Maidenford in that way." Evan laughed. "I think we're a bit larger and a little more modern here than some of your fictional villages. I assure you, Maidenford is quite safe."

Evan parked the car in one of the reserved parking spots along the park. "You have your own parking space?" I asked.

"One of the privileges of being the local marquess, Gemma." He smiled.

We exited the convertible and walked around the perimeter of the park, enjoying the beauty of the gardens and statues. Evan pointed out two of them specifically. "These are memorials that were set up for the local veterans who were killed in World War

I and World War II. Plaques at the base of each list the names of those killed."

We crossed over to Saint Mary's church and walked in. I was struck by the beautiful stained-glass windows and stonework on the walls. "How pretty. It's amazing to me that these structures have been here for so long. They're older than the United States," I joked as we toured around. The vicar entered the church and warmly greeted Evan.

"Gemma, please meet Vicar Hawthorne. He's the vicar here at Saint Mary's and one of our biggest supporters for the competition," Evan said. "My cousin, Vicar, Dr. Gemma Phillips. Gemma is one of the more educated members of our family. She's just arrived from America and will be helping us win the competition for Cherrywood Hall."

"So glad to meet you, Dr. Phillips," Vicar Hawthorne said. "We're so excited about the competition. Can you imagine Maidenford being the setting of the new *Castlewood Manor* series?" he asked excitedly. "We can't wait to see who wins. By the way, isn't your mother Jillian Phillips, the actress?"

I laughed at his barrage of comments and questions. He was very enthusiastic, I had to admit.

"Yes, Vicar, my ma-ma is Jillian Phillips. She'll be so excited to know that she has a fan here."

"A longtime fan, Dr. Phillips—I've followed her career for years." Rev. Hawthorne guided Evan and me outside to see the cemetery grounds. It was beautifully kept, with symmetrical rows of graves. I looked down at the headstones. Many were hard to read, having been there for hundreds of years.

We came to a large crypt surrounded by wrought-iron gates. A carved marble angel stood over the crypt, raising its wings to the sky. "This is our Lancaster family crypt, Gemma," Evan said. "My father is buried here with his father. Aunt Pippa is here too." I saw fresh white roses and blue orchids in the vase at the door of the crypt. "Aunt Pippa's favorite," Evan said.

"I'm surprised they're not buried on the grounds of Cherrywood Hall. Isn't that what most estate owners do?"

"Our ancestors wanted to be seen and included as part of the township. The grounds and estate of Cherrywood Hall are important, of course, but the decision was made long before me to reach out and be a part of the community, not just recluses on an estate."

"How very forward-thinking. It must have been Pippa's American West Coast ideology making a mark."

"This happened even before Pippa's time. We Lancasters were not all stuffy aristocrats, you know. Even now we're trying to break new ground—in more ways than you know."

We finished our tour and said our good-byes to the vicar. We crossed over to the businesses around the park. We stopped and looked into the market, clothing stores, and tailor shop lining the street across from the church. Several of the store proprietors came out to say hello to Evan. He introduced me to them, and I soon had many invitations to take tea here in town.

We went into the village hall to meet Mayor Brown. "Very nice to meet you, Dr. Phillips. Lord Evan has told me great things about you. Thank you for coming over to help us win."

"My pleasure, Mayor Brown. We have such an amazing opportunity here with the competition; I can't wait to get my part of the efforts started." I smiled.

Evan took me next to his solicitor's office, Gowen and Gowen. Evan's family had used this firm for years to look after the Cherrywood Hall estate matters. We were met by "young" Mr. Gowen, who was in his sixties.

"Oh, I'm glad you came by, Lord Evan," Mr. Gowen said. "I have some contract items I want to discuss with you if you have a moment."

"Of course," Evan said as they left me in the lobby and went into his formal office.

I waved him on as I went to look out the window to the park. Mommies were strolling, with their children in prams, doing their daily shopping. Some riders strode by on their grand horses. I loved being here in this quaint little village. As I turned away from the window, I caught a glimpse of someone in a dark hoodie and black pants standing on the opposite corner, looking as if he or she was watching me. I went back to the window to look again, and the person was gone. Strange, I thought, but shrugged it off.

Evan soon came out of Mr. Gowen's office. "All done now," Mr. Gowen said and smiled. "Very nice to meet you, Dr. Phillips. Be sure and say hello to the old man."

"How old is 'old,' Mr. Gowen?" I asked Evan as we left.

"You'll see him at the Howling Pig. He's in his eighties, but you wouldn't know it. He has an early pint at the Pig every day. Claims it keeps him young."

We stopped for a quick visit to the village newspaper office, the *Maidenford Banner*. Evan introduced me to the editor, Mrs. Sally Prim. "Sally has been terrific working with us. She's been pulling some of the historical records and pictures for us that the production company requested early on in its evaluation."

"We want Cherrywood Hall to win, so anything you need, Lord Evan." She smiled.

"Sally and her staff will be covering our formal dinner event, along with some of the press from London," Evan said.

"I'd like to come back someday, Sally," I said. "We have many photos and documents on Cherrywood's history that Evan has pulled for me to read, but it would be great to see some of your archive documents as well."

"Anytime, Gemma, just give me a ring. I'm usually here." She laughed.

We finally made our way into the doors of the Howling Pig. I was enchanted immediately, loving the smiling faux pig's head that stood over the bar.

"That's our Patty Pig," Henry the barkeep explained. "She was my first love," he said, making the whole pub laugh.

"I'll take a pint, Henry," Evan ordered. "Give Gemma a pint of the apple cider. It's the house specialty," Evan said to me. We took our filled pints and headed over to a table by the window to wait for Charles. Sure enough, old Mr. Gowen sat a few tables down, carefully nursing his one pint for the day. Evan stopped to introduce me, and we took our seats.

"Cheers, Gemma," Evan said as we clinked our glasses. "Welcome officially to Maidenford."

Charles Linford joined us a few minutes later. He was a tall, serious young man with dark brown hair and a pale complexion. He carried a messenger bag hung across his chest that held his laptop and papers. Evan introduced us, and Charles blushed when Evan praised his previous work on the Cherrywood website.

"Thank you, Lord Evan," he said. "I appreciate the opportunity to do it. Cherrywood Hall is a major coup for me on my CV." We ordered lunch: fish and chips for Evan and me, and bangers and mash for Charles.

"I've pulled a lot of the house inventory booklets and specifications that have been compiled over the years, Charles," Evan explained as we waited for our lunch. "We also have many of the house drawings that detail new additions and repairs. We'd like to have these captured and digitized if possible. We also want to take inventory of each room's contents so that we formally document what we have. It needs to be done for future generations of Cherrywood, and if we win the competition, we could more easily market and brand some of the content for any new business ventures."

"I've done some initial archiving of Cherrywood documents," I said. "During my dissertation, I started some work to organize and archive some of the materials Evan sent to me. I've been reading some new materials as well. I'd be glad to show you what I've done—hopefully this will give you some ideas on how to design the data archive. We have also discussed taking videos of each room for a virtual web tour of the hall and grounds. I know you've been working with Kyle on the winery rooms. Are you up to taking on the whole of Cherrywood Hall too?"

"I'd be honored to do it. What an amazing project," Charles said. "I'd love to see some of your work too. I've never done anything on this scale." We cleared the table as our lunches arrived.

"How is the competition going, Lord Evan?" Charles asked, changing the topic.

"Well, we're down to the final three estates, Charles, now that Ainsley Abbey has been withdrawn," Evan explained. "Each of the estates will be hosting an event that will be part of the selection criteria. Cherrywood Hall has been slated to host a formal dinner gala."

"Tragic about Lord and Lady Hemsworth. I've heard the other estates are Longthorpe Manor and Shipley House. Do you think Cherrywood Hall can beat them?" Charles asked innocently, between bites of his bangers.

Evan smiled. "Well, we're going to try. They are some formidable competition. We have a secret weapon with Gemma, though." He winked.

Charles looked at me and smiled nervously. "I'm glad to help, Lord Evan. I'll do the best I can."

We finished up our lunch and went over a few more items. We said our good-byes and left. Charles was going to come over to Cherrywood Hall the next day to see some of the new materials and the work I did on my dissertation. As I walked, I turned to wave a last time. Charles was already on his cell phone, waving his arms and walking in circles. It looked serious.

We climbed into Evan's convertible and headed back to Cherrywood Hall. A dark fog was rolling in, making for an early evening. Evan turned on his lights as we went through the curving road back to the estate. As we rounded the last curve, a dark sports car sped into our lane, driving us off the road. Evan steered madly to avoid hitting the trees lining the side of the road. The car bumped and swerved until we finally skidded to a stop.

"Bloody hell," Evan yelled, more panicked than angry.

"Who was that?" I asked, shaken but OK.

"I have no idea. Did you see the make of the car? I wasn't really paying attention until it came right at us," Evan said.

"Not really. It was small. I'm not familiar with car models here, but it looked like a dark coupe, maybe British or German?" I suggested. I hadn't gotten a clear look, but I would have sworn the driver was cloaked in a dark hoodie.

We were able to back the convertible out of the woods and climbed onto the road leading to Cherrywood Hall. As we pulled in front of the hall, we saw Kyle walking up to the house. Evan waved at him and told him to meet us in the sitting room. "I need a drink after that," he said.

Kyle met us in the sitting room and poured himself a whiskey. "It's five o'clock somewhere, right?" he teased. He then saw that we were a bit shaken. "What happened?"

"Some idiot just ran us off the road—deliberately. We could have been killed. I know they saw us. It was no accident."

"Did you see anyone or recognize the car?"

"No. Gemma thinks it looked like a British or German dark coupe."

"The driver was wearing a hoodie. I don't think they wanted to be seen," I said.

"Well, there's not many of those types of cars around here. It was probably just a fluke or maybe a teenage kid or weirdo pranking. Very stupid," Kyle said. "I'll have Constable Jones keep a lookout, though, just in case."

Who was the person in the hoodie watching me and why? Was that who was driving the car? I shivered at the thought of anyone purposely wanting to harm us. Maybe Maidenford village wasn't as innocent as it seemed.

8

Danger on the Sea Path

Evan, Kyle, and I met for breakfast early the next day. We wanted to take Kyle up to the closet room areas and discuss what needed to be done to preserve and showcase the garments. Today our time together was limited. Kyle had meetings with the Cherrywood wine distributors, and Evan was going to London this afternoon to meet with the Rosehill Production executives. I was going to meet Charles in the early afternoon to go over some of the new materials we wanted to include in the archive and film projects.

We went upstairs to the closet rooms, where Kyle closely examined the room dimensions and contents. "Do you have any of the drawings for these specific rooms?"

"We do, but they're quite old and haven't been updated. I don't know how accurate they are," Evan said.

Kyle continued the examination around the room, feeling the paneling on the walls and knocking on them. "What are you doing?" I asked.

"Well, I'm trying to listen to see if there's a solid wall or perhaps another room or corridor on the other side. Listen to this." He knocked on one section of wall and then another. There was a definite difference in the sound of his knocking. "If I had to guess, I believe there is some type of space behind this wall. It sounds hollow. If it is a room, there is probably a hidden way to get in, like the panel in the library that leads to the servant corridor."

"How do we find that?" I asked.

"Well, we could get incredibly lucky and touch the right panel. I think an inspection camera might save us some time, though. I just have to drill a few holes around the room and insert the camera probe to see what is behind the walls. I can use a stud finder as well to determine the room structure."

"What would you suggest we do with the closet rooms?" Evan asked. "Right now they're just four interior rooms with no special protection. Gemma thinks many of the garments are very valuable, if not priceless. High-quality gems adorn many of the garments. Should we think of expanding the vault?"

"Unless you're really set on keeping the four rooms separate, I'd suggest combining the rooms into one and adding in some climate-control features for the preservation. We can construct some built-ins for more storage space as well as displays in whatever configuration you want. Room access can also be controlled for the valuables, so no, we wouldn't necessarily have to expand the vault. I'll bring some of my tools up here in the next few days to see what we have to work with and put some drawings together for you to see the options. Once you choose what you want, my construction team should be able to get things built fairly quickly."

"I like the idea of one giant room," I said. "The built-ins would be great for the accessories and shoes. I'd like some glass-enclosed cases too for display of some of the more fragile and valuable items, if possible. I can't wait to see what's behind the walls. We may find Pippa's collection and who knows what."

"Sounds great, Kyle," Evan said. "Let us know what you find and come up with. I'll let you and Gemma figure out what's best. Right now, though, I need to leave for the drive to London."

Kyle took some pictures and made a few more notes. When he finished, I walked him to the front entrance. "Are you going to be around this evening? Evan will probably be in London until late. I'd like some company if you have time."

"You would? My meetings should end by early evening. I'll come up to the hall after we finish. Maybe we can take that swim." He smiled.

Charles arrived at Cherrywood promptly at one. I took him into the library to show him the house charts and documents that we wanted to include in the data archive. I pulled out my laptop and showed him how I had deployed some of the video and multimedia techniques to bring my dissertation research to life with pictures, videos, and animations. Many were actual clips from historical Cherrywood films that Evan had let me use for my research.

"I was thinking we'd make a virtual tour of the rooms here at Cherrywood Hall to allow visitors to see and experience some of the grander rooms in the hall and how they were used. We could highlight specific paintings or architectural details with close-ups and narration. What do you think?"

"I like the idea. We can take a video tour of the rooms using a roving camera stand. I can pan in on the room contents, so we kill two birds with one stone: one clip for the inventory archive and one for the visitor website. It should be easy to splice in the historical pictures and films with the video tour footage. I can totally work this." He smiled.

"I'm glad you're so confident. Let me know what you're going to need with respect to cameras, video equipment, and computers. Evan has generously offered to get any equipment and help we need for this. I'll ask Evan and Kyle to prioritize any areas they want to feature on the website as well. It's going to be quite a production in itself, so let's make sure we set it up right the first time."

After Charles left, I decided to go back up to the closet rooms. I took my laptop and camera with me to take pictures and notes. In the large closet room, I looked at each of the dresses and gowns in the garment bags. The beading, sequins, and materials were exquisite. I imagined myself wearing these garments at the lavish parties and dinners held here at the estate. In the shoe closet, I couldn't resist trying on some of the shoes and boots that looked to be my size. To my delight, I was able to wear many of them.

"Must be the Lancaster genes." I smiled. I had some ideas of how I wanted to tackle this very special inventory to highlight the advantage of Cherrywood Hall to the production company. The thoughts of a major fashion show swam through my head.

"The villagers could model, and we could film it for the website," I said to myself, thinking of the possibilities. I looked at my watch and saw it was just past four. I wanted to take a walk outside before dark to get some exercise and fresh air. And I was hoping to spend some time with Kyle this evening. I went downstairs to grab my jacket and hat and headed out.

I walked around the side of the hall and headed down to the sea path where Kyle and I had ridden a few days before. It was another cloudy day, but the view of the sea made up for the gloom of the clouds. The sea path was paved in decomposed granite. The long path took the walker or rider along the cliffside down a swerving, back-and-forth journey. There were several resting stops along the way, with benches to stop and look at the beautiful views. When you reached the woods, the path turned upward, and you had the choice of continuing out on the grounds, as Kyle and I had done before, or head back to the hall.

I was glad I had decided to take my shearling coat for the walk. The winds were picking up quite a bit as I made my way around the path. I pulled on my leather gloves. "Should have brought a flashlight," I muttered to myself.

I pressed on and thought about the many walks that had been taken down this path. I gasped as a fox zigged and zagged erratically across the path in front of me, running up into the woods. "Better run, little fellow," I said, glad that we would be hosting the formal dinner gala rather than the hunt. I decided to sit for a while on the last bench area before making my way back up to the hall.

The North Sea waves were cresting whitecaps and crashing against the cliffsides with more frequency. I sat for a long time, mesmerized by the waves and thinking of all the wonderful treasures I had seen today in the closet rooms. I couldn't wait to see what designs Kyle would come up with to showcase some of the more spectacular pieces.

The chill of the air started to get to me, so I decided to head back. It was turning darker and colder by the minute, and I

cursed myself again for not bringing a flashlight. I hadn't realized how steep the path was uphill. "The horse was doing all the
work last time," I lamented.

I heard some branches crunching behind me.

"Is anyone there?" I turned and shouted against the wind. I
squinted to see down the path, but the wind was blowing so hard
that it was tough to focus. No one answered my call. I shook myself and decided to continue up the pathway. I was getting a little
spooked and just wanted to be back inside Cherrywood.

It was now pitch-black outside. My progress up the path was
much slower now because I couldn't see where I was going. I
struggled to walk against the wind for another twenty minutes
or so, not sure of the distance I was covering. I heard another
crunch of leaves and sticks and turned around again.

"Is that you, Mr. Fox?" I asked, trying to calm my nerves and
see if I could see anything.

Once again, nothing. I turned to start back up the hill
when I was tackled hard, directly at my knees. The force threw
me totally off guard, and the next thing I knew, I was half
flying, half skidding down the steep hillside in between the
curves of the pathway. I picked up more and more speed and
was heading down to the edge of the cliff. I grabbed at anything I could find, but my momentum was so great, nothing I
did manage to catch held.

"Grab something, Gemma," I yelled to myself as I continued
to plummet. It felt like I slid a hundred feet, and the edge of the
cliff was fast approaching. I took one last tumble and finally was
able to grab a tree root that held. My heart was racing. I tried
to look up and down to see where I was and if there was any secure footing to be found. The root I was holding gave way a little
bit at a time. I stayed put, trying to be as still as I could. I was

thoroughly chilled. My hat was gone, and my jeans and gloves were ripped to shreds.

I tried to huddle down closer to the earth, using every climbing skill I could think of. I raised my head every now and again to shout, "Help!" But with the wind, I doubted anyone would hear me. My fingers were growing numb, holding on to the tree root. I didn't know how much longer I could hang on, but I knew it would not be good to get panicked.

"Hold on, Gemma," I heard, a soft voice whispering to me. By now the shock of the fall was setting in, and I was starting to lose consciousness. I tried to see who was whispering to me, but all I saw was darkness.

"Help!" I screamed again. I sank my head back to the ground and started to cry.

"Hold on, Gemma," the voice whispered to me again.

My fingers were beginning to slip, and I could feel my body start to move again. The branch cracked in half, splintering at its roots. My body slipped from the hillside and was once again airborne, heading to the cliff.

"Gemma!" I heard my name being called loudly. I tried to turn my head, but I was frozen, until I fell into Kyle's arms, fainting dead away.

Kyle carried my wilted body over to the four-wheeled Gator utility vehicle he had driven on the path. He carefully placed me in the back seat and covered me with some blankets.

"Hold on, Gemma," he whispered to me. "We'll be back at Cherrywood in a just a few minutes." He started the Gator, and we climbed bumpily up the path. My body ached terribly from the fall, but I thought I could move everything. I had scrapes and cuts, and for sure some bruises would materialize. I was still drifting in and out. The cold air had chilled me to the bone.

Kyle pulled up in front of the house and lifted me out of the back seat. Bridges and Mrs. Smythe were waiting at the front door, looking concerned.

"I found her," Kyle told them as he carried me inside. "Let's get her to her room. Bridges, can you please have some whiskey and tea brought up, and perhaps some soup?"

Mrs. Smythe led the way up the staircase. Kyle followed, carrying me. Bridges headed off to the kitchen to get the drinks and food. Once in my room, Kyle placed me on my bed, where he and Mrs. Smythe removed my torn and tattered clothing. Kyle examined me to see if there were any broken bones.

"I think I'm OK," I whispered, looking into his eyes.

"You've had a bad fall, and you're chilled to the bone. Let's get you washed up and into some warm clothes," he said.

I was able to sit up in bed as they gently washed my scrapes and cuts. I moaned a little when Kyle's hands touched the lace of my bra and panties, wishing that he was not seeing me for the first time all cut and bruised. Mrs. Smythe brought over my cozy terry robe and slipped it over me. Bridges discreetly knocked on the door and was summoned in. He wheeled in a cart carrying whiskey, a pot of hot tea, and a soup terrine.

Mrs. Smythe brushed the knots and debris from my hair as Bridges and Kyle arranged the cart tray in front of the chairs by the fireplace. Bridges stoked the fire and soon had its raging warmth filling the room. Kyle carefully picked me up and sat me down in the chair closest to the fire.

"Here, drink this first." He handed me a glass of whiskey. "That's all, Mrs. Smythe and Bridges," he commanded. "When Lord Evan arrives, have him come up here, please. I'll sit with Gemma for now." Kyle poured himself a whiskey as Mrs. Smythe and Bridges left the room. He pulled the other chair next to mine and sat down.

"What happened, Gemma? Do you remember?" he asked, gently moving a fallen strand of hair from my face. "If I hadn't arrived when I did—"

"I don't know, Kyle," I whispered. "I was heading back to Cherrywood Hall on the path. I kept hearing noises, like someone was following me. At first I thought it was a fox I had seen earlier. It was hard pushing against the wind on the trail, and I couldn't see in the dark. I didn't bring a flashlight. Someone clipped me on the knees, and I went falling down. It was a deliberate push. Someone wanted me down that cliff. How did you end up finding me?" I asked, sipping my whiskey.

"I was just leaving the winery and heading up to Cherrywood to see you. I wanted to take you up on your offer to visit," he said, smiling at me. "I heard a car squealing off on the drive. I ran up the hill and saw a small dark car swerving around. Whoever was here was leaving in a hurry. I went to the hall to ask for you, but Bridges told me you had gone out for a walk on the sea path earlier. He was worried you hadn't returned yet. I went to the barn to get the Gator to go look for you." He took my whiskey glass and handed me a bowl of split-pea soup with a Parmesan crostino floating on top.

"Thank you." I smiled. The soup smelled delicious, and I tucked in, loving the creamy warmth.

"I'd driven down the sea path right as it turned by the forest," he explained. "Some rocks and debris were falling in front of the Gator. I stopped and looked up, and there you were tumbling down toward me. I was just able to catch you." He smiled, touching my hair once more. "And here we are. How are you feeling now?"

I looked up from my soup bowl. "Much better now. I think the whiskey and soup are kicking in." I tried to smile. "Could I have my whiskey back?"

"Of course," Kyle said, handing me my glass. "Sip slowly. It slips up on you, as we know."

"After today's events, I don't quite care. Can anyone get on to the estate, Kyle?"

"Well, right now we have a lot of workers helping on the polo field construction as well as the winery. They have the codes to enter into the gate when they arrive and leave. I suppose the gate could have been left open or malfunctioned."

"Did you recognize the car that you saw?"

"No, but I really couldn't see. They were driving with their headlights turned off. I could only see the taillights when they braked. It looked like a sports car of some type, but I couldn't tell the make."

Evan knocked softly and came into the room. "Hey, Gemma," he said, coming over to me and kissing my forehead. "What happened, love?" he asked, looking up at Kyle worriedly. Evan pulled up a third chair and sat with us. Kyle poured him a whiskey, and we recounted the story of what had happened.

"I can't believe it," Evan said angrily. "We've never had a problem here at Cherrywood. And why would they attack Gemma?"

"There's more," Kyle said. "I didn't get a good look at the car that raced out, but I'm pretty sure it was a small sports car—a dark sports car."

"Like the one that tried to run us off the road? This is getting worse and worse."

"I'll have the police come over in the morning to look for tire tracks on the road to see if we can nail down the type of car. I'll also walk them around the sea path to look for anything out of the ordinary. We'll find them," Kyle said, trying to reassure us.

"Do you think it's this damn competition?" Evan asked. "I'd rather pull out—I don't want anyone to get hurt. The Hemsworths have already died. We don't need to be next."

"We don't know that, Evan," I said. "The car running us off the road could have just been a fluke accident, someone checking their cell or texting. As for me being pushed, well, I don't know. Kyle said the workers have codes to the gate. Maybe it was just some kids who were drinking or..." My voice just drifted off. I didn't know what to think. I was afraid to think these were deliberate attacks.

"Let's see what the police find out tomorrow," Kyle said. "I'll put some new measures in place for entering and leaving the estate and change the gate access code for the workers."

"How was your meeting with the production execs, Evan?" I asked, wanting to change the subject.

"They're still reeling from the loss of Ainsley Abbey. The good news is that the company wants us to come to London on Saturday and Sunday. They have us booked at the Beauchamp. We're going to meet the other competitors and the selection team."

"Oh, I can't wait. I've heard so much about these people. I can't wait to meet them," I said excitedly.

"I'm sure they're curious to meet you as well, Gemma. I don't think they were expecting an American in their midst. I'll have Bates drive us to the Beauchamp Saturday morning in the Royale limo. They have a meet-and-greet session planned for us on Saturday afternoon. They also want to go over some of the final details for our respective events. Saturday evening they are hosting a dinner for us with some of the actors and selection committee members. It's going to be quite the affair, I've been told, so, Gemma, feel free to wear any of the Lancaster jewels you want. We can go down to the vault tomorrow to pick out some things."

"Yes," I said loudly and smiled. It was amazing how the thought of wearing magnificent jewels made my injuries subside. "I'll make sure to do the Lancaster ladies proud."

"I have no doubt of that, cousin," Evan said. "Look, it's getting late, and you need to rest. I'm afraid you're going to be sore tomorrow." He came over to kiss my forehead.

"I'll get up," I said, wobbling to my feet. Kyle walked behind me.

"Good night, Gemma," Evan said, nodding to Kyle.

"I'll let myself out, Evan. I'll see you in the morning," Kyle said. He closed the bedroom door once Evan left.

He walked over and lifted me in his arms. He carried me over to the chair and sat me in his lap, holding me softly. He ran his fingers through my hair and gently outlined my face. We sat looking at each other in the firelight of the room. I closed my eyes as he continued running his fingers through my hair. Kyle softly kissed my closed eyelids. I lifted my wet lips to his, wanting to kiss him. He put his finger between our lips.

"Not yet, Gemma," he whispered. "I want to kiss you properly, but you're sore tonight. Later," he said, kissing my eyelids again.

I sat in Kyle's lap, feeling his arms around me. I snuggled my face near his neck, smelling his warmth. We sat in each other's arms until I fell asleep. I felt Kyle lift me and carry me over to my bed. He drew back the covers and gently placed me between them, taking off my robe and leaving me in my lace underwear with my hair spread out over the pillowcase. He traced his finger over my bra, barely touching me.

"I like your lace." I tried to push up, responding to his touch. I wanted to kiss him, badly. "I see some things weren't hurt." He smiled, gently pushing me back down on the pillow.

"Stay with me, Kyle, until I fall asleep," I said softly. He lay down by my side, making sure the thick comforter was placed between us. He kept stroking my hair until I was starting to finally nod off.

"Kyle, did you have Mrs. Smythe with you when you found me?"

"No, it was just me," he answered. I was really starting to fade out. I felt Kyle get out of bed and kiss me gently on my forehead.

"Sleep tight, Gemma," he whispered, slipping out of my room.

I rolled over to the side of bed where he had lain. I wanted to breathe the last smell of him before I slept for the night. A nagging question kept bubbling up. I knew I had heard a woman's voice telling me, "Hold on, Gemma," as I hung on to the hillside. In my confusion, I thought it had been Mrs. Smythe, there with Kyle. But if it wasn't her...then who? I finally drifted off to sleep for good, smiling at the thought of Kyle's warm hands. The fire shifted, and some sparks flew against the fire screen. If I had been awake, I would have seen a warm twinkle appear on Pippa's face in the painting over the fireplace.

9

Fresh Change of Scene

woke the next morning sore from head to toe. My legs had taken the brunt of my fall. There were cuts and scrapes where my jeans had torn. A few bruises were starting to form. My knees hurt from where I'd been clipped, but all in all I was OK. I was going to be moving slower than usual. Mrs. Smythe had brought a breakfast tray into my room, so I could take my time this morning. The tray was loaded with lots of goodies, including my favorites, sautéed mushrooms and grilled tomatoes. I tucked into the food. I had only eaten a half bowl of soup and a glass of whiskey last evening. I blushed thinking about last night, being held in Kyle's arms. We had been so close to kissing each other. He was so warm and enchanting. He was definitely starting to open my broken heart.

When I was through with breakfast, I rang for Mrs. Smythe. She saw my bruised legs and drew me a nice hot bath in the soaking tub. I sank into the tub, fully enjoying the warmth of the water against my battered body. I soaked for almost an hour and finally emerged a somewhat new woman, still sore but definitely refreshed.

"Lord Evan and Mr. Kyle are having tea and a light lunch in the conservatory in a half hour, Miss Gemma. They wanted me to tell you to join them if you felt well enough," Mrs. Smythe said, laying out my clothes options for today. "I didn't know exactly what you might want to wear, but hopefully some of these things will do."

"Yes, thank you so much, Mrs. Smythe. I'm feeling much better now after the wonderful bath you drew for me. I can take it from here. Thanks so much for your help and kindness today."

I wanted to get downstairs and see if Evan and Kyle had learned anything this morning from the police search around the grounds. I pulled on the black jeggings, white shirt covered with a black cashmere sweater, and my black boots that Mrs. Smythe had laid out for me. I braided my hair in a single braid down my back and tied a cravat scarf around my neck. I gave myself a last glance and slowly made my way downstairs to the conservatory.

It took me a bit longer than I had planned to walk down the grand staircase and through the dining room to the conservatory. I took a grateful seat at a table overlooking the waterfall and helped myself to a nice strong cup of tea.

Kyle and Evan walked in just a few minutes later, smiling when they saw that I was back to the living. They both were dressed in turtlenecks, along with riding pants tucked into their leather boots. Kyle's thick hair was curled just a little from the wetness of the fog outside. Evan kissed my cheek. Kyle sweetly pinched my chin with his fingers.

"There's my girl," he said, smiling. They sat down at the table and helped themselves to a cup of tea.

"Tell me what's going on," I demanded. "Have the police found anything?"

"Unfortunately, we're socked in this morning," Evan said. "It's pea soup outside. Hard to see more than a few feet in front of you."

"I did take them to the estate road to show them a few areas that look suspicious where the car had swerved when it was racing out," Kyle said. "I rode Sir Lad along the road earlier to see if I could find anything. There were several tread marks in the road; I think they may be able to get some tire tracks. That would at least narrow down the type of sports car we're looking for. I've changed the access codes for the workers as well and given strict instructions to the managers that no access is permitted after work hours unless permission is given. They will keep a close eye on things from here out."

"Constable Jones said he would let us know as soon as they were able to gain any details," Evan said. "I've told him to contact the county authorities as well to let them know of our road attack. Your attack last evening may or may not be connected, but I want them to understand what we've been exposed to. They are investigating the Hemsworths' deaths as well, even though it has been ruled an accident at this time. Our attacks may or may not be related, but since we were both in this competition, I felt they should be made aware. I want to talk with the production executives when we're in London as well. They need to know and up security."

"It's so hard to believe these attacks are related, just because of this competition," I said. "I would have never believed this would be so cutthroat, much less involve deadly violence. Is there anyone in the village or county who is against this competition? So much to sabotage it?"

"There are always going to be factions that are against anything that involves commercialism, and I suppose some of them could use violence. I haven't had any complaints registered that I know of. Have you, Kyle?" Evan asked.

"No, I haven't heard anything either, and I've been working very closely with the businesses and local government officials for months now. Everyone is quite excited at the prospect of their businesses growing and the new potential for the village. The only negative comments I've gotten are when I couldn't guarantee some of the locals that they would be cast in the *Castlewood Manor* series if we are selected. I never knew so many people wanted to be actors." He laughed. "Vicar is the worst!"

"Gemma and I could see that from our visit to Maidenford the other day." Evan smiled. "I'm glad you're stepping up security around the grounds. I'd feel better if we had some folks assigned to the hall too, Kyle. I don't want us to feel as if we're being watched at all times, but for now I'd rather be safe than sorry."

"That's being taken care of as we speak, Evan. I've also expedited some enhancements to the security system that's in the hall. Big brother will be watching—discreetly, of course," Kyle said, smiling at me.

Bridges brought in a light lunch, which included a tureen of watercress soup, ham and fish tea sandwiches, and fresh-out-of-the-oven strawberry scones with cream. Our appetites didn't appear to suffer from all the talk of intruders and security. The yummies on the trays soon disappeared, and we sat back to enjoy our fullness and listen to the water rushing down the falls.

"So what do you feel like doing this afternoon?" Evan asked as he finished his tea, breaking our little food coma.

"Well, I for one would like to go to the vault," I said cheerily, trying to keep up our newly refreshed spirits. "I have some absolutely fabulous outfits picked out for our trip to London tomorrow, Evan, and I want to dazzle our competitors with the Lancaster family gems."

"Gemma, you can pick anything you desire." Evan smiled.

"You're going to dazzle them with or without diamonds, Gemma. Knowing our elite British girls, you are going to stand out quite a bit," Kyle said.

"True," I said kiddingly, "but I am the only American participating in this competition. I'm not so sure how that's going to go down with your lovely British aristocratic families."

"You two have fun choosing your baubles. I'm going to go out to check up on my security team and our police friends," Kyle said, finishing his tea. "I'll see you both later today."

Evan and I made our way down to the corner jewel vault. I was still pretty achy from my fall, but the walking was doing me good. As we entered the vault, my spirits immediately perked up once I saw the sparkling jewelry.

I had decided to wear a sage-green sweater dress tomorrow to London for our meet-and-greet session. Evan picked out a stunning emerald ring for me to complement the green of the dress. For the evening dinner, I was wearing an elegant evening gown, this one a shimmering nude with faux fur collar. I picked some diamond drop earrings and bracelet for this ensemble.

"This should do it." I smiled as we gathered my choices in a Francois travel jewelry case and headed back upstairs. I was starting to hurt a bit and decided to go back to my room to rest and pack. I called for Mrs. Smythe's assistance to help pack my clothes for our London trip. I opened the jewelry case to show her the gems I had picked to go with the evening dresses.

"They're lovely, Miss Gemma," she said. "You'll do us proud." We spent the next hour pulling shoes, purses, and accessories for the evening outfits and figuring out my daywear. Mrs. Smythe had the packing well under control and insisted that I sit and rest as she finished up.

I chose the chair closest to the fire, with my feet propped up on a leopard print ottoman. I had pulled out one of Pippa's early diaries to read to get her perspective on living and managing the events at Cherrywood Hall. Even in the early days, Pippa was planning improvements for Cherrywood: "Must speak with Charles about opening up the grand hall with a terrace addition. We could do some spectacular fireworks displays that everyone could enjoy after a dinner party."

She was also speaking her mind about some of her husband's friends: "Some of the young dukes and earls are behaving most inappropriately. Must speak with Charles and insist on no overnight stays by their so-called lady friends. Cherrywood Hall is not a brothel! And I do not care if one is a duke or earl or prince."

The word *prince* was underlined and upped my curiosity. Who was this wayward prince who'd obviously gotten under Pippa's skin?

"Poor Charles." I smiled. I had a feeling Pippa "spoke" to him quite often.

Her next entry made me a bit sad:

> Just received a nice long letter from Lillian. I'm so proud of her. She's just entering medical

school. Papa, of course, is not totally in favor
of this path, but Lillian has stood her ground.
Imagine having a doctor in the family, and a female at that! My only wish is that we could live
close to each other. It's always been my dream that
we remain close. We must promise to always cor-
respond and spend what time we can together, for
I am certain she will remain in America. Sweet
wishes, my dear sister...

I ran my fingers over this sweet entry, trying to picture Pippa
and Lillian as young women, each venturing into totally un-
known paths, yet obviously loving each other very much.

I drifted off for a nap, made cozy by the warmth of the fire.
I woke to find a wool blanket had been pulled over me. To my
delight, I saw Kyle sitting in the chair opposite me. His eyes were
closed, and his head was leaned on his upright arm propped up
by the side of the chair. His long legs stretched out across the
floor, the reflection of the fire dancing off the glistening surface
of his leather riding boots. He smiled and looked up when he
heard me stirring.

"Hey," I said, smiling groggily. "What are you doing here?"

"Just came up to take you to dinner." Kyle smiled, getting up
to stretch. "You were still asleep, so I decided to wait for you to
wake up. I drifted off myself. I've been out all day in the cold fog.
Your fire felt great."

"Did the police find anything else from this morning?" I asked.

"Not a whole lot. They did lift the tire tracks for prints and
sent them off to the crime lab. We found a few footprints that
could have come from your attacker, but the prints were from
British Wellies unfortunately. About a million people have those

boots, hundreds in this area alone. We'll find them, Gemma," he said reassuringly.

"So where are we going for dinner?" I asked, getting up to stretch myself. I wobbled as I stood, and Kyle grabbed my arm to help steady me.

"Easy now. Evan and I didn't want to have you move too far. We're having pizza over in his room tonight." He laughed. "Evan is a pizza aficionado, or at least he thinks he is. Chef Karl has prepared some of his favorites. If we're lucky, the fog will have broken enough tonight for us to take a look through his telescope. We may see some stars tonight."

We walked over to Evan's room and found a buffet table had been set up with the pizza creations. Evan had chilled some of the Cherrywood sparkling wine and offered us both glasses. We took our seats by the fireplace, and Bridges served us plates filled with the tasty slices.

"This is almost Californian American—sparkling wine and pizza. I am impressed," I said, snuggling into a comfortable armchair with an ottoman to stretch my legs.

Thai chicken pizza with cilantro pesto, barbecued chipotle rib pizza with arugula garnee, and a quarto cheese pizza with sliced tomatoes made up our selections. The crusts were thin and crunchy, allowing the pizza fillings to stand out.

"Yummy," I said, pulling a long string of cheese into my mouth.

"See, my time in America paid off." Evan smiled. "I do like American pizza. You tend to up the taste levels quite a bit from what we know here traditionally. Chef Karl is a wizard with concocting new taste combinations."

There wasn't a lot of conversation as we ate. We each enjoyed savoring the different slices and ended up eating the buffet plates clean. It was good to be relaxed tonight, given the circumstances of the past twenty-four hours. Another wonderful food coma enveloped us.

"I told Gemma about the tire tracks and finding the footprints in the area where she was attacked." Kyle stood and refilled our wineglasses. "I also found some footprints around the perimeter of the hall, specifically where some of the security cameras were installed. Unfortunately, they were wearing Wellies too, so we aren't going to be able to identify them."

"Do you think someone was trying to disable the cameras, Kyle? Were you able to get video of them with the cameras?" I asked.

"Could be, although there didn't seem to be any physical damage that I could see. It was almost as if someone was more interested in studying how the cameras were physically networked. Unfortunately, these were new cameras that were just installed, so they weren't operational. If someone is up to no good with this competition and wanted to sabotage us, hacking into our security network would give them access to what was going on in and around the hall. If they could track us inside and out, that would open up a whole new category of sinister things they could plan. I've informed the police so that they have this added information for their investigation."

"I never thought about a cyberattack. Kyle, can they really hack into our security system? We definitely need to let the police know about this, and I will speak with the production executives when we're in London as well. I want to know if the other estates are experiencing anything similar to what we have been exposed to the past few days. If they have not, why not?" Evan said suspiciously.

"I doubt the other estates have the infrastructure we have here at Cherrywood," Kyle said. "I know Longthorpe Manor doesn't. I'm putting some extra measures and manpower in place. I've also placed some calls in to friends who work at the Biz." Kyle smiled knowingly at Evan. "I wanted to get their input on some technology we might want to consider."

"What biz?" I asked innocently.

"*The Biz*, my dear, is how the royals refer to their business. Kyle, fortunately for us, has some excellent connections that he won't even disclose to me," Evan explained.

"Actually, I work with them quite a bit. One never knows when a royal will attend a polo event or party. Security measures have become quite common at our British estates these days, and we all are being enticed to up our capabilities. I'm leading a task force to ensure that the technologies used are not demeaning to these old homes. We have to live with all kinds of rulings and guidelines for any other architectural change we make. I want to make sure the security measures are no different. Must keep up our appearances, and heaven forbid, we can't have security cameras spilling out into film productions supposedly set in the eighteen or nineteen hundreds!"

"Wow. I'm amazed at all the talents you two have. Community relations, security, new business ventures, the 'royals'...I really don't know what I can add here, gentlemen. You surprise me at every turn," I said.

"Ah, but see, cousin, you add in a much-needed feminine touch to our efforts, not to mention a bright American point of view. You can shake up our staid British thinking, Gemma. I would have never thought of the ideas you have with the filming and archive. And who knew about the clothes in the closet rooms? You have a multitude of ideas I would have never even thought of."

"Speaking of which, I have some drawings for the closet revisions, if you'd like to see some of them. They're still a work in progress, but I can show you some of my initial thoughts," Kyle said as he pulled out his tablet and started it up. He sat down between Evan and me and showed us the screen. He pulled up some of the designs that would combine the four rooms into one. He filled the room with glassed-in cases that had humidity and climate control for the more delicate and valuable garments. With his design, one could walk around the cases and get a front and back view. Shelving around the perimeter would highlight and showcase the shoes and accessories that were currently stuffed into boxes. The lighting could be switched to highlight a specific garment, or combinations making for a spectacular, one-of-a-kind viewing experience.

"We could open this part of the floor up to the public once we get the cases and systems installed," Kyle explained. "I'm sure there would be a lot of people who would love to see the fashions, especially if we are selected for the series."

"Kyle, these designs are wonderful. I know everyone will want to see the collections. I'm sure the wardrobe designers, seamstresses, and tailors would love to have this kind of access. I'd love to film the construction of this for the archive and room footage. It will be exciting to include this on the Cherrywood Hall website too for everyone to get to see these fashions. Many are one-of-a-kind garments. Are you going to be able to secure this area, though? I don't want to give any ideas to anyone who has negative intentions, especially with what's been going on."

"These rooms will be access controlled if we invite the public in, much like the jewel vault. Since I'm enhancing the security system, it won't be that much to include this in the construction. Don't worry, Evan. The budget won't be that affected." Kyle laughed.

"I was starting to worry there a bit, chap. But let's do it right, as I know you'll do. I want to minimize our chances of catastrophe if we can." Evan stood to look out the French doors opening to his balcony. "Hey, I think the fog has broken. Do you all want to go out and see some stars?"

Kyle pulled a wool wrap from one of the storage shelves in Evan's wardrobe and put it around my shoulders as we made our way out onto Evan's balcony. The fog had broken, and we could see several pockets of bright shining stars through the clouds. It was still quite chilly, and Evan lighted a tower gas heater standing in one of the corners to ward off the chill.

Evan made some adjustments to his telescope and invited us over to take a look. He pointed out some of the more significant stars he knew as we took turns looking through his telescope. "That's one of the benefits of living out here in the countryside. The stars are quite bright, and we don't have any competing city lights. I've always loved looking at them and thinking of the nights I've spent in Africa doing the same. The skies are quite different in the two hemispheres, but I've enjoyed learning each of the skies over the years. The African skies can be spectacular. I miss them," Evan said whimsically.

I looked at my cousin and knew he was thinking about more things than just stars. He hadn't opened up to me yet about his love interest. I gave him a hug around the waist. The clouds were almost clear now, and the sky above was lit with stars and a quarter moon. A shining blaze appeared right overhead.

"Look, a shooting star!" I gushed, pointing at the falling light.

"Make a wish, Gemma." Kyle smiled.

I closed my eyes and made a wish, opening them to see Kyle's smiling face looking at me. I was hoping he could read my mind.

10

Sizing Up the Competition

We left Cherrywood the next morning at ten o'clock. Bates, Evan's chauffer, was driving us to London in the Royale limousine. It was one of Evan's pride and joys. It was a 1958 Silvertron and had belonged to his grandfather. Bates was to be commended for its care. At almost sixty years old, it was still beautiful. The seats were covered in gray leather that had melted to soft perfection. Burl walnut trimmed the doors and accessories. It was plenty spacious enough for us to sit back and relax for the drive to the Beauchamp hotel.

We wanted to get to the Beauchamp early enough to get to our suites and freshen up before we met the competitors at the meet and greet at two o'clock. Mrs. Smythe had left earlier that morning, taking our luggage up to the Beauchamp. I had protested her having to come up on her weekend. The Beauchamp was providing us with maid and valet services. She insisted, though, being concerned that I was not quite 100 percent recovered from my injuries. I felt honored and a little relieved that she had wanted to take care of me.

We headed off, and I looked at the invitation that Rosehill Productions had sent to us. The invitees were listed at the top of the invite:

> Longthorpe Manor—Lord Frederick Paunchley, Count of Woodley; the Honorable Lady Jane Paunchley; Miss Althea Jones
> Cherrywood Hall—Lord Evan Lancaster, Marquess of Kentshire; Dr. Gemma Phillips; Mr. Kyle Williams
> Shipley House—Lord James Hampton, Earl of Wooster; the Honorable Francis Hampton; Mr. Christopher Madden

"So who can tell me more about our competitors?" I asked, looking at Evan and Kyle.

"Longthorpe Manor is a huge house nestled on over three thousand acres of wooded land southwest of London," Evan began. "Lord Paunchley is nearing seventy years old, and his daughter, Jane, is set to inherit the estate as countess upon his passing, a change to the primogeniture laws of the past. Jane is my age, as Mother said the other night. She is an accomplished rider and was an alternate for the British equestrian team in the 2012 London Games. I believe the estate is fairly well maintained. However, Jane's primary focus is horses, not the care of an estate. I'm not sure how much Lord Paunchley is going to be able to do in the competition. He had a mild heart attack last year and is still recovering. Althea Jones is Jane's cousin, I believe. I don't know her background, but I am fairly certain she doesn't have any experience with the estate."

"She's not a titled relation," Kyle said. "I met her once when I was going out with Jane. She's rather shy and not athletic at all, which used to upset Jane, who expected everyone to be able to ride and jump. I'm surprised she is helping them with the competition. It doesn't seem her sort of thing."

"Why do the Paunchleys want to participate in the competition? Do they support the local community like you do? Do they support the arts?" I asked.

"I would expect the Paunchleys' incentive is more monetary. As I said, Jane's focus is horses, and the ones she admires most cost a lot of money. She does participate in several polo clubs and events, but I never saw her as a community maven when I was with her. Longthorpe Manor is maintained, but they are doing no business expansions, and I would doubt they fund many architectural or technical improvements for their estate. You need to realize that just keeping up with normal maintenance on these estates is ultimately a losing proposition—and a very expensive one at that. There will always be something to be fixed if you don't make a concerted effort to get ahead of the curve."

"Did you ever go to Francis's estate when you were in school with Christopher?" Evan asked. "I've heard Shipley House has an extensive garden area and a magnificent waterfall fountain that spans the hillside in back of the house. It's been pictured in magazines globally and is a perfect choice for the formal tea and garden tour."

"I did go up a few times with Christopher while we were in the architecture program. Francis preferred that he come to the estate as much as possible. They loved to throw some extravagant parties that lasted for days. They were known for giving a good time, and most of their guests were the who's who of the homosexual elite of London—not that any of us were supposed to know this, of course." He smiled.

"I liked them, although Francis can be a prig when he wants to. He knows he's inheriting a title and Shipley House, and he tends to remind people of that often. Christopher loves him very much. I was quite impressed with their relationship. As Lady Margaret told us, Francis and his father are estranged, to say the least. I'm very surprised that Lord Hampton agreed to have Shipley House participate in the competition."

"He's not supportive," Evan said. "I've been in several of the production meetings that he has attended. It's obvious he does not want to be a part of the competition, and most times he seems a bit loaded. I'm not sure how Francis and Christopher got him to agree unless they're keeping him liquored up. It seems that Christopher is pressing Francis to be in this, but I'm not sure of what their main interests are. They seem very close to one of the competition judges in particular, Lady Sarah Effington."

"I've heard of her. I'm surprised she's an event judge. Sounds like Christopher may be star or royal struck." I smiled. "I know the type well and see it all the time in Ma-ma's filming efforts. She has groupie followings that troop to her film locations just to get a peek at her. It's mad at times. A lot of people will do anything just to get a piece of so-called fame."

I was thrilled when we arrived in London. The streets were bustling, and it was exciting to see the skyline, both new and old. We drove by Parliament and Trafalgar Square. I loved seeing the famous buildings and statues. The history was ever present, juxtaposed against the present. We arrived at the Beauchamp promptly at noon, its main tower glistening in gray glass.

We were shown to our adjoining suites on the top floor. We had magnificent views of the London skyline, and the London Eye was just across the Thames. Mrs. Smythe was finishing unpacking my luggage and getting my evening gown ready for the dinner event later tonight. She had her own room at the Beauchamp. While we were attending the meet and greet this afternoon, she was going to do some shopping in London, before coming back to help me dress for dinner.

I freshened my makeup and hair and gave my emerald outfit and jewels a last glance. I wanted these British competitors to know this American meant business. Kyle and Evan knocked on my door, and we headed down to the private meeting room that had been reserved for our group.

We were greeted by Byron Brown and Lucy Etheridge, members of the production executive team that headed the estate selection. We were further introduced to the other selection team members, including Lady Sarah Effington, Dame Agnes Knight, and Sir James Dennison. I was familiar with Dame Knight and Sir Dennison. Both were established, well-loved actors in the film and theater industries. I had met them previously at a gala given by the famous director Richard Claire at his estate in Malibu a year before.

"Gemma," Dame Agnes said as she air-kissed my cheek, "how lovely to see you. How is your wonderful mother?"

"Fine, thank you. It's very good of you to remember me. This is quite the change from Malibu." I laughed.

Dame Knight continued introducing me. "Sir Dennison I think you know," she said as he and I nodded to each other. "Let me introduce you to Lady Sarah," she said, guiding me over. Lady Sarah Effington was a goddaughter of a royal prince and princess. She had made the headlines often the past few years, many times in a not-so-flattering manner. She was now quite the celebrity herself, taking a high-profile position managing stock funds and dedicating her time to worthy charitable and artistic ventures. Her royal connections approved her endeavors these days, and she kept her activities nonscandalous, at least as far as we knew.

"Lady Sarah darling, please meet Dr. Gemma Phillips. She is Lord Evan's cousin from America," Dame Agnes explained.

"Lovely to meet you, Dr. Phillips. I've heard about some of your work," she said, smiling. "I was surprised when Evan told us that you would be helping him. I can't imagine what an American would know about grand British estates. If you need any help, please let me know."

"Gemma, please." I smiled. "It's an honor to be here working on the competition. Evan called me at just the right time. I'm excited to be in on this. I really wouldn't want to bother you with any questions. I wouldn't dream of trying to get any inside information from you." Ouch. I had to say that the cat fur was flying.

I looked across the room and saw Kyle speaking with a stunning woman with jet-black hair. She was laughing quite a bit and had her hand clamped on Kyle's waist. I walked over to them.

"Jane, let me introduce you to Evan's cousin, Dr. Gemma Phillips," Kyle said.

"Hello. Very pleased to meet you," I said, extending my hand. Jane looked at me and ignored my handshake.

"Oh yes, you're the American we've been hearing about," she said, looking down at me with her aristocratic eyes. "Daddy, Althea, come meet Evan's little American," she said, motioning her father and cousin over.

I bristled at her rudeness but kept my temper in check. "Lord Paunchley, Miss Jones, how very nice to meet you both," I said, determined to be nice in spite of Jane's rude behavior.

"Welcome to London and the competition," Lord Paunchley said kindly. He was a frail man with a pale pallor, obviously still recovering from his heart attack, as Kyle had mentioned.

"Thank you, sir," I said. "I'm so pleased to be here."

"Please meet our cousin, Miss Althea Jones," Lord Paunchley continued. "She's been ever so kind to help us with this. I'm afraid I'm not much use these days. Althea has been wonderful leading things for us." Althea blushed at his compliment.

Kyle's description of Althea as shy was an understatement. Miss Jones was very polite, but her shyness made talking with her awkward. She kept her head down low, her mouse-brown hair hanging down over most of her face as if to camouflage her. She dressed in a conservative, outdated brown suit with clunky brown oxfords, a far cry from the bright red Parisian suit her cousin Jane was wearing. As vain as Jane appeared to be, I was surprised she had not arranged a fashion makeover for her cousin, so she wouldn't embarrass her.

"Do you live at Longthorpe Manor?" I asked Miss Jones.

"I do now, of course, with the competition," she said slowly. "Jane insisted I come down so that I could better get things ready. It's exciting, really. I'm not used to all the glitz and glamour, though. My village is quite tame compared to all this."

"Well, I'm sure you're going to do well. I've heard nothing but great things about Longthorpe Manor. I look forward to seeing it."

"Althea, be a dear and fetch me a glass of wine from the bar," Jane ordered, apparently not wanting me to get any details from her cousin. "Daddy, Kyle's invited me down to Cherrywood to see the work being done on their polo field. He's going to give me a personal tour," she said slyly, looking at me. She still had her hand on his waist. I could tell Kyle was getting a little tired of that placement.

"Gemma, Kyle, come over here, please." Evan waved at us from across the room. Kyle and I were glad to make our getaway. "Gemma, please meet Lord Hampton and his son, Francis, and Mr. Christopher Madden. Kyle, I think you already know these gents," he said, smiling.

Lord Hampton made a loud "Harrumph" and nodded at us, and then quickly turned and made his way over to the bar, walking a bit unsteadily. Francis gave me the same aristocratic once-over that Jane had.

"Hello, Gemma," he said, not even pretending to acknowledge my degree title. "Wonderful that you've come over to help out Evan here. He's going to need it." Francis laughed, making the remark in a snide manner.

Christopher was much kinder. "Is your mother Jillian Phillips the actress?" he asked. "I just love her. She's divine."

"Yes, Jillian is my mother," I answered.

"How is Malibu? I told Francis he must take me there next summer. We'll come visit you," he said. I didn't have a chance really to reply. Kyle was looking at me, smiling at my being plied with questions and visit demands.

"Ladies and gentlemen, will you please take your seats," Byron and Lucy said, talking in unison. We took our assigned seats at the U-shaped table they had arranged for us.

"Thank you all for coming down for our meeting here today," Byron said.

"We wanted to have you meet one another in person, now that we're in the final three competition," Lucy said, smiling. "I want to first thank you for all your support and sympathy given the tragic circumstances of the Hemsworths. It was a tragic loss for us, but we must press on and do them proud."

"And of course, you've met our wonderful selection committee members," she said, pointing at a smiling Lady Effington, Dame Knight, and Sir Dennison. "They will do a superb job, I'm sure. I'm honored to make a secret announcement. Dame Agnes and Sir James will not only be part of our selection committee, but they also have starring roles in the *Castlewood Manor* production." We all clapped in admiration. This was a major coup, casting two veteran actors on their level as the stars of the show.

"Now, we have just a few details to go over before we let you go today. We just want to remind everyone of the upcoming events and schedules that you will be hosting," she continued. "I've taken the liberty of putting together a chart that shows our timeline of events."

Byron spoke up as we were shown the slide. "As you can see, Shipley House will be hosting our first event in four weeks," he said, looking at a smiling Francis and Christopher and Lord Hampton, who was aggressively gulping his whiskey—his third, I believed. I saw Lady Sarah give Christopher and Francis an air kiss and wink at this announcement. "They will be hosting the formal tea and garden tour. The production house has sent out invitations to all of your events in advance. You all will be hosting VIPs and the actors for the *Castlewood Manor* series," he said, emphasizing "VIPs."

"Longthorpe Manor will be hosting the traditional breakfast and hunt two weeks after the tea," Lucy continued. "And last but certainly not least"—she smiled a little too brightly—"Cherrywood Hall will host the formal dinner gala two weeks after the hunt, which will put us in early December. Now, I know everyone has their schedules absolutely booked with the upcoming holidays. I must remind you that you must be guests at the competing events. No skipping," she said, trying to be serious but chipper.

"And of course, the final selection will be announced New Year's Eve," Byron finished. "We will have loads of publicity that night. It's going to be a fabulous announcement." Byron and Lucy beamed as they finished up some details and dismissed us until the dinner later that evening. "Cocktails will be served at eight, and dinner begins at nine," they said in unison. "We will meet in the Grand Salon."

We said our good-byes and made our way back to our suites. Evan, Kyle, and I agreed to meet in Evan's suite before we headed down for cocktails. My joints were beginning to ache, but I was determined to give Jane a run for the money this evening. I was surprised at how much I had not liked her hand on Kyle's waist. I settled in for a long hot bath to rest my bones and calm down. The warmth of the water soothed my aches and pains and calmed my churning brain. I liked Lord Paunchley. He seemed kind despite his poor health. Althea was nice as well, though carefully controlled by overbearing Jane. Lord Hampton seemed gruff, and I agreed with Evan's assessment, a bit drunk. Francis was a prig, as Kyle had called him earlier, but I liked Christopher despite his star gawking. I had several gay friends in Malibu and enjoyed being with them immensely.

Mrs. Smythe came into my room at six thirty to help me dress. The nude shimmering evening gown I selected had a turtleneck halter top that highlighted my tanned shoulders. The soft faux fox collar in tans and grays gave me an elegant appearance. Mrs. Smythe and I arranged my long hair into a regal, messy-looking bun with long tendrils curling around my face. The diamond drop earrings I had selected framed my face and just hit the top of the fur collar. I slipped on the diamond bangle to complete my look.

"Lord Evan told me to show you this," Mrs. Smythe said, holding out a huge pear-shaped diamond ring set in platinum.

"Oh, Mrs. Smythe, that is stunning," I said, taking the ring from her and slipping it on my right forefinger. "I can't believe he picked that for me," I said, thinking sweet thoughts of Evan.

"Lord Evan is a true gentleman." Mrs. Smythe beamed. "There aren't many gents who would take the time he does. No sir."

I slipped on my matching nude pumps and looked in the mirror to make sure I was ready to give Jane a run for her money—Lady Sarah too, for that matter.

"You're gorgeous, miss," Mrs. Smythe said, looking with me at my reflection. "You do Cherrywood Hall proud." Tonight I did look rather stunning. I was glad, because I was not only out to put Jane in check and show Lady Sarah that I was not a bumble head American. I wanted Kyle to see that I was recovered from my injuries. I wanted his promise of a proper kissing, soon.

I knocked on Evan's suite door right before half past seven. Evan answered, and I saw Kyle standing by the fireplace, whiskey in hand. "I say, Gemma, well done," Evan gushed as he led me into his suite. Kyle turned and smiled when he saw me.

"How do I look?" I asked both of them, turning slowly. I was glad my dress clung to my body in all the right places. I wanted Kyle to notice in particular.

"You're gorgeous, Gemma," he said, looking into my eyes.

"Stunning." Evan poured me a whiskey and handed it to me. "Well, here's to us," he said, "and may the best estate win!" We clinked glasses and laughed. Tonight was going to be fun.

We made our entrance into the Grand Salon room promptly at eight. A butler was announcing guests as they entered the room.

"Lord Evan Lancaster, Dr. Gemma Phillips, and Mr. Kyle Williams of Cherrywood Hall," he boomed as we made our way in. The Grand Salon was decorated in elegant shades of gold and silver. A string quartet was playing in the corner. Waiters were serving flutes of champagne and hors d'oeuvres to the guests in the room. Lucy and Byron took us around to meet more of the Rosehill Production executives and their spouses as well as some of the other actors who would be appearing in the series.

"Kyle," Jane shouted from across the room, obviously a bit lubed from too many cocktails. She made her way over and threw her arms around him. "Isn't he the most handsome man," she said to us all, gushing very loudly. "You should see him ride," she said very pointedly and suggestively to me. I was beginning to think she wasn't quite as out of it as she had first seemed.

"I've seen him ride, Lady Jane," I answered firmly. "I agree. He's magnificent." There was no doubt in my mind at all that Lady Jane knew my meaning exactly. Lord Paunchley came over and led his daughter away from us, highly embarrassed by her loudness.

"Magnificent, hey," Kyle said, smiling down at me. I punched his arm playfully.

"I'm sure you enjoyed that," I said.

"It's rather flattering to have two lovely ladies complimenting me on my 'ride,'" he said.

"I'm sure your horse loves having your legs around it," I said, walking away from him and over to meet some of the actors Dame Agnes was waving me over to.

As I walked across the room, I saw Lord Hampton had whisked Jane away from her father and was engaged in some bawdy talk with her. He had his hands all over Jane as they were talking. I glanced over at Lord Paunchley, who was watching this from across the room. I thought for a second that the frail old man had turned into a slithering snake. His eyes narrowed, and I could sense that if he could, he would have struck Lord Hampton in the neck with a deadly bite. He dispatched Althea Jones over to lead a wobbly Jane away from Lord Hampton's lecherous grasp.

The dinner gong sounded, and we took our seats at the long table that had been set up in the room. I was seated next to Lord Hampton, who continued to harrumph and drink whiskey all evening. Francis and Christopher were seated across from me.

"Evan has told me you have a wonderful waterfall fountain that streams down a hillside at Shipley House. It must be magnificent," I said.

"It was built as a monument to honor my late mother and sisters," Francis said. "My father had it constructed after their untimely deaths."

"Waste of good garden space," Lord Hampton harrumphed, taking yet another swig of whiskey.

Francis half stood in anger but was held back by Charles. "Now Lord H," Christopher started, trying to cool things down, "you know that fountain is spectacular. Why, it's just been featured in the *Royal Architecture* guide. Shipley House is famous. Your wife and daughters would have been proud."

"Shipley House is mine," Lord Hampton growled, giving Christopher and Francis an ugly scowl. Francis's jaw clenched and turned a bright red. I could tell he was seething in anger. There was no love lost between this father and son.

"Shipley House is yours, Father, for now," Francis hissed, breaking a breadstick.

"Christopher, have you been to the States?" I asked, trying to lighten up the discussion.

"Oh yes, lots of times," Christopher gushed. "New York, Hollywood...I love your country, Gemma. And I meant what I said earlier. You must invite us to your Malibu house after this competition concludes. We're going to be awfully busy with *Castlewood Manor*, but I'm sure you will want to hear how the series progresses," he teased.

"Well, I'd be glad to have you visit, but I am afraid that I will be busy here in England with the filming of *Castlewood Manor* at Cherrywood Hall," I answered, smiling sweetly, batting my eyelids.

Jane's laughter unfortunately grew louder as the evening wore on and now sounded like more of a hyena yelp. We started when we heard a crash of glass down where she was seated. She had knocked to the ground the wineglasses of both her and the young actor sitting next to her. Lord Paunchley leaned over and whispered harshly in her ear. Jane's drunken look darkened, and she stood, glaring at him. Althea stood and went to her cousin's side, loosely grabbing her arm and leading her away. She asked Jane to come with her in an attempt to quiet her down before she made a bad scene in front of everyone. Kyle stood ready to go over to her as well. He had been watching Jane's disintegrating behavior. Luckily Jane went away with Althea calmly, and the dinner conversation started once again. Lord Paunchley watched his daughter exit the room, his eyes narrowed in disgust.

Thankfully the dinner came to an end. Christopher and I had continued our not-so-subtle jabs at who was going to win the competition, but we soon found ourselves laughing together. Even Francis joined in once in a while. Lord Hampton had drifted off and was snoring next to me. I was afraid he was going to fall in his uneaten dessert when a valet came and subtly took him by the arm to escort him up to his room. Francis and Christopher seemed relieved they wouldn't have to deal with him anymore this evening.

Evan and Kyle made their way over to me. "Wow, that was interesting," I said. "I thought we were going to have a few fights right at the dinner table. I was looking for the nearest exit just in case." I laughed. Evan grabbed us some champagne from a passing waiter.

"I think I need something stronger," Evan said with a big gulp. "I'll go find us something that has a bit more bite." Evan left us to go up to the bar.

"Do you think Jane is OK?"

"She's had too much to drink. That's obvious. She wasn't in a good mood either, which I'm sure the alcohol didn't help."

"Lord Paunchley looked like he wanted to throttle her, and you should have seen him earlier when Lord Hampton had his hands all over her. I thought he was going to hit him."

"There's definitely tension there. How are you? I'm sorry, Evan and I were seated so far away."

"I'm fine. We had a few tense moments between Francis and Lord Hampton, but Christopher is great fun."

Evan returned bearing drinks. "Managed to get this terrific cocktail they serve at the Yankee Bar here. It's called an Eye Spy." We sipped the bourbon cocktail with great relish.

We were led out onto a large balcony overlooking the river after dinner. The lights of the city shined brightly, and we could see the stunning London Eye shimmering on the Thames. It had grown chilly outside, and I could feel goose bumps harden on my body, showing through my body-hugging dress. Kyle came up from behind me and gallantly placed his tuxedo jacket around my shoulders.

One of the famous Italian cantanti had been brought in to serenade us in the evening light. I snuggled back slightly against Kyle, his arms holding on to my shoulders. I wrapped my hand on top of his, softly caressing his strong fingers, wanting to never let go of his hand.

11

Surprises and Plans

The events of the night before hadn't ended until almost two o'clock. When we came in from the balcony after being serenaded by the Italian cantanti, to our surprise, Sir Wesley James himself was setting up in the salon to rock us into dancing the rest of the evening. It was so enchanting to hear Sir Wesley singing his hits, many of which I had grown up to. My mother's favorite song of his was "Shooting the Bad," the theme song of the Killer Agent McGuire movie. She played it many times throughout my childhood. She had tried out for the McGuire girl part in the movie but didn't get the role, which seemed to get to her for some time.

All of us, even a reemerged Jane, managed to get out on the dance floor to rock to the magical music. She was hanging on to just about anyone who would let her, and I could tell she was going to have a difficult time in the morning. Lady Sarah was hanging on to Christopher and Francis in a very friendly manner. They made sure her champagne glass was never empty, which I was sure she would regret in the morning.

During a break, Evan led me up to the stage where Sir Wesley was removing the guitar strap from around his neck. "Tell your mother hello. She would have made a great McGuire girl, you know." Sir Wesley winked at me as Evan and I shook hands with him. I had been star struck tonight, a very unusual thing for me. Ma-ma won't like missing this, I thought.

Evan, Kyle, and I danced our way back to our suites once the event ended. We were all a little more the worse for wear from the generous servings of champagne that flowed and flowed throughout the evening. Evan and Kyle, in true gentlemen fashion, delivered me to my room safely, unscathed. I managed to undress and put the beautiful Lancaster jewels away in the safe. Then I promptly collapsed in my bed, fast asleep.

Mrs. Smythe gently woke me at eleven the next morning. I showered and dressed, and the two of us packed up my clothes. I had decided to wear one of my favorite fall outfits today, a gray cashmere sweater and wool pants covered with a gray duster jacket. I left my hair long. I was a bit tired of the formality of the British and wanted to be the California girl I was today.

I called the valet to take down my bags, so Mrs. Smythe could get our luggage back to Cherrywood. Evan, Kyle, and I had planned to meet in the beautiful tearoom downstairs, the Crown Foyer, for some tea and scones (pronounced "scons," I had learned) before we left.

This morning I was the first one down and took a table in the back of the beautiful tearoom, so I could admire the lavish decor. The walls were painted an elegant gold with softly lit sconces around the room. The centerpiece was the beautiful glass and wrought-iron gazebo that sat in the center of the circular room with a gorgeous black baby grand piano. I was enchanted by the elegance of the room as I looked around.

Across the room I saw Jane Paunchley talking with Althea Jones in a rather animated fashion. I was surprised she was up. They seemed to be arguing, but why? Jane turned and saw me looking at her. She stopped her talks with Althea abruptly and glared back at me. I smiled and gave a quick wave and quickly looked down at the lovely menu. I peeked up and saw Jane leave. Althea stayed seated and started texting on her phone. She did not look pleased.

Kyle and Evan joined me a few minutes later.

"Did you see Jane?" I asked.

Kyle smiled back at me. "We did, just as we were entering the tearoom. She said to say good-bye to you."

"Was she OK? I saw her sitting with Althea a while ago. They seemed to be arguing."

"She seemed more than a little under the weather from last night," Evan said. "And probably was embarrassed for her behavior. I don't think there were many men at the party last night that she didn't put a move on."

"Tell me about it." Kyle grimaced. "I do hope she's all right, though. She typically isn't like that."

Our waitress came, and we ordered a selection of their pastries and cakes with our tea.

"Oh, these are yummy," I said, stuffing a crème-filled puff into my mouth.

"This is one of Mother's favorite places to have tea," Evan said. "She used to bring me here all the time when we stayed at the Belgravia house. By the way, I hope neither of you will mind.

I told Mother we would stop for a quick visit before we headed back to Cherrywood. I'm sure she'll want to hear the latest details from the dinner last night."

We finished our tea and went out to our limo, which Bates had waiting for us.

"I love this house," I said as Bates pulled up to the stately front of the Belgravia house. It had white marble columns that stood on either side of the front door. The sidewalk leading up to the door was tiled in an elegant black-and- white marble design. Ma-ma and I had stayed here several times when I was growing up. I was glad to be here again.

Aunt Margaret's butler, James, let us in and took us to the drawing room, where Aunt Margaret was waiting for us. She stood and came over to give us a welcome kiss.

"Gemma darling," I heard a voice calling in the corner of the room. I turned and could not have been more surprised. It was Ma-ma, Jillian.

"Ma-ma, what are you doing here?" I asked, kissing her cheeks, my mouth open.

"Evan," she said, walking over to kiss him, ignoring my question. "And you must be Kyle," she said, making her way to him to shake hands.

"Very nice to meet you, Ms. Phillips," Kyle said graciously.

"Jillian, please, darling," she admonished him. "Ms. Phillips sounds so, well, old," she said, laughing.

"Please, everyone, have a seat," Aunt Margaret directed. We settled in, and Aunt Margaret asked James to bring us some sherry.

"Ma-ma, why didn't you tell me you were coming to London?" I asked, trying to get an answer this time.

"Well, darling, I didn't know, at least not before you left Malibu. I didn't want to say anything to you—bad luck, you know—and I was sworn to secrecy. But well, I'm going to star in *Castlewood Manor!*" she said excitedly. All our mouths opened on hearing this.

"Well done, Aunt Jillian," Evan congratulated.

"Ma-ma, I didn't even know you knew of this series," I said. "Why weren't you at the dinner last night? Several of the actors were there."

"Darling, don't be daft. Do you really think any actor would not know of the newest British period series? After the success of *Upton Park*, everyone wants to have a role in this type production," she admonished. "I just arrived here last evening. I had to close some things up in Malibu before traveling here."

James brought in the glasses of sherry, and we toasted. "To Jillian," we said in unison.

"And to Cherrywood Hall being selected as the series estate," Ma-ma said.

"Hear, hear!" we answered.

"So, Ma-ma," I said, "will you be staying in London? What is your schedule?"

"Margaret has graciously offered to let me stay with her, at least for the next few months. As you know, filming won't begin until early next year. I've been given my scripts to learn and will be measured for my costumes. Guess what part I have?" She didn't wait for our answer. "I'm the American mother living at *Castlewood Manor* who's trying to get her daughters married off to aristocrats. I also just happen to be best friends with the queen!" she said enthusiastically. "I think my character is fantastic. She's beautiful, determined, and pretty spiteful, I must say. She needs to hold her own against these established British ma-mas, including the queen," she said proudly. "The drawings of clothes I've seen are divine. I can't wait to get started."

We listened to her talk and talk and talk. Being the child of a film star, I was used to listening to the gushes of Ma-ma anytime she had a new part. I was happy to see that her talking was fascinating to Aunt Margaret, Evan, and Kyle, at least for the time being.

"We learned that Dame Knight and Sir Dennison are going to be in the series as well," Evan said. "They are on the estate selection committee with Lady Sarah Effington. We got the secret casting news yesterday."

"Yes, I heard that as well," Ma-ma said. She was more than a little jealous of Dame Knight's fame and reputation. "She will be playing the role of the queen, best friend to my character, as I understand. They needed an older woman for that role, of course," she said, not so subtly throwing some shade.

"Ma-ma, Sir Wesley said to say hello to you. He played for us last evening at the Beauchamp. He said you would have made a very fine McGuire girl," I said, wanting to get her in a good mood again. She immediately lit up in a smile.

"Oh, how dear he is. I've always known they made a mistake in not selecting me," she gloated, glad to be the center of attention again. I hoped Aunt Margaret was up to having the highs and lows of an actress with her the next few months.

"I cannot believe Sarah Effington is on the selection committee. She's nothing. Tell me," Aunt Margaret asked, "how did Lord Paunchley act with Lord Hampton?" Evan, Kyle, and I looked at one another before I answered.

"Jane was drinking quite a bit," I started. "She was making the rounds of the room, I'm afraid, going after a lot of the men who were there. Things got a bit out of hand, especially when Lord Hampton was groping her unabashedly in the center of the room. I saw Lord Paunchley's face when he saw them. He was seething, I'm afraid."

"Not good, not good," Aunt Margaret muttered. "Please, I want all of you to stay away from them as much as you can," she said worriedly.

"Mother, we are in the midst of a competition with them. We will be spending time in their company. It's required," Evan said.

"Just be careful, son. That's all I am saying. Deep sorrow sometimes turns into deep hatred. In this case, I am sure of it."

We told them about the events scheduled at Longthorpe Manor, Shipley House, and Cherrywood Hall. We were a bit apprehensive about the short schedule but extremely excited to get on with it. We finally left to head back to Cherrywood Hall, covered in good-bye kisses from both Aunt Margaret and Ma-ma.

"Gemma, I would have given anything to have a picture of your face when your mother popped around the corner." Kyle laughed.

"I know. Her face was priceless," Evan said, and we all laughed.

"Ha-ha. Real funny, you two," I teased back. "She was very eager for me to come over here. Now I know why!"

"Well, we're...I'm glad you came, Gemma," Kyle said, smiling.

"Yes, we are," Evan joined in.

Our glee slowed with the soft hum of the car. The late night before and the surprise at Aunt Margaret's soon took its toll on us. We all fell asleep for the rest of the ride back to Cherrywood.

The next day Lucy called and asked to meet us tomorrow to go over the preparations for our formal dinner gala. "I'll send you the details tonight to go over before we meet," she said. "We can go over any questions you have then."

Since we didn't have a lot of time to prepare, I decided to continue to go through the stacks of boxes that contained the archive documents and booklets that had been saved by the ladies of Cherrywood throughout the years. I hit a gold mine when I found some more diaries belonging to Pippa.

I grabbed the new books and went into the front parlor to read them, hoping to find some new "Pippa words of wisdom" to help in planning our upcoming dinner gala. It turned out to be a treasure trove. It was fascinating to see my aunt's elegant handwriting across the pages. She had a beautiful scrawl, easy to read and perfectly executed. Pippa was meticulous in planning the activities at Cherrywood. Afternoon teas, dinner parties, breakfast hunts, formal balls—it didn't matter what the event; she described each one and what was to be done morning, noon, and night.

She listed the visitors and invitees as well for each event, and I marveled at the aristocratic list of lords and ladies, dukes and duchesses, and princes and princesses. My heart warmed when she listed our family members that traveled over from the United States. I ran my fingers over her handwritten pages when she described being visited by her sister, Lillian, and her family. She was particularly excited by this visit, for she was to meet her niece and nephews for the first time. She took particular pride in making sure that these US "commoner relatives" received as much attention as any royal or aristocratic guest.

I found one entry of particular interest. I couldn't believe my luck. In 1934, Pippa was organizing a three-day party that included the Prince of Kingwood and his newly found "friend," the actress and dancer Sofie Jenkins.

Care must be taken with these two. I must have Longworth [her butler at the time] have their rooms in close proximity to each other. I know the prince will reside in the Anchor Room. I suppose that woman will have to be put in the Sky Room or the Tapestry Room. I'll have Longworth decide. I'd rather not even know... Really, the prince needs to settle down and quit dallying with such women, especially an American actress and dancer who's been married seven times!

I laughed as I thought of my aunt's disdain over having to cover for the prince and Miss Jenkins. Their affair was one of those dirty scandals of the day that caused much consternation to the ladies who had to entertain them and pretend not to know. Their relationship in particular eventually led to his abdicating the British throne. He received a title of duke, and when he became the eighth husband of Miss Jenkins, she became a duchess. They formed a dance duet called the Dancing Duchies, traveling around the world until their deaths. Prince Joey and Sofie seemed very happy with their choice to leave royal life behind. The current queen, Queen Annelyce, had been only a girl at the time of his abdication, becoming queen at the age of thirteen, with her mother, the Duchess of Argyle, Duchess Eugenie, acting as queen regent until she became of age.

I continued reading the planning details of the prince's visit and got to the evening of the formal dinner. I was amazed at the elaborate grandiosity of the event. Pippa was definitely pulling out all stops when it came to this dinner.

Dinner for one hundred is being arranged by the staff. I have instructed them to use the Seascape china and Irish stemware. Longworth has ordered the staff to bring out the Georgian silverware to serve. He informed me that he was able to obtain sixty pounds of rare oysters to arrive in time. They are the prince's favorite, although very expensive! I have instructed that five hundred tea candles be set around the room interspersed in gold and silver beads. I know we all will glow in radiance. I'm excited to say I was able to get Duchess Eugenie to attend as well. I know how much she loves the softness of candlelight. I just hope no one slips on an errant bead. That would ruin the glow! Except, of course, if it's Miss Jenkins—I'm sure the Duchess Eugenie might have a laugh at that.

I laughed again at my aunt's comments dosed with a hint of cattiness and her sincerity in making sure her event and menu would be perfect in every way. What an impressive dinner to have some of the highest royals in the land attend. I kept leafing through the diary and to my delight found a folded menu for the festive dinner. It included seven courses, a feat and expense for one hundred people that would have been truly significant in 1934.

Oyster on the Half Shell
Lobster Bisque
Wilted Salad
Raviolis Beurre Blanc
Crab-Stuffed Halibut

Rack of Lamb with Root Vegetables
Almond Cake, Strawberries, Poached Pears

My mouth watered as I went down the list, and I had a burst of inspiration for our dinner gala event. Why not duplicate the dinner down to every detail Pippa had so meticulously prepared? I thought. We still had all the china, crystal, and silverware that were used at the prince's party. I was sure we could duplicate the table settings and "candles interspersed in the silver and gold beads." I was also thinking we could frame pictures of some, if not the majority, of the guests invited to that special night in 1934, so our attendees could relive the splendor of the evening.

I was so excited by this idea that I grabbed the booklets and ran to the library, which housed many pictures of events that had taken place at Cherrywood through the years. I ended up finding several pictures taken that evening in 1934. One contained Pippa smiling with the prince and Miss Jenkins and the Duchess of Argyle. What a find! The dress Pippa wore was a sequined creation I recognized from the closet room. Could I fit into the dress? I was brimming with anticipation.

That evening at dinner, I told Kyle and Evan of my afternoon find. I had brought down some of the writings and pictures to show them when we took our after-dinner cocktails in the sitting room, as was becoming our habit. They loved looking at Pippa's writings and thought that the idea of recreating that famous dinner and showcasing the guests would be brilliant.

Evan congratulated me. "I can't believe you found this. Well done, Gemma. I think we have our plan!"

We went over the instructions Lucy had sent. The production company had requested a multicourse meal for seventy-five to one hundred guests. The instructions also cautioned that security at the dinner event was of utmost importance, for some of the VIP guests would have strict requirements.

"I can handle the security. In fact, I've just ordered another drone to fly over the estate. It has an attached thermal video camera that will canvas the grounds. We'll know if anything is out of the ordinary. I wonder what royal they have in mind for our event?"

"Do you think it's the queen?" I asked.

"I don't know about the queen, Gemma," Evan said. "She's not doing as many events these days. But it could be the Prince and Princess of Kingwood. They have been avid supporters of the British period productions. He is the heir apparent to Queen Annelyce, you know."

"Wouldn't that be a coup! The party of the two Princes of Kingwood—no one will be able to top that." I grinned. I kept secret my plan to wear Pippa's dress, assuming it fit. I wanted to keep an element of surprise for them.

The next morning promptly at ten o'clock, Lucy met with Evan, Kyle, and me to go over the content from her e-mail. She did disclose to us the guest list the production company had arranged for our event. It included the actors and actresses from the series, the production executives and their spouses, the selection committee, and to my delight, our VIPs, which included not only the Prince and Princess of Kingwood (Prince Hadley and Princess Alyce) but also his son and his wife, the Duke and Duchess of Nexton (Prince Camdon and Duchess Priscilla): ninety guests in total.

"Obviously the guest list attendees must be held in the strictest confidence since we have the royals attending. Kyle, I will have you as the point of contact for Their Majesties' protection services," she told us.

"I am familiar with some of the protocols, Lucy," Kyle said. "Evan had Prince Camdon and Duchess Priscilla here at Cherrywood last year for a charity event. I'm sure there are additional requirements now, though." I was confident Kyle would ensure that every detail would be covered, especially since I had been attacked. He wasn't going to have another accident on his watch if at all possible.

Evan, Kyle, and I had agreed the night before to not divulge to Lucy too many details about our plans. We wanted to surprise the guests with our charming "Two Princes of Kingwood Dinner Gala." Before she left, she handed us the printed invite to the Shipley House Formal Tea and Garden Tour to be held in four weeks.

"Don't forget to come," she kidded. "You have the advantage of being the last event, but the disadvantage of having to exceed some pretty high thresholds to be set by the others! Kidding aside, I am sure the Hamptons want you to attend."

"I will tell them we accept today," I promised. To my word, I sent an RSVP to the Hamptons on behalf of myself, Evan, and Kyle. I couldn't wait to attend, really. I was sure Francis and Christopher were planning a wonderful event, although I couldn't quite picture the role Lord Hampton would have.

The next four weeks, Evan, Kyle, and I each were consumed with planning our dinner gala event. Evan worked with the village and county representatives to determine who from their constituency would attend. We wanted to make sure they felt as included and important as the royals and other guests. Kyle coordinated on the security efforts in addition to overseeing the distribution of the Cherrywood wines, which sadly meant we didn't get much time to see each other.

The production company had set up a press interview with Sally Prim, the editor at the *Maidenford Banner* newspaper, to get the details of the completion and Cherrywood Hall's formal dinner gala into the news. Social-media posts were also made and managed by the production company.

Evan and Mayor Brown had been working with the village and county administrators to get the village and outlying roads in top shape to put our best foot forward for the royals, actors, and executives that would be making the drive from London and surrounding estates. Maidenford was making a tremendous effort to put the village in tip-top shape for the event. The village and park monuments and sidewalks were all freshly power washed. The Ladies' Guild had volunteered to work with the village park and recreation office to make sure flower beds and public gardens were in full bloom with fall flowers and fauna.

I was responsible for working with Bridges and Chef Karl to go over the details of the dinner and solicit their input and guidance. Chef Karl was delighted with the menu from Pippa's 1934 party.

"I can put a modern twist to each course to bring it a bit more up-to-date. I want to make sure that only organic, locally sourced produce and meats are used. I know that the Prince of Kingwood is a champion of this. I don't want to insult His Royal Highness; that's for sure." He smiled. "I need to get orders in with my suppliers now."

"I have full confidence in you, Chef." I smiled. "I know that Lady Pippa would be pleased." Chef Karl and I agreed to meet weekly to go over the status and daily the week before the event to ensure that no detail on the menu suffered.

Bridges and I went over the table settings and decor we would showcase at the dinner. To my delight, Bridges was able to show me all the china, crystal, and silverware that would have been used at the 1934 party, now housed in a storage room off the kitchen area. He showed me rows and rows of beautiful sets of china and glassware. Many had sufficient number to easily handle the dinner for ninety guests. The sterling-silver serving dishes and platters were magnificent in their shine and would give our dinner the regal presentation needed.

"I'm so glad we are using the Seascape china, Miss Gemma. We have not used it for many years," he said. Bridges and I inspected the Seascape dishes. They had an ivory center surrounded by navy enamel and gold gilding. These, coupled with the Irish crystal settings, would make a wonderful table setting.

"We have matching gold flatware as well, Miss Gemma," Bridges said as he took me over to the flatware drawers. He pulled open the top drawer, which was lined in blue velvet. The gold flatware shined as the light hit it. I knew it would be brilliant next to the Seascape china.

"Oh, Bridges, this is going to be so lovely!" I exclaimed. My excitement pleased Bridges. I could tell he took great pride in caring for these treasures.

I tasked Charles Linford with searching for pictures of guests attending the 1934 party, starting with the *Maidenford Banner* archives. Bridges had many silver frames we could use for the pictures, and I was sure their shiny surface would add to the glow of the room. Charles had made a lot of progress on filming the rooms of Cherrywood for our archive and film projects. I was confident we would have much usable footage for the website to give visitors a chance to see and experience Cherrywood Hall and its magnificent contents.

I had one final detail to work out: finding the dress Pippa had worn that evening and hoping it could be fitted to my frame. I had the picture of Pippa with the royals and Miss Jenkins. The dress she wore was an early twentieth-century Parisian design.

From her notes, I knew it was covered with blue sequins. The photo showed it had small straps with a V-shaped neckline. The skirt flared at the knees, giving a long and elegant profile. Pippa wore a splendid diamond and sapphire drop necklace with matching earrings and the Lancaster diamond tiara I could see in the photo.

"Where is this gown?" I asked as I went through each of the rows of formals in the large closet room. The rows had been pushed together as Kyle's construction crew had begun framing for the new combined closet room. The garments would soon be moved to one of the spare rooms when construction began in earnest. I was about to give up when I saw the final garment bag. I could see vivid royal-blue sequins in the clear view window.

"Can this be it?" I asked excitedly as I hurriedly unzipped the bag. I drew my breath as I took the elegant dress out to look at it more closely. I could tell the dress sparkled in the photo of Pippa, but I was not prepared for the brilliant sapphire-blue color and the sparkle of the gown in person. The sequins and beading were exquisite.

"The work that went into this dress," I marveled. I ran my hand over the elegant dress and held it up to my shoulders. I was lucky to have inherited the American Lancaster girls' physique. All of us were on the tall, slim side. I was sure that with Mrs. Smythe's help, we could size the dress to fit me. It was going to be just a bit short, but I thought with some tailoring, we could make it work (especially if I wore flats).

During my search, I had found some wonderful dresses for Aunt Margaret and Ma-ma to wear as well. We can be the Lancaster Ladies, I thought, pleased at my idea. I knew Aunt Margaret had probably worn many of these dresses, but Ma-ma would be ecstatic to wear one of the Lancaster treasures.

I decided to take the dresses up to my room, so I put inventory place cards on the racks where the dresses had been. When I got to my room, I put the blue sequined gown on the dress form next to my wardrobe. The dress was even more dazzling against the blue walls of Pippa's room.

How beautiful she must have looked, I thought as I gazed lovingly at the dress. "I hope to make you proud, Auntie Pippa," I whispered. To my amazement, I felt a slight warmth on my cheek. I was sure Pippa had given me a kiss.

12

Shipley House Tea, Tours, and Tragedy

The day of the Shipley House Formal Tea and Garden Tour arrived. Evan, Kyle, and I decided to drive the Balmore convertible to take advantage of the rare day of fall sunshine. The tea was scheduled from four to seven, so we planned to leave Cherrywood Hall a few hours before to allow enough time to get to the event. It was getting to be the moment of truth now that the events were starting. Production crews had been at each of the estates, taking pictures, measuring rooms, and scouting locations, preparing to start building mock-ups at the studio once the final estate was selected. Excitement was in the air!

It was good to have a day with Evan and Kyle again. Our schedules had been so crammed with preparation for our own event and the day-to-day operations at Cherrywood Hall; we hadn't had a lot of time to be with one another. We had breakfast and dinner together at times and managed to take some horseback rides around the estate every now and then. The launch of Cherrywood Wines had successfully occurred, and orders were flowing in, making Evan and Kyle happy with their new business venture.

I hadn't had the chance to be alone with Kyle since our trip to London. Our friendship had continued to grow, which I was glad of. We had not had the opportunity to pursue a more romantic angle to our relationship yet. I kept telling myself to relax and let things develop as they would. I decided to help things along today by dressing in a romantic ivory-lace maxi-dress with a wide leather belt. It had the look of romance with a little cowgirl spunk thrown in. I finished my look with some brown leather lace-up boots and fedora hat—not exactly English-tea style, but I wanted to make an impression. I threw on a faux fur vest to keep the November chill at bay.

I walked outside where Kyle and Evan waited by the Balmore. The air was brisk today, but the sunshine was a welcome luxury—it had rained most of the past month. Kyle was striking in black wool pants, black turtleneck, and black suede jacket—setting off his jet-black hair. Evan chose dark green wool pants with matching turtleneck and black watch plaid blazer and looked very much the "lord of the manor." Both men had scarves carefully wound around their necks, as only European men seem to pull off.

"I'm so glad to see the sun!" I yelled as I joined them outside.

"You need to toughen up, California girl," Kyle teased as he climbed in the back seat of the Balmore, letting me ride in front with Evan, who drove. The wind in my face felt glorious as we cruised up the roadway to Shipley House. Evan had turned on the heater, and I switched on the seat heater to ward off the chill.

Cherrywood was only about sixty miles from Shipley House, but we had to travel much of the distance on two-lane roads, which slowed our drive speed significantly in some areas. Evan and Kyle both pointed out estates and landmarks as we made our way, and I was impressed with the beauty of the towns and countryside that we passed.

Kyle and Evan had brought a case of the newly bottled Cherrywood sparkling wine to present to Lord Hampton, Francis, and Christopher as a way to congratulate them for this first event.

"I'm sure Francis and Christopher must be running around madly with last-minute preparations," Evan said.

"And no doubt Lord Hampton is well into his second bottle of whiskey," I said, laughing.

"Well, if it lightens up his attitude, it will be worth it," Kyle added. "The gardens should be beautiful today. We don't need any stormy flare-ups out of him."

"I wonder who their VIPs are. Did Lucy drop any hints?" I asked.

"I'm sure they will have some fairly significant royals," Evan said. "If we have the Prince of Kingwood and Duke of Nexton attending our event, you can be sure that the other estates will have members of the royal family attending theirs. Garden tours and formal teas are a mainstay of the royals too. Mother goes to similar events held by the queen several times a year."

"Prince Thaddeus, the prince consort, is a personal friend of Lord Hampton. I wouldn't be surprised to see him in attendance. And if he is there—"

"Do you think the queen will be there? I would so love to see her."

Evan and Kyle both laughed at my enthusiasm.

"Well, you know, Gemma, the queen supposedly loved watching *Upton Park*. She was said to take particular pleasure in pointing out details that were incorrect," Evan said.

"Duchess Priscilla visited the set of *Upton Park* as well when she was pregnant with their twins. The royals must love these series as much as the rest of the world," Kyle said, smiling.

"That's why the production company is putting so much effort into the estate selection," Evan said. "Details can make or break the series, so the selection process and expense is serious business for them. I've read that each episode of *Upton Park* cost over a million pounds to film."

"Well, I am very proud of both of you," I said to Evan and Kyle. "Your work at Cherrywood Hall and the surrounding communities has been first-rate as far as I'm concerned. I have to tell you I have thoroughly enjoyed working on this. I never appreciated all the work and effort that goes into a production before the first bit of filming is done. Ma-ma is going to be thrilled at my changing attitude. She always thought I went the academic route because I thought acting was frivolous."

"You've been stellar too, Gemma," Kyle said. "Charles showed me some of the filming you two have been doing for the archive project and website. Your ideas have been brilliant." He leaned up and whispered in my ear, "I still owe you a proper kissing, you know. I haven't forgotten." He squeezed my shoulder, sending ripples through my body.

I turned back to him and whispered, "I haven't forgotten either," and smiled at him.

"Well, here we are," Evan said as he slowed and pulled into the grand entry gate of Shipley House. The estate was about three-quarters the size of Cherrywood and was surrounded by magnificent rolling hills. Guards greeted us at the gate, checking our invitation, the car, and us on the inside as well as examining the outer and undersides of the car. I could see that security was heavy, so perhaps the queen would be here. I smiled to myself. We drove down the long drive and were asked to park in a section of land that had been cordoned off for parking for the event. Shuttles were running from the parking area down to the house and gardens for the visitors.

Unlike Cherrywood Hall's imposing presence on the cliffsides overlooking the sea, Shipley House was set in a valley surrounded by hills on every side. A small river cut through the property in back of the house. The hillside behind the house had been carved into a dramatic tiered waterfall fountain that ran from the top of the hill to the river's edge. Topiary gardens were placed on the front and right side of the house, with huge walking paths for visitors to enjoy. On the left side of the house was a stately orangery, where the formal tea was to be held later that afternoon. Shipley House was structured out of limestone blocks that had bronzed with age and had huge columns framing its front entry. It was very elegant in appearance and certainly a formidable competitor to Cherrywood Hall.

"At the Beauchamp dinner, Francis told us that the hillside waterfall fountain was built as a tribute to his late mother and sisters," I said. "But I'm afraid Lord Hampton said it was a waste of space. That did not go down well with Francis."

"Lord Hampton obviously was drunk. The waterfall fountain has been featured in numerous media outlets, putting Shipley House on the map from an architectural landscaping perspective. Wait until you see it, Gemma. It's stunning," Kyle said.

We got on the shuttle bus that took us from the parking area down to the house and garden venue. We were dropped off at the front of Shipley House at the columned porch. Lord Hampton,

Francis, and Christopher stood at the entrance to welcome guests as they left the shuttle. Evan and Kyle carried each end of the case of wine they had brought as a congratulatory gift as we waited in line to greet them. Francis and Christopher seemed touched as Evan and Kyle presented the wine to them and said hello. Even Lord Hampton harrumphed in appreciation. Francis summoned a butler, who hurriedly came over to take the case of wine into the house.

"Gemma dear, you look gorgeous," Christopher said to me, air-kissing both of my cheeks. "We're so lucky to have this beautiful day. It's almost like Malibu." He laughed. "Wait until you see who's here," he said teasingly.

"Christopher," Francis admonished, "let our guests get refreshed and have a chance to see the gardens. They'll know soon enough who is here for our event," he said smugly. We took our cue of dismissal and began our walk around the topiary gardens.

Guides had been placed strategically around the paths to answer any questions the guests might have. Waiters were serving glasses of champagne and water to guests as they made their way around. We saw the judges—Dame Agnes Knight, Sir James Dennison, and Lady Sarah Effington—walking the grounds with Lucy Etheridge and Byron Brown, looking at every detail and taking notes. We waved at them and stopped to say hello.

"Isn't the garden lovely?" gushed Lady Sarah. "The Hamptons have set the performance bar very high," she gloated. "I knew they had excellent taste."

"It is stunning, Sarah," Evan said. "I'm sure that Gemma, Kyle, and I have our work cut out for us. We'll leave you to your judging."

"I wouldn't have been so diplomatic," I teased Evan as we made our way down another pathway.

"Mustn't raise a fuss publicly, especially in front of the other judges." He smiled. "Sarah seems to be rather biased, I think. We'll have to win her round."

"I think we should focus on Dame Agnes and Sir James. Sarah doesn't impress me. I'm rather surprised she is on the judging team. She must have called in some royal favors to get this position," Kyle said.

"Kyle, Evan," Jane Paunchley shouted as she made her way down the path over to us. "You two look dashing," she gushed, pushing her cheeks forward to both of them to be kissed. I noticed that her hands were once again on Kyle's waist.

"Oh hello, Gemma," she said in a dismissing voice. She wedged herself between Kyle and Evan and steered them away from me. I saw Lord Paunchley heading to the front door of the house with Althea Jones holding on to his arm. He didn't look well today. Althea was doing her best to steady him.

Fed up with Jane's rudeness and not wanting to cause a scene, I gave my excuses and decided to make my way to the back of the house alone to see the tiered waterfall that ran down the hillside. I turned the corner of the house, admiring its perfectly manicured walkways and lawns and the striking statues that were placed strategically for viewing.

When I reached the back of the house, I went to the center to look up at the striking falls. The hillside was at least two hundred feet up. Rock tiers had been laid in the hillside for the water to splash down to the river, where pumps would continuously recycle the flow back uphill. The falls were an amazing piece of architecture, and many of the guests stood in front with me, taking pictures and commenting on the splendor.

I decided to go up the staircase leading up to the back terrace of the house to get a better picture of the falls with my camera.

As I got to the top terrace stairs, I heard angry voices coming through a window on the first floor of the house.

"You stupid prig," an angry voice shouted. "How dare you bring people into my private library? Get out, all of you. This isn't yours yet. Out!" I turned to see who was shouting, but the drapes were hastily being pulled shut.

A minute later Francis was showing some men out of the house and onto the terrace about twenty feet away from where I stood. "I'm sorry," he said. "Please enjoy the falls and the side garden. I'll join you in a bit." He pointed the men down the stairs.

Christopher ran out the door and clasped Francis on his shoulders. "Are you all right, darling?" he said, trying to calm Francis's angry looks.

"I hate him," Francis seethed. "I wish he was dead. I didn't bring them into his room, Christopher. I saw them go in on their own and was just trying to get them out of there before Father saw them. But I was too late." Francis wept in frustration. "I can't do anything to please him. I've had enough."

"Let's go inside, darling," Christopher said, looking around nervously. He stopped when he saw me. I tried to smile back encouragingly as they went indoors. Just as they entered the house, Lord Paunchley and Althea came out and made their way down to the riverbank and falls. I couldn't help but notice a smug smile on Lord Paunchley's thin lips. Althea looked a little out of breath.

Poor girl, I thought, she needs to take a rest herself it looks like. I wonder why she doesn't ask Jane for some help—probably because Jane wouldn't consider it.

I took my pictures of the falls and started down the staircase. Kyle, who was standing in front of the falls, called out to me. "Aren't these magnificent?" he said, appreciating the architecture and engineering that had gone into their design and construction. He placed his arm around my shoulders. "I hope you haven't been too lonesome. I plan on being with you the rest of the afternoon. I'll see if I can whisk you away into a dark corner."

"You've let the sunshine and champagne go to your head. I think I'd rather wait until we get back to Cherrywood Hall, away from any disturbances." I smiled. "I've already seen some fireworks between Francis and, I believe, his father. He's very upset. Apparently some of his friends went into Lord Hampton's library uninvited. He tore into Francis."

"It sounds like Lord Hampton," Kyle said. "The man's an ass with Francis—always has been. And from his breath I smelled at our greeting, I would say he's already three sheets gone."

"Christopher took Francis inside to calm him down. Hopefully he can get his spirits up for their lovely event, Lord Hampton or no Lord Hampton."

We decided to go find Evan before we made our way to the orangery, where the tea was to be held. As we made our way around the corner of the house, Evan shouted out, "Hey, you two, look who I've found!"

We made our way over to him and saw that my ma-ma was standing behind him. She was looking beautiful today in a peach chiffon tea dress with matching hat and pearls.

"Gemma," she said, and smiled, coming over to kiss me, "I'm so glad to see you, darling. Isn't this lovely? Hello, Kyle darling," she said, kissing his cheeks as well. "Evan found me out front and has graciously been introducing me to his peers. He even introduced me to Prince Thomas and his wife, the Countess of Minton. Isn't it a lovely day?" Ma-ma was in one of her nonstop actress modes. I knew better than to try to interrupt. Kyle smiled at me and gave my hand a soft squeeze.

A gong sounded to announce the start of the formal tea. We made our way along the path to the orangery on the left side of the house. It was a magnificent rectangular building with floor-to-ceiling glass windows and doors that went around its perimeter. At the entrance, Francis, Christopher, and Lord Hampton greeted the guests as they were led to their tables. A large rectangular table had been set up on one side of the building, raised up on a platform to oversee the round tables. To my amazement, I saw not only the queen's youngest son, Prince Thomas, and his wife, but also Queen Annelyce and Prince Thaddeus.

This time I gave Kyle's hand a hard squeeze in my excitement and turned to Ma-ma. "Look, Ma-ma, there's Queen Annelyce," I whispered.

"Let me take you over to introduce you before we get started," Evan said, leading Ma-ma, me, and Kyle over to the royals. We waited for our turn with the queen.

"Hello, Evan," the queen greeted in a sweet voice.

"Your Majesty, Your Royal Highness Prince Thaddeus," Evan said, bowing slightly. "May I present my aunt, Ms. Jillian Phillips; my cousin, Dr. Gemma Phillips; and my business partner, Mr. Kyle Williams." Kyle bowed, as did Evan. Ma-ma and I, being American, did not curtsy but lowered our head in respect. "Aunt Jillian is an actress who will be a part of the *Castlewood Manor* series, and Gemma and Kyle are helping me with the estate competition," Evan explained.

"Oh, the American Lancasters," the queen said sweetly. "Your Aunt Pippa had lovely parties at Cherrywood Hall. My mother went there many times. We did too when we were younger. Welcome, and good luck to both of you." She looked at Evan.

"Please give my regards to your mother, Evan. I'll be seeing her at the palace tea in a few weeks."

"Yes, ma'am, I will," Evan answered. Queen Annelyce and Prince Thaddeus nodded their good-byes, and we moved off to the side to let others greet them.

As we sat down at our table, we laughed at being able to meet the queen and Prince Thaddeus. Ma-ma was particularly happy. As an actress, she could now legitimately name-drop to her friends and foes. Soon everyone was seated at a table. Francis welcomed everyone and asked us to stand as a small band in the corner played "God Save the Queen."

It was an amazing sight to see this diminutive woman standing so close by, listening to a song that was in her honor. My eyes misted in appreciation. After the anthem, Francis made some welcoming remarks and introductions of the production executives, judge, and actors sitting at the head table with the royals, Francis himself, Christopher, and Lord Hampton. At his direction, the formal tea began.

The Shipley House Formal Tea and Garden Tour had more invitees than our event would. There were twenty-five round tables seating ten guests that were set in front of the raised table seating the royals, distinguished guests, judges, and hosts. Butlers ushered in silver tea carts and came around to each of the tables to first serve luscious savory pies, crisp sandwiches, and canapés. The details on the baked goods were magnificent; they had obviously been baked with great care and diligence. No decorative detail was spared. Delicious cups of hot teas were poured, and the room conversations soon quieted to a murmur as the guests enjoyed the wonderful treats.

"Francis spared no expense for this tea," Evan said. "These pastries were prepared by some of the best participants in *The Great*

Bake-On series, which also happens to be produced by Rosehill Productions. I'm sure including these bakers was a step to get in the company's good graces."

"I'm sure Christopher thought of that angle. He doesn't miss a beat." I laughed. Or maybe he had help, I thought, looking over at Lady Sarah.

"I adore that show," Ma-ma said. "I wonder if they will be catering for us at the studio? Really, the only thing that does concern me is bland English food the next few months as we film."

I rolled my eyes at her last remark, for she had a very modest diet, especially during filming. She wouldn't care if the food were bland. I looked around the orangery as tea was being served to the other tables. It was an elegant building, more sparsely decorated with plants and foliage than the conservatory at Cherrywood Hall. It was beautifully appointed with crystal chandeliers that sparkled in the sunlight streaming in through the windows and doors. The floor was polished ivory marble inset with black marble keystones that gave it a very elegant look.

I glanced up at the head table. Christopher was seated at one end with Sir James, Prince Thomas, and his wife, the Countess of Minton. Francis was seated at the center of the table among some of the production executives, Dame Agnes, and the queen. Lord Hampton was seated at the other end next to Lady Sarah and his friend Prince Thaddeus. Lady Sarah was laughing and teasing both men, enjoying being the center of attention. I saw Lord Hampton take his whiskey flask out and pour the golden liquid into his teacup.

I guess he prefers a stronger cuppa, I thought, shaking my head.

I was glad to see that Francis had calmed down from his earlier argument with his father. He was even laughing and smiling.

The band continued to softly play songs and was joined by several birds tweeting in the aviary located at the other end of the orangery. I could see several men and women whom I assumed were part of the royals' protection services scattered around the room, keeping close eyes on everyone.

"So what do you think of this, Gemma?" Kyle asked.

"It's beautiful, isn't it? We're going to have our work cut out for us. Are those people standing around the room the Royal Protective Service?" I asked Kyle, trying to discreetly nod at them.

"Yes, that would be them," he said. "You would not believe how well this room is being monitored." He pointed to several cameras that were discreetly hidden behind plants. "Her Majesty's finest are here today."

Waiters were coming through once more to offer fresh tea and champagne for those who preferred it. Fresh pastries, tarts, scones, and jugs of fresh creams followed close behind. I finished making my way through the savory pies and sandwiches and couldn't wait to get started on the tarts and scones. I looked over at Ma-ma's plate and grinned. She was in true form, eating the typical actress diet of air and air, having barely taken a bite of the wonderful food.

"Doesn't your mother like the food?" Kyle asked, seeing me look at her plate. "Is she well?"

"She's well, Kyle. You have to remember that she is an actress being fitted for costumes," I explained with a smile. "It's a tough life," I said, biting into a crème-filled éclair. "Ah couldn't do it." I laughed and covered my puff-filled mouth.

"I prefer women who eat." He smiled back. "They tend to have more strength and stamina."

I looked into his deep green eyes and wished I could have my proper kiss with him right then and there. He took his napkin and dabbed a spot of powdered sugar from my cheek.

"Thank you," I said graciously.

"My pleasure," he answered. His knee rubbed up against mine beneath the table, and I didn't bother to move. Our eyes locked, and we each started to smile, taking another bite of éclair.

A loud scream came from the table where the royals and VIPs were seated. Everyone in the room looked up to see what was wrong. The scream had come from Francis, as it turned out. He was staring at his father. Lord Hampton was standing and grabbing desperately at his throat, his face turning a dark shade of purple. The royal protection members ran to the table to protect the queen and her family and to try to offer assistance to Lord Hampton. He lashed out at anyone who tried to get near him. He let out one final harrumph before collapsing on the table right in front of Lady Sarah and Prince Thaddeus.

The protective service members quickly rushed the queen and her family from the main table and out backdoors they had screened beforehand to use in case of an emergency.

Several of the ladies started to scream as they realized they had just witnessed Lord Hampton's death. He lay on the table where he'd fallen, his eyes staring wide open. His tongue protruded hideously from his gaping mouth. We couldn't believe what we heard next. Francis was standing and pointing at his now dead father, but his scream had turned to hysterical laughter. Lady Sarah collapsed, her head falling into her slice of cream pie.

13

Tea Turns to Terror

Christopher ran to Francis's side and tried to turn him away from the ghastly sight of his father lying on the table. Evan and Kyle, along with a few other men, had run up to the head table to see if they could do anything for Lord Hampton. Byron and Lucy ran to Lady Sarah to revive her and clean the cream off her face. She was sitting up now, very upset. I grabbed Ma-ma, who had stood and was now crying softly into my shoulder. Several people were trying to leave the orangery, but the protection service members were blocking the exits, asking the people to please return to their seats.

I looked over to the next table, where the Paunchley party was seated. Jane was awkwardly trying to comfort a sobbing Althea. Lord Paunchley sat and quietly finished his scones and crème and sipped his tea. He showed no reaction at all and even filled his plate with a second helping of scones.

I guess we all have our own way of coping, I thought. He didn't even raise an eyebrow.

Kyle came back to our table, shaking his head; nothing could be done for the now dead lord. Evan stayed up at the front table to be with Francis and Christopher. The protection services and butlers had brought in several large screens to put in front of the main table to shield the ghastly sight from view.

"Drinks—we need drinks here," Jane yelled from the next table. A butler came rushing over with a bottle of champagne. "I need something stronger than that," she said, sneering and having the man run back to get a whiskey. Lord Paunchley was still seated, quietly eating his scones.

Althea had quit her sobbing but looked as though she was frightened. "Why can't we just leave?" she moaned. "I don't want to be here."

"Oh shut up, Althea," Jane said crossly.

"Jane!" Lord Paunchley admonished. "Please lower your voice. We're likely to be here some time."

Ma-ma was looking a bit pale herself, and I realized she hadn't eaten anything the past few hours. "You must have something, Ma-ma," I said, piling some sandwiches and tarts onto a plate.

"Oh no, I couldn't," she said, but quickly changed her mind and popped a sandwich into her mouth. I noticed that several of the actresses who had been observing the "air diet" were now also taking in some calories.

Kyle was able to corner a waiter and have them bring fresh tea and a bottle of sherry to our table. "Medicinal purposes." He smiled, handing me and Ma-ma a glass.

The police and medical examiner soon arrived and made their way to the front table area, now screened from view. Evan came back to our table. "Francis is a mess," he said, taking a glass of sherry. "Christopher had to give him a Valium. What I'm not sure of is whether he's upset about his father's death or because his formal tea was ruined."

"Scotland Yard has arrived," Kyle said, nodding at a new set of police now entering the orangery.

"I'm sure with the royal family here, they were dispatched pronto," Evan said. One of the Scotland Yard contingencies soon took to the microphone to speak with us.

Chief Inspector Marquot was a tall man in his fifties with salt-and-pepper hair and an imposing mustache.

"Ladies and gentlemen, thank you for your patience in this difficult time. As you can see," he said, pointing back at the screened area behind him, "we will be processing the scene for some time." A large groan came from the audience. "Please, I understand that you want to leave as soon as possible. My staff is setting up a table." He pointed to the end of the room next to the aviary. "I'd ask that you line up and head back there to give them your names and contact information. You may leave after that. The shuttles are outside to take you back to your cars in the parking area." A sigh of relief came from the room.

"I would ask that all of you involved in the estate competition, and those who are with the production company, stay behind. I would like to speak with you personally," he said with emphasis.

Dame Agnes came to our table. "Jillian dear, come with me to give our names to the police. We actors are not required to stay. You may ride with me back to London. You're staying with Margaret, aren't you?" she asked.

"Yes, thank you, Agnes," Ma-ma said gratefully. "I'd appreciate it." I kissed Ma-ma good-bye as she left with Dame Agnes to go to the line. Kyle, Evan, and I went back to a corner of the room where the Paunchleys and Althea were standing. Lucy Etheridge and Byron Brown were there as well with Lady Sarah, who was now visibly angry because she had not been ushered out with the royals. Waiters had set up a new table for us to sit and wait for Chief Inspector Marquot to come over and question us.

As we took our seats, Christopher slowly led Francis over to the table to sit with us. I got up to give Francis a hug. "I'm so sorry for your loss," I said.

"Thank you, Gemma. I'm all right now," he answered, wiping his nose. Jane just stared into her whiskey glass. Althea still looked and acted as if she would jump out of her skin. Lord Paunchley stared straight ahead, avoiding looking at Francis or Christopher.

Lucy and Byron tried to make small talk to lighten the mood, especially since Lady Sarah's anger was evident. "I'm sure we won't have to stay long," Lucy said nervously. "They can't possibly think any of us did something wrong."

"I don't know why I have to stay," Lady Sarah yelled. "The other judges left. I'm sure there was some oversight explaining why I wasn't taken with the royals. I'll be sure to tell this to the production owners," she threatened.

"You drove here with us, Lady Sarah," Lucy whispered, trying to calm her. "We'll get you home as soon as possible. Why don't you have a drink," she said, motioning for a waiter to bring the sherry over. "You've had a shock, you poor dear." Sarah gulped her sherry down and then grabbed a second one.

"We didn't do anything," Jane said angrily. "Why can't we leave? Lord Hampton just died. People do that every day," she said, rolling her eyes and taking a large gulp of her whiskey.

"I'm afraid it's not that simple," Chief Inspector Marquot said as he came up to our table, responding to Jane's comments. Evan and Kyle rose to introduce themselves and me to Chief Inspector Marquot. He then went to the Paunchleys and Althea, Lucy, Byron, and Lady Sarah, and finally to Christopher and Francis, whom he had met earlier. He sat down at our table.

"It appears that Lord Hampton did not die of natural causes," he said.

"What?" Francis shouted. "He had a heart attack. Everyone could see." Christopher grabbed his hand to try to quiet him down.

"I'm afraid not, sir," Chief Inspector Marquot said. "We won't know the exact cause of death until the medical examiner gives us official results, but it appears that he has been poisoned."

"Poisoned," Jane said with a sneer. "Great. Now we'll never get out of here."

"Jane, please," Lord Paunchley snapped, irritated at her behavior.

"Lady Jane, we will not hold you much longer. I wanted to meet you because, as competitors, you have motive. And as competitors, you too may be in danger. We're exploring everything," Chief Inspector Marquot explained.

"Are you out of your mind?" Francis yelled, ignoring Christopher's attempts to quiet him down. "These people had nothing to do with Father's death. Competition motive—that's insane."

"It may seem so, Mr. Hampton. But we're going to do a thorough investigation. I will remind you that you too are a key suspect."

"Me? Are you accusing me?" Francis kept asking.

"You are now to become Lord Hampton, am I not correct?" Chief Inspector Marquot said, pausing for emphasis. Francis's jaw clenched, but he stayed quiet.

"Miss Etheridge and Mr. Brown, I will need you to review the list of attendees the police are collecting to verify they were indeed invited by Rosehill Productions. Sir Hampton and Mr. Madden, I will need you to assist in verifying all the estate personnel and extra help. We will respect this difficult time for you, but this verification must be done."

"Of course, Chief Inspector." Christopher spoke this time. "We will do whatever you need us to do."

"Lady Effington, you were sitting in between Lord Hampton and Prince Thaddeus. Did you see anything out of the ordinary or see Lord Hampton take something?"

"I didn't see anything," Lady Sarah answered defiantly. "Lord Hampton seemed perfectly fine. We were having a fine conversation with Prince Thaddeus at this beautiful event."

"Lord Hampton took no pills. Secret drinks perhaps?"

"Oh for goodness sake, this is ridiculous. He may have taken a sip of whiskey from his flask. What's the harm? I need a glass of whiskey myself. Waiter!" Lady Sarah stood and pointed to her drink glass, wanting another drink.

"The *harm*, Lady Sarah, is that Lord Hampton is dead. We are trying to determine how and when he might have taken the poison."

Lady Sarah rolled her eyes but stayed quiet. A waiter brought her a third drink, which she gulped down once again.

Chief Inspector Marquot turned to us and the Paunchley group. "I would like to speak with you at your estates in the next few days, to go over any details you may remember. I would ask that you not leave the country without letting me know personally."

"Leave the country?" Jane sneered. "Do you realize I have the next competitive event in two weeks? Father, Althea, and I will be at Longthorpe Manor if you need us. Please call first," she warned.

Chief Inspector Marquot ignored her snipe and turned to us.

"Please let us know when you'd like to come to Cherrywood Hall, Chief Inspector," Evan said. "We will be at the estate working on our upcoming event as well—assuming the competition continues." He looked at Lucy and Byron.

"Of course the competition will continue," Francis squawked. "Just because Father died...I mean, he would have wanted us to continue." He was trying to be calmer now. We all looked at him in disbelief. Was he really going to stay in the competition now, given what just happened?

"I agree. Why should the competition be stopped? We are absolutely going to continue, particularly after this magnificent formal tea event," Lady Sarah slurred loudly. "Christopher and Francis have done an excellent job."

Byron and Lucy looked at her sternly to try to quieten her. She was becoming noticeably intoxicated.

"Ladies and gentlemen, please remain calm and let us do our job. I am sure everyone would like to continue with the competition, but your safety is of utmost importance, and finding the killer or killers, of course," said Chief Inspector Marquot.

Chief Inspector Marquot dismissed us, and we went out to find a shuttle waiting to take the Paunchleys and us back up to the parking area to retrieve our cars. Before we got in the shuttle, I approached Francis and asked him to please let us know when Lord Hampton's service would be held.

"We won't be having one," he said abruptly. "Father didn't believe in that nonsense. I will respect his wishes."

Evan, Kyle, and I gave each other raised eyebrows as we entered the shuttle. No one said anything until we arrived at the parking area.

"I'll drive, Jane," Lord Paunchley said, taking the keys away from her. They said good-bye and got into her sedan. Althea shyly waved at us, her head held down.

Kyle volunteered to drive the Balmore back, and Evan gratefully accepted. We decided to put the convertible top up for the ride home. The sun was down now, and it was cold. Our spirits were dampened as well, as the gravity of the afternoon was settling in.

We followed Lord Paunchley as he drove Jane's sedan out the estate road. We were all surprised when a car raced in front of us to get in between us and the sedan.

"What the—" Kyle braked the Balmore to let the car pass.

"Evan, Kyle, look!" I yelled. "It's a small sports car." Althea Jones was driving the navy-blue coupe.

"Do you think it is the sports car that ran us off the road, Evan? What about the car on the drive the night I was attacked, Kyle?" I asked incredulously.

"I can't believe that," Evan said. "Why, she doesn't even look like she can drive, much less skillfully run us off the road. That car could have been the one, though."

"She passed us pretty capably, old man. She knows how to speed up and cut through traffic," Kyle said.

"But why in the world would she want to go after us? We've only just met her, and as far as I know, until now she has never had anything to do with the estate."

"What do you think about Lady Sarah?" I asked. "I'm sure Lucy and Byron are having a miserable drive back to London with her."

"Looks like she's very protective of Francis and Christopher," Evan said.

"She's back to old habits, if you ask me," Kyle said, "lots of drink and a big mouth. She has always been trouble. Just mark my words: her kind never changes."

We sat in silence for most of the drive home, thinking about the events of the day and the unanswered questions regarding Althea and new questions about Lady Sarah's behavior and growing bias toward Christopher and Francis. Kyle dropped Evan and me off at the Cherrywood Hall doors. Evan said good night and left us alone, standing in the drive.

"Want to take a walk?" Kyle asked. "I need to stretch my legs; I've been sitting much too long today." He smiled.

"I'd love to," I said, pulling on the faux fur vest to keep off the night-chilled air. We headed down to the sea path to watch the waves glisten by the beautiful starlight. We walked down the path until we got to the first observation deck.

Kyle stopped and turned to me. He put his arm around my waist and pulled me close to him. Our faces were almost touching, and we wrapped our arms around each other, staring intently into each other's eyes. The magnetism between us was pulling us closer and closer until we could stand it no more.

His lips caressed my eyelids and nose and finally made their way to my mouth. He kissed me gently and caressed my mouth with his tongue. I responded intensely, pushing my body closer and closer to his as our passion grew. Kyle lifted me in his arms and held me against him, my feet dangling. We finally stopped, both breathless now, looking at each other and giggling.

Kyle cupped my chin in his fingers. "I've been wanting to kiss you for so long," he said softly, pressing his face in my hair and breathing in deeply. His lips found mine again, and we locked in another long kiss. We took no notice of the chilled sea air, finding warmth in our soft embrace.

"Now I know what a proper kiss is," I whispered, kissing Kyle's neck. We were gearing up for another long kiss when we heard footsteps.

"Gemma," Evan yelled as he walked down the pathway toward us. Kyle and I reluctantly pulled apart from each other.

"Over here, Evan," I yelled back, trying to straighten my dress. Kyle adjusted his pants and combed back his hair. He tried to straighten out my locks too.

"Saved, for now," he whispered, patting my bottom. We laughed as Evan finally came into sight.

"Beautiful night," Evan said, laughing, being a gentleman and trying to not say anything about our somewhat disheveled appearance.

"We were just taking a walk, trying to get our minds off things," Kyle said, smiling.

"I see that you were." Evan laughed. "Gemma, sorry, but your ma-ma has been ringing my phone. She wants you to call her to let her know you're OK."

"She gets worried during a crisis," I said. "I better get up to the house and call her. She won't stop until we talk."

The three of us headed up the pathway to the main door. Evan said good night to us again and left. Kyle and I stood in the light of the stars and looked at each other. He grabbed my hand and kissed my fingers.

"Sleep well, Dr. Phillips," he said, holding my hand tightly.

"I will," I replied, softly touching his cheek with my hand.

We parted, and I made my way up the grand staircase to my room. Mrs. Smythe had lit the fire in the fireplace, making the room nice and toasty.

I looked up at the portrait of Pippa and jumped up in the air, squealing, "Yes!"

I sank down in the chair by the fire and started taking off my boots. I dialed Ma-ma to let her know I was fine and then listened to her worrying about the future of the series, given this terrible event. She finally stopped talking as I reassured her that everything would be fine. We said our good nights, and I finished undressing and sank down between the covers on my bed. I was still tingling from Kyle's touch as I turned on my side and closed my eyes. Tonight I could finally dream of our first proper kiss.

I skipped down to the breakfast table the next morning, hoping to see Kyle. I wore a denim blouse tucked into my blue jeans and brown leather riding boots, my hair hanging in a long braid down my back. To my delight, Kyle and Evan were already seated, eating breakfast. They both rose as I entered, wishing me good morning.

"Did you sleep well?" Kyle asked mischievously.

"Yes, I did, like a rock," I teased, wanting to act nonchalant.

"Yes, I slept hard as a rock myself," Kyle teased back.

Evan, who was reading a paper, lowered it and gave us both a look of *really?* We tucked into our breakfast to stop Evan from giving us more looks.

"Was your ma-ma OK?" Evan asked politely.

"Yes, she was fine," I answered. "She rode back to London with Dame Agnes, as you know. Of course, all the actors are now worried that the series might somehow be delayed or canceled, even worse. I guess Lord Hampton is now gone and forgotten as far as they're concerned."

"Well, you can tell her everything is still on. I received a call from Lucy Etheridge this morning at seven. She was anxious to make sure we were still OK to continue the competition. It seems the production executives had a last-minute panic thinking we might all pull out, leaving them high and dry. Lucy also said that both the Paunchleys and Hamptons had agreed to continue. She emphasized that Francis was adamant that his father would have wanted them to go on. I find that a bit hard to believe, since it never seemed he wanted to be in the competition at all. Seems like Lady Sarah made sure to give a choice story this morning too," he explained, waving the newspaper. "She made sure to mention how pleased everyone was, including the royals, about the Shipley House formal tea and garden tour. Her bias is showing a bit."

"He's not even having a service of any kind for his father. I don't think Francis is going to let his death stop him," I said, a little shocked.

"Are you still fine with being in the competition, Evan?" Kyle asked.

Evan took a deep breath. "I told Lucy that we would still be competing," he said softly. "I am concerned, though, given everything that has happened. This was supposed to be a fun and meaningful challenge. We've had three people killed now and Gemma attacked. And maybe even our being run off the road was part of this."

Bridges entered the dining room. "Chief Inspector Marquot is in the sitting room, my lord. Should I tell him you will be with him shortly?"

"Yes, Bridges, thank you," Evan said. "Please offer him some coffee or tea. That was my second call this morning. Lord Hampton was poisoned. It's been confirmed. Chief Inspector Marquot wanted to see us first thing. I hope you all don't mind. I thought it was important that we speak to him as soon as possible." We quietly finished our breakfast and went into the sitting room to be questioned. We were much more somber now.

"Good morning, Lord Lancaster, Dr. Phillips, Mr. Williams," he said, standing to shake each of our hands. "I'm sorry to bother you so early."

"I've told them about Lord Hampton's death," Evan said.

"Thank you, sir. It appears Lord Hampton was poisoned by strychnine. Most unpleasant," he said. "I wanted to see you while things were still fresh in your mind. We're questioning everyone who attended. Can you tell me anything you may have seen or heard that was out of the ordinary yesterday?"

Evan, Kyle, and I looked at one another.

"I heard them fighting," I said to the chief inspector. "I had gone off to the rear of the house shortly after we arrived to see the waterfalls built into the hillside. I wanted to take some pictures, so I went up the stairs to the back terrace to get a better view. I was standing next to Lord Hampton's library. I could hear him and Francis yelling. Lord Hampton was very upset that some of Francis's friends were in his private room. He was not happy in the least."

"Were there any threats made, either by Sir Francis or Lord Hampton?" the chief inspector asked.

"No, I didn't hear any threats. Lord Hampton was calling Francis names and yelling at him to get out. The curtains in the room were closed suddenly. I saw Francis come out on the terrace with the interloping guests. He pointed at some other garden areas for them to go see. Christopher came out shortly after and hugged him. Francis was very upset."

"Did you hear what he said?" the chief inspector asked. I closed my eyes, trying to remember the scene.

"He told Christopher it wasn't his fault. His friends had gone into the room. He was just trying to lead them out when Lord Hampton barged in," I said.

"Anything else?"

"Yes," I said nervously, "Francis said that he hated him, referring to his father."

"Lord Hampton had been drinking. Heavily I would suspect," Kyle added.

"Yes, there was quite a copious amount of alcohol in Lord Hampton's system," the chief inspector said. "It was quite likely why he didn't taste the bitterness of the strychnine. The whiskey can mask it, especially when one has been drinking as much as he apparently had."

The chief inspector stood and walked to the window. "We've learned from quite a few people that relations between the two of them were not good," he said. "Did you see anything else, Dr. Phillips?"

I debated but decided to tell him that I had seen Lord Paunchley and Althea walk out of the house just after the argument. "I thought Lord Paunchley wasn't feeling well," I started to explain. "They had gone into the front of the house when I went around back to see the falls. When they came out of the house, I..." I stopped for a minute to consider my words.

"What, Dr. Phillips?" the chief inspector asked, prodding me to answer.

"Well, I thought Lord Paunchley seemed to have a smirk on his face. Althea seemed a bit out of breath," I finished. "It seemed odd, but I thought maybe they had just heard the argument. I didn't think anything wicked. It just seemed odd."

I stopped myself from saying anything more. I didn't tell him about the lack of reaction Lord Paunchley had during Lord Hampton's dramatic death—that he had just kept eating scones as if nothing had happened.

"There is more," Evan said to the chief inspector. "A few weeks ago, Gemma and I were run off the road when we were returning from a visit to Maidenford. A day after that, Gemma was pushed off the footpath near the cliffs. We don't know if either was related but given Lord Hampton's death and the automobile accident of the Hemsworths, I wanted you to know."

"Constable Jones of the local force is leading that investigation," Kyle said. "I will get you his contact information. They took some prints on the estate road, but I don't think they've had any results yet."

"I know Constable Jones. I will stop and see him after I leave here," Chief Inspector Marquot said. "Please keep your eyes and ears open and be very careful. At least one man has been murdered with this competition. Your added attacks are very coincidental, and I do not believe in coincidences."

We walked him to the front entrance and said our good-byes. We hadn't told him about seeing Althea driving a dark small car last evening. The seriousness of having an honest-to-goodness murder right in front of our eyes had us all in shock. We were under attack. And one or more of us was a murderer.

14

Longthorpe Manor: Let the Hunting Begin

The second competition event, the Longthorpe Manor Breakfast and Hunt hosted by the Paunchleys, was occurring tomorrow. Since it was located eighty miles north of London and the weather forecast called for a chance of snow, Evan, Kyle, and I had decided to drive up to the local village outside Longthorpe, appropriately named Houndston, to spend the night and arrive early at the estate for the breakfast and hunt.

We were staying at the Black Fox, a local pub, which let rooms. Jane Paunchley had invited Kyle to spend the night at the estate as her guest, but he had declined, saying he would be traveling with Evan and me. We had laughed about Evan and me being slighted by Jane as we drove up the roads to Houndston. Obviously we knew where we rated with Jane.

Secretly I was ecstatic at Kyle's refusal. We had taken many private walks the past two weeks, enjoying each other's company and building our friendship. And oh, we did like to properly kiss. Each night we retraced our walk along the sea path and ended up in a swirl of arms and more proper kisses, not minding the cold sea air at all.

During our drive up to Houndston, I had asked Evan and Kyle to tell me about the rules of a hunt. I was glad to hear that the British Parliament had passed a law that prohibited the hunting of wild animals with dogs. I didn't think I could stomach seeing a cute little fox being shredded by hound dogs. It sounded disgusting. For the Longthorpe Manor hunt tomorrow, they were going to have a drag hunt, where artificial scent is actually dragged around the grounds by a human, in patterns that simulated the run of a wild fox.

"So what do we all do? Just follow the dogs once they are set loose?" I asked.

"Well, there's a bit more to it, Gemma," Kyle answered. "The hunt is very structured, with many governed protocols to follow. The hunt is led by the master. I'm sure Jane will assume this role, although given that this is a competition and she will need to socialize more than normal, she may elect to have a joint master. The master has a staff to assist with the duties. The huntsman controls the hounds and directs the whippers-in, who assist with managing the dogs. We're part of what's known as the field. We need to abide by the ground rules set by the master and huntsman."

"Remember, you must follow the path set by the master," Evan said. "No going through fields or woods—just the path set. We don't want you to get lost. If you do, head for the nearest road, and stay there. We'll find you."

"Wow, I never knew there were so many key players involved," I said. "I'll keep to the rear and watch; that's for sure."

"Well, it is proper for the more inexperienced riders to keep to the rear," Kyle said. "And when there's a jump, remember that it's protocol to try twice, and if you don't make it, go off to the side to let the other riders proceed. If you knock down a rail, remember to put it back in place."

"That I do know. I have done equestrian jumping," I said, trying to show a little experience, though I was way out of my league with this event.

"The main thing is to have fun and commune with nature and the experience," Evan said. "We'll be out early, and the terrain at Longthorpe Manor offers some stunning views. Personally, I love hearing the horns mixed with the sounds of the horses running and dogs barking. It's really quite invigorating. And you won't have to worry about seeing a little fox torn to shreds," Evan kidded.

"Of course, we have this in case of an emergency." Kyle laughed, pulling out a silver flask filled with whiskey. "I brought you each one just in case you forgot. One must always be prepared."

"We may have to take a nip soon," I said, looking at the dark clouds through the window. "The sky has turned very gray, and the temperature has already dropped fifteen degrees. Are you sure this isn't going to be a formal skating party?"

"We're going to have to get this girl to grow some thicker skin, Evan," Kyle teased. "You're not in Malibu anymore, kiddo. Welcome to Britain, where the weather can change in a moment."

"I'm prepared," I muttered. I was glad I had packed some extra layers in my bag. The sky continued to darken, and the winds were definitely picking up.

We arrived at the Black Fox and were shown to our rooms to unpack and freshen up. Since it was late and now very cold outside, we decided to grab dinner at the pub. We ordered savory shepherd's pies with mash and pints of refreshing hard apple cider. Spirits were high at the Black Fox, and we heard lots of conversations going on about the hunt tomorrow. Everyone was guessing who would be in attendance. It was whispered that a prince or two would attend, causing the ladies of Houndston to swoon.

The ciders arrived, and we toasted to a successful hunt. "Have you heard any more from Chief Inspector Marquot?" I asked Evan, taking a long drink of the delicious cider.

"I did see him in London yesterday. He and his staff are still investigating Lord Hampton's death. The strychnine used to poison him was manufactured in China. It's illegal to buy strychnine here in the UK, so someone had to order it or bring it into the country. They are making transaction inquiries on everyone to see if they can find any trace of who might have bought it."

"It could have been stolen from a university or lab. Some of these old estates have huge stores of chemicals that can no longer be purchased as well, hundreds of years sitting on an old shelf," Kyle added. "And of course, there are always underground channels. One can buy anything today if you have the connections and money."

"I can't believe this," I said. "I bet there's less than one death a decade caused by strychnine, if that many. Who in the world would plan a death by strychnine poisoning? It was so horrible for Lord Hampton. I can't imagine the pain he must have gone through. Someone wanted him to suffer tremendously—and right in front of the queen and Prince Thaddeus at that. I bet she never attends another tea."

"Sorry, Gemma. Mother attended a tea with her at the palace this past weekend. A little murder is never going to stop our regal tea tradition and reputation." Evan laughed. "I'm sure they checked everything more than once, though, just to be safe."

Our shepherd's pies arrived, and all talks of poison and death ceased. The rich pies were full of lamb and beef covered in thick, rich gravy. Carrots, parsnips, and onion gave a refreshing bite, with the mashed potatoes baked to a crisp on top. We drank one more pint of cider and decided to call it a night. I had a sweet dessert kiss from Kyle and went to bed, eager to ride the next day.

The following morning, we woke early and left our rooms at the Black Fox to head over to Longthorpe Manor. To our surprise, we saw it had snowed two inches overnight, making for a beautiful white landscape all around. We wore our traditional hunting attire. Evan had taken me to his tailor in Maidenford to have a riding outfit made for me, since I had never been on a hunt. We wore tan riding pants, white shirts with stock ties, black riding jackets, black leather boots with brown oxford tops, black leather gloves, and riding hats. I was glad I had decided to bring the extra layering garments. It was going to be cold today, especially with the snow.

After showing our invitations to the guards and being subjected to a search, we pulled into the Longthorpe Manor estate gates, our tires crunching in the fresh snow on the drive. Longthorpe Manor is a grand estate nestled on over two thousand acres of wooded land and sprawling fields. It has been in the Paunchley family for over two hundred fifty years. The four-story house was clad in white marble and granite in an L-shaped configuration. A two-story fountain with bronze cherubs and horses towering over a splashing pool stood in front of the entrance of the house. Evergreen, oak, and maple trees surrounded the house, standing like columns protecting the house from harm.

We parked our car and walked up to the grand entrance of the house. Jane, Lord Paunchley, and Althea were dressed in formal attire befitting the master of the hunt and staff. Their coats were a magnificent scarlet red, with white riding pants and shirt. Jane especially looked stunning, with her long black hair cascading down her back. Today she was truly in her element, and she was indeed not only the mistress of the house but also the master of the hunt. They greeted us as we went through the doorway, and we were led to the dining room for a traditional English breakfast.

The dining room had been set up for the buffet breakfast in grand style, and the food had been prepared by two of the UK's more famous celebrity chefs, Jacob Godfrey and Luella Clifford, who stood behind the buffet warmly greeting the guests as they filled their plates. Several members of the hunting field were already there, enjoying the fine breakfast of eggs, bacon, kidneys, mushrooms, tomatoes, and baked beans and toast. Photographers took lots of pictures of the food and guests attending this morning.

"Get ready to read all about it in the papers and tabloids this evening," Evan whispered to Kyle and me as we stood in line to get our food. "Jane's outdone herself with the publicity. No telling how much they paid her to open these doors. The fees alone probably paid the full expense of the hunt."

"Is that legal?" I whispered back. "I mean, wouldn't the outside publicity put off Rosehill Productions?"

"Gemma darling, they're probably kicking themselves for not having this done themselves." Kyle laughed. "She ought to be careful, though. These people will cover anything, and the worse the news is, the better the coverage. Our British press is ruthless, as many in this room know. Scandal sells." Kyle handed me a warm plate.

Today's field included several young actors set to star in the *Castlewood Manor* series. I was glad to see Ma-ma was not at this event—riding in cold weather early in the morning was not her forte. Lucy and Byron attended from the Rosehill Productions. The judges—Dame Agnes, Sir James, and Lady Sarah—were here, although only Lady Sarah was dressed to ride. And of course Longthorpe's competitors—Evan, Kyle, and me from Cherrywood Hall, and Francis and Christopher from Shipley House—were there.

Francis was his usual arrogant self, making snide comments about the house and breakfast. Lady Sarah and he were whispering to each other and rolling their eyes as they looked around the room. I was sure he was upset that his event had abruptly ended with the ghastly death of his father. Christopher was a delight as usual, and I particularly admired his bold statement of riding jacket—not traditional attire by any means, but a gorgeous, loud red-and-pink plaid. We made our way around the room to greet everyone and then took our loaded plates to our table to tuck into the delicious food.

I was just putting a carefully loaded bite into my mouth when everyone in the room stood. I looked up and saw why. At the entrance of the dining room stood Jane, and she had Prince Andres and his cousin Sir Timothy Oxmoor by her side.

"Ladies and gentlemen, lords, may I present His Royal Highness Prince Andres and his cousin Sir Timothy Oxmoor, MBE," she introduced. The British subjects in the room, which turned out to be everyone but me, bowed and curtsied as Prince Andres entered. Prince Andres was the son of the queen's second son, Prince Simon. He was rumored to be her favorite grandson. Timothy Oxmoor was Her Royal Highness Princess Zane's son and also the queen's grandson, but he was not an HRH himself. His mother wanted her son to not be burdened with titles and royal responsibilities but to have a more normal life it was said. Bravo, Princess Zane, I thought. Timothy was an experienced and avid equestrian in his own right and had received a silver medal in the 2012 London Games, where Jane had been alternate.

Prince Andres and Evan shook hands, and Evan turned to introduce me. "Your Royal Highness, please meet my cousin, Dr. Gemma Phillips, from America. She is helping our Cherrywood team in the estate competition, and we need her by our side very much, sir." Evan laughed. I was struck by how tall and handsome Prince Andres was.

"Dr. Phillips, very nice to meet you," Prince Andres said. "I'm glad to hear you'll be helping these two renegade gents out."

"Gemma, please, sir," I said with a big grin.

"Then Gemma it will be." He smiled. "I love America. I've been there quite often recently. Are you ready for the hunt today?"

"Well, sir, this is my first one, so I'm afraid I'm at a bit of a disadvantage."

"Well then, we'll have to make sure you are taken care of." He smiled. I thought I would melt then and there. "Kyle, old man," Prince Andres said, moving from me to Kyle, "glad to see you made it. Looking forward to giving you a run," he joked.

"Glad to see you, sir." Kyle smiled. "I suppose we could have a little wager on today's event..." They all laughed.

Sir Oxmoor was introduced next by Evan. "Timothy, please meet my American cousin Dr. Gemma Phillips," he said.

"Pleasure to meet you. I'm a fan of yours from the London Games. It must have been a thrill to participate and win a medal for your country," I said.

"Thank you so much. Very nice to meet you as well," he said. "Keep these gentlemen in line today," he teased, looking at Evan and Kyle.

"You didn't tell me you were friends with Prince Andres and Timothy. And I found it slightly alarming that they both hinted for me to keep you in line," I scolded both Evan and Kyle as we sat and resumed our breakfast.

"We've got to keep some secrets from you, Gemma," Evan said.

"We don't want you ditching us and falling for the prince," Kyle added.

"From what I've read in the tabloids, he's taken. How did you meet him?" I asked Kyle.

"Polo fields, of course." He smiled. "Prince Andres is a fine player. I've had the honor of playing on his team and against him with other clubs many times. He travels around the world playing for different charity events and fund raisers. He's quite dedicated to his causes. He's a fine man."

I noticed several formal-looking men standing around the room, obviously guarding the prince and his cousin. I assumed they were with the Royal Protection Services. I'm sure the thought of the prince in open fields with guns was very concerning to them, especially with this competition event and given the death of Lord Hampton a few weeks before.

As we finished breakfast, we heard the loud toot-toot of the horns in the back of the manor beckoning us to mount our horses. Longthorpe Manor was providing the rides for the hunt today—a welcome convenience, especially since it had snowed last evening. Before we mounted, we were served silver hunting glasses filled with a rich, sweet port the butlers shuttled through the snow. The crisp air showed our breath as we listened to Jane's toast.

"To a most glorious day. Enjoy it and all it brings. Especially if it brings Longthorpe Manor the *Castlewood Manor* series," she toasted, giving us a snide smirk. I could hear the snap of several cameras in the background. Lady Sarah was fawning over Prince Andres and Sir Timothy, having temporarily forgotten her apparent alliance with Francis and Christopher. I was sure Jane's statement and the pictures of Lady Sarah and the prince would be in the evening editions tonight.

"Hear, hear!" the field answered in unison, drinking our ports. Glasses were collected, and we mounted our horses. My mount today was a beautiful, dark-brown filly named Gannymede. She was light on foot and had a certain sassiness—just like me. I smiled to myself.

The hounds were starting to bark and eager to start. There was an air of excitement, and Lady Jane as master was looking at everything to make sure nothing was amiss. She nodded when satisfied, and the horns blew.

"Tallyho!" And off we went.

We rode along the back of the estate, and I was entranced by the beauty of the fields and surrounding forest. The snow made it a winter wonderland, with crystal ice hanging off the trees. The horses huffed and ran as a group, following the barking hounds. I stayed in the rear of the group, minding the protocol for less experienced riders. Kyle stayed back with me, and I was glad of his company.

We turned to go uphill and were facing the first jump. Rider after rider took off and cleared the hedge, airborne and magnificent.

Gannymede was biting at the bit, waiting her turn. As we were beginning our run to the hedge, I felt something hit the rear of my horse, causing her to rise up on her hind legs, whinnying in distress. She landed and began to run off course, through the trees and up a hill. I kept low and tried to slow her down, but to no avail. I heard thundering hoof sounds coming from behind me. To my relief it was Kyle, running his steed to try to get in front of us to bring Gannymede to a halt. It seemed forever before he could finally get in front of us and safely get us to a stop. We dismounted the panting horses, and I inspected Gannymede's rear quarters.

"What happened?" Kyle asked. "Come here," he said, taking me in his arms and holding me until my breathing calmed.

I hadn't realized how frightened I was. Riding a new horse in a strange land with snow was dangerous, even for the most experienced rider.

"I heard something whiz by and strike Gannymede's rear," I said, turning to look at my horse. She was calm now, nuzzling with Kyle's horse. "Look," I said, pointing to a small red mark on her left rump. Kyle examined it closely and smoothed the mark with his hand.

"There, there, girl," he whispered softly to Gannymede. "It looks like a pellet mark. Who in the devil would shoot at you or a horse? You could have been killed running on this slick ground." We let the horses rest a bit and tried to get our bearings. Kyle was looking around the fields and surrounding hills to look for any clues of the shooter. In the distance, we heard horns begin blowing and blowing very ominously.

"That's odd," Kyle said as he helped me remount and then mounted his own.

"Did they catch something? Is that why the horns are blowing? Isn't it too soon? The hunt can't be over yet, can it?"

"It's not normal, Gemma. It sounds as if they're blowing an SOS. Let's go. Something's wrong, I'm afraid."

We made our way down the hill and listened for the direction of the tooting horns. Kyle and I took our horses to a run, trying to get closer to the sound of the horns. They ran and panted, and we finally found the trail of the other horses to follow. The sound of the horns was growing louder, and we turned through the woods, drawing closer. We made our way to the clearing and saw the riders stopped dead in their tracks. They were in a circle formation. Several of them had tears streaming down their faces.

We rode closer to the stopped group and heard a wailing man cry in desperation. I looked frantically at the crowd, finally sighing with relief when I spotted Evan.

"Thank God you're OK," I said to him. Evan saw Kyle and me approach and rode slowly over to us. "What's happened?" I asked, afraid of the answer.

"There's been an accident," Evan said sadly, "a terrible one. Christopher has been killed. Trampled to death it looks like."

Several of the riders had broken circle and were being told to ride back to Longthorpe Manor. In the break, I could see the bright red-and-pink plaid coat lying in the snow on top of Christopher's still body, now turning dark red from his bleeding body. Francis was kneeling beside him, crying and yelling his heart out.

"Why, oh why?" he cried in despair. Lady Sarah stood behind him, her face as white as the snow. I was surprised she was not comforting Francis but instead seemed to be assuming poses. My assumptions soon proved correct as we heard the click of a camera. One of the photographers who had been allowed to ride with the field was snapping pictures left and right of the royals and the scene at Christopher's body, including Lady Sarah.

Prince Andres was getting ready to dismount and go over to Francis, but I saw a protective service member extend his hand, motioning for the prince to stay put on his horse. They soon surrounded the prince and Sir Timothy and led them away from the group, separate from the other returning riders. I could see their royal SUVs coming up the side road to gather them safely away.

Evan, Kyle, and I dismounted and joined the other riders who were trying to comfort Francis. He was sobbing now, in shock.

"I loved him so much," he cried. "He was so good, so good..." Francis was now racked with pain. Jane had a blanket, which she laid over Francis's shoulders. Evan took out his flask and ordered Francis to take a drink. I put my arms around Francis, trying to comfort his sobbing body.

The joint master quietly asked the remaining riders to please remount and ride back, following him in single file. Lady Sarah, still white as a sheet but prancing a bit knowing she would be featured prominently in the evening news, went back with this group. Jane and Evan decided to stay with Christopher's body until the police came to the scene. Evan asked Kyle to take Francis and me back to Longthorpe Manor and call for a doctor. Kyle boosted me up on Gannymede and then helped Francis on behind me.

"It will be better for him to hold on to you, Gemma, for the ride back. He's pretty broken up."

"Thank you." Francis wept, holding on to my waist tightly. I could feel his sobs shaking through his body. He was oblivious to the outside world, clearly overcome with grief.

"Evan, try to find their horses," I said. Christopher's and Francis's rides had galloped away during the frenzy.

"They'll come back, Gemma. Don't worry. Just get back to the manor safely, all of you."

I whispered over to Kyle, "Do you think someone shot at him as well? Christopher's body was so trampled, like a madman had gone over and over him."

Kyle's look of concern confirmed my thoughts. "This was no accident, first your horse being shot and then this. Someone wanted this hunt to end badly. The fox was never in danger here." Kyle raised a finger to his lips as a sign to save this conversation for later. We didn't know who might be listening and maybe still hunting. Our ride back began. We kept our eyes and ears on high alert, afraid of another devious attack.

15

Hunting the Hunter

Kyle, Francis, and I made our way slowly back to Longthorpe Manor through the crunching snow. Francis's hard sobs had subsided to a soft whimper, and his shoulders hunched down in sorrow. He was still miles away mentally, and I was very worried for his well-being. Kyle and I had our horses riding side by side, and he reached over to me often to give me a reassuring pat on my arm. The temperature was dropping rapidly, and it was beginning to snow again. The horses were panting heavily, their breath outlined in the cold. I felt Francis's head drop down on my shoulder and heard a soft snore against my back.

"Is Francis all right, Kyle? I think he's sleeping."

"He's either asleep or passed out—more than likely shock and a combination of draining Evan's flask. He might be a bit smashed."

"I can't believe this has happened, first my horse and then Christopher. The Royal Protection Services sure whisked Prince Andres and Sir Timothy out of there quickly."

"They must, Gemma. If there's any chance of danger or scandal, it's protocol for them to be removed from the scene. This scenario is a worse nightmare for them."

"I would venture to say that there won't be any royals attending our event, if we even have one. With the deaths at Shipley House and now Longthorpe Manor, I can't imagine things will continue. I couldn't believe that photographer was snapping pictures. How awful for Francis. Lady Sarah seemed to be posing."

"Lady Sarah is nothing but a shameless tart. It wouldn't surprise me if she is already giving an interview. Don't worry about her now. Chin up. Let's see what the details turn out to be. I'm sure there will be changes, especially now, but we Brits have a very strong fortitude in bad times. Keep calm and all that." He smiled.

"Ma-ma always says to never let them see you sweat." I giggled, tears welling up in my eyes.

"Hang on, Gemma. We're almost at Longthorpe. You've had quite a few shocks yourself today," Kyle whispered, his hand reaching over to hold my arm.

We could finally see the side pavilion at Longthorpe Manor, and soon our horses were clip-clopping on the cobblestone path at the doorway. Groomsmen came up to assist us as soon as we stopped. Kyle dismounted and then came over to help me down first. We eased Francis down next and flanked each side, walking him inside Longthorpe Manor.

Lord Paunchley was standing in the doorway, motioning for us to take Francis to the library to sit on an oversized leather couch. Althea joined us in the room, taking a wool blanket over to Francis and putting it over his legs. Lady Sarah stood in the corner of the room, talking on her cell phone. She looked somewhat sheepish as she saw us enter and quickly rang off her phone. Lord Paunchley poured each of us a tumbler of brandy that we gratefully accepted.

A fire had been started in the grand fireplace across the room, and soon, with the help of the brandy and the fire, we started to thaw from our cold morning's ride and shock. Lady Sarah sat down by the fireplace and took back to her phone, texting now and remaining very quiet. The other riders were being sequestered in the dining room until the police arrived.

"I've called Dr. Cooke," Althea said quietly. "For Francis," she added.

"The police are on their way," Lord Paunchley added. "Along with the medical—" He stopped, not wanting to make Francis cry again.

"Thank you," Francis said graciously. "I need for my boy to be taken care of."

I put my hand on his knee to comfort him. I looked over at Lord Paunchley and Althea, who were sitting in chairs across from us. I noticed that their white riding pants had grass and mud stains on them.

"Did you fall?" I asked. Lord Paunchley and Althea looked at their stained pants.

"Um, yes, silly me—I'm too old to ride these days," Lord Paunchley explained.

"And I slipped as I tried to pick him up," Althea added nervously.

"Well, you should have Dr. Cooke look at you too," I said to Lord Paunchley with concern. I didn't remember seeing them start the ride with us. I had assumed that given Lord Paunchley's health and Althea's timid nature, they had elected to stay back.

I gave Kyle a quick look across the room. He seemed to be studying Lord Paunchley and Althea as well. Did he remember seeing them?

"No fuss, no fuss," Lord Paunchley said, going over to refill his brandy snifter. "Would anyone like another?" I nodded over to Francis's glass, now empty. He took the carafe over and refilled Francis's snifter.

Francis was looking down at his glass, a tear splashing into the amber liquid. "Thank you all," he said softly, squeezing my hand.

The Paunchleys' butler came into the doorway of the library and announced, "Chief Inspector Marquot, sir," as the chief inspector made his way into the room, nodding at us. He had a very solemn look on his face, concerned that he was seeing us just two weeks later because of another death. No introductions were needed.

We saw the medical examiner's van and a police car pass by the window to go into the field where Evan and Jane were waiting with Christopher's body. "I told them to have Lord Evan and Lady Jane return to the house at once when they reach them. I appreciate them staying with the body until we arrived," Chief Inspector Marquot said. "I have some of my men questioning the other riders in the dining room. We will be taking their statements and information."

"I should make sure they're taken care of," Althea said, starting to rise.

"They're fine, miss. Your servants have brought in drinks and some sandwiches. We will try to not keep them long," the chief inspector said. He focused his attention to us. "Now, who here can tell me what happened?"

The room was quiet until Francis began. "I was with him. We were riding with the field at first, but Christopher..." His voice began to shake. "Christopher said, 'To hell with them,' and started racing in front of the field group. He was laughing hard as he raced out in front of everyone. I yelled at him to slow down. I knew it was going to upset Jane with Christopher racing ahead like that."

"Did you go after him?" Chief Inspector Marquot asked.

"I started to. But with the prince in the field, I didn't want to cause a scene. Christopher was so flashy at times, not caring about protocols. But he was so happy with the snow this morning. He said it made him feel like a small boy." Francis sobbed. "I should have gone after him. I could have maybe prevented this." He started to cry heavily now, tremors shaking his body. I grabbed his snifter just as it was about to crash to the floor. Kyle quickly took the glass from me and sat down next to Francis. He put his arm around him, and Francis hid his face in Kyle's shoulder. I gave Kyle a grateful glance.

"I didn't see anything," Lady Sarah said, finally taking her attention away from her phone. "I was back with Prince Andres." She went back to her texting.

"Lady Sarah, I'm going to ask to see your phone. I don't want any news of this meeting leaking out. We're still investigating," Chief Inspector Marquot said.

"What? How dare you—" Lady Sarah started.

"We weren't there," I began, cutting Lady Sarah off before she made a rude statement. "My horse bolted before the first jump and ran off through the woods and up a hillside. I was trying to stop her, but she was frantic. Kyle ran after me with his horse and was finally able to get in front of us to stop us. We ended up very far away from the field I'm afraid."

"What frightened your horse, Dr. Phillips? Aren't the riding horses used to the sounds of the hunt?" the chief inspector asked.

"It wasn't the sounds of the hunt, Chief Inspector," Kyle said. "Gemma's horse was shot."

"Shot!" the chief inspector exclaimed. "By what and from where?"

"It appeared to be a pellet gun, from the welt on Gannymede's rump," I said. "She's out in the stable now. You can check on her."

"There is a hill beside the first jump area," Kyle said. "It would give someone a vantage point to fire without being seen. I looked once we stopped, but I couldn't see anyone."

The chief inspector looked very serious. "Were you harmed, Dr. Phillips?"

"No, just my horse. I was terrified we were going to slip and fall on the snow. She was running so fast. I don't know why someone would shoot at me." The room grew very quiet.

Our group silence was broken when Evan and Jane walked into the library. I jumped up from the sofa and went to Evan to hug him. Jane headed straight to the bar table and poured herself a generous whiskey. She gulped it down and poured another before she asked Evan if he wanted a drink.

"Yes, please," he answered. She poured him one and took it over to him. Kyle brought two more chairs over for them. Chief Inspector Marquot let them take a seat and drink a few sips before continuing his questioning. Kyle and I sat back down on either side of Francis.

"Dr. Phillips was just telling us about her horse being shot," the chief inspector said.

Evan looked over at me, his mouth wide open. "Are you kidding me? This stops now! We're done," he said angrily.

"Shot!" Jane screeched. "Bloody hell," she said, taking a gulp of whiskey.

"Jane," her father cautioned.

"Hell, Daddy, everything has been ruined—in front of Prince Andres," she wailed. Althea cringed at her harsh tone and sank her body down low in her chair.

"Are you OK, Gemma?" Evan asked, trying to regain his composure after his outburst.

"Yes, I'm fine, Evan. It was a pellet gun. Kyle was able to catch up to me and stop the horse. She's fine," I said, looking at Jane, knowing she cared more about the horse's condition than mine. "Did you find Christopher's horse yet? I was afraid his horse might have been hit as well, causing the accident."

"The bloody fool," Jane started angrily. "Why was he running his horse ahead of the field? He knows better." She glared at Francis. "And in the snow, his poor horse must have slipped and crushed him. Now who knows where the poor animal is."

"Stop it, stop it—Christopher is dead," Francis cried.

"Jane, be quiet. How dare you speak ill of Christopher," Lady Sarah yelled. "It wasn't his fault your substandard event failed."

"My event did not fail, bitch. What are you doing in this room? You should be in the dining room with the other riders. Who invited you?"

"I'm here supporting Francis, of course," Lady Sarah said, trying to squeeze out a tear. "Christopher and he are dear friends of mine."

"Please, all of you calm down," the chief inspector said. "We're going to find the horse." He looked at Jane. "And we will find out what happened to Mr. Madden," he finished, looking at Francis. "I need to know what anyone saw once Christopher disappeared from sight. And who found him?"

"I'm afraid I was talking with Prince Andres and Timothy when that stupid...when Christopher went running past. I tried to slow a bit and let the other field riders pass. I was embarrassed by his outburst," Jane muttered.

"I was with Prince Andres too," Lady Sarah said once again. Jane scowled at her, clearly disgusted.

"I was midfield," Evan explained. "As I got to where Christopher lay, there were already several riders surrounding him. You were there," he finished, looking at Lord Paunchley and Althea.

"We didn't see anything," Lord Paunchley said. "I've explained that I took a fall. Althea was helping me up. Christopher was down before we got to him."

Althea stayed quiet, nodding her agreement and then whispering, "The estate truck guided the Royal Protection Service SUVs up the side road to where we were to get Prince Andres and Sir Timothy away. I thought it best that I get Lord Paunchley back to the manor, especially after his fall. Another rider took our horses back. We walked over to the truck and came back here."

"Daddy," Jane started but stopped abruptly. Lord Paunchley looked at her sharply. Is he willing her to keep quiet? I wondered. Chief Inspector Marquot noticed the look as well but kept silent.

"Did you hear anything before you got to Mr. Madden? I would think a man being trampled or crushed would have cried out," Chief Inspector Marquot asked.

"No," Evan said. Jane and Lady Sarah shook their heads no as well.

"We heard nothing," Lord Paunchley said, glancing at Althea.

"I didn't hear him cry out," Francis joined, now looking perplexed. "Christopher had no tolerance for pain. I'm sure he would have screamed."

"There was a photographer there who took pictures," I said. "He may have some pictures that could give you more details."

A policeman entered the room and whispered into Chief Inspector Marquot's ear. When he finished, he left the room. The chief inspector stood silent, gathering his thoughts with the new information.

"I was just informed that Christopher Madden likely did not die of being crushed or trampled," he said slowly, looking around the room at all of us. "He died of a gunshot wound to the neck," he finished gravely. "He wouldn't have had an opportunity to scream."

Francis stood up from the couch and cried out in true pain and sorrow.

"Noooooo," he sobbed, falling to his knees with his head to the floor. Evan and Kyle both got up and knelt down by him, their hands on his shoulder, trying to comfort him. Lady Sarah even put her phone down to go stand by Francis. Althea turned her head and started to cry softly. Jane got up and went to the bar table, pouring herself another whiskey. I noticed that Lord Paunchley, once more in the midst of death, showed no emotion. He sat stone-faced, calmly taking a drink of his brandy.

To our relief, Dr. Cooke finally arrived and went straight over to the fallen Francis. Althea shook off her tears and went with the butler to make a guest room ready for the doctor to properly examine Francis and hopefully administer something to calm him down. She came back a few minutes later and motioned for Dr. Cooke to bring Francis to the guest room the servants had prepared. Evan and Kyle each took a side, lifted Francis to a standing position, and walked him to the room with the doctor. They returned to the library with Althea as soon as they had gotten Francis settled.

"I can't understand it," I said to the group. "Why would someone shoot my horse with a pellet gun and then shoot Christopher with a rifle? It doesn't make sense," I said, shaking my head.

"Maybe shooting your horse was a diversion, Gemma," Kyle said, "to take attention away from Christopher's shooting. You and I were at the rear of the field. If we were out of the way, there would be fewer eyes and ears as witnesses."

"We were so early into the hunt," Evan said, his brows raised. "I didn't even know your horse had been hit or you had left the field. I didn't hear anything, and no one said a word."

"I was in the back, Evan. It happened so quickly before the first jump; there wasn't time to yell. Gannymede was racing away after she was hit. Kyle was able to get to me because he was behind me and saw my horse take off. Less experienced hunt members like me are expected to stay in the rear of the field to let the experienced hunters be in front," I explained, looking over to Chief Inspector Marquot.

"I see," the chief inspector said, rubbing his chin. We noticed a large veterinary van pass by the window.

"Have they found Christopher's horse?" Jane asked, looking out the window. "Francis's horse ran away too."

"I'm afraid they have, Lady Jane," Chief Inspector Marquot said. "My men located the animals about a couple of hundred feet away from Mr. Madden's body. One of the horse's hooves was bloody," he said quietly.

"Then it was the horse who trampled Christopher," Jane said. "He must have been spooked when Christopher was shot. Is he all right?" she asked hopefully.

"I'm afraid he has been shot as well, Lady Jane. The van that just passed is going to collect its body," he said. Jane cried out and began crying. Althea ran over to try to calm her. I looked at Lord Paunchley. A tear ran down his cragged cheek. For the first time, he was showing emotion.

"Good God," Evan swore, visibly upset. "That's it. We're pulling out of this blasted competition. I'm not having you and Kyle in danger anymore. There's a maniac around."

"Evan, no, please," Jane cried, surprising us. "You've got to continue. You have no idea what this means to us. If the production company stops the competition, we'll be ruined!"

"Jane, enough," Lord Paunchley yelled. "Lord Evan is right. If he is concerned, they should pull out. It's not worth people getting hurt or worse."

"Yes, if he wants to quit, by all means he should," Lady Sarah agreed, smirking. "Your Aunt Pippa's previous friendship with the queen regent really doesn't carry any weight with the judges, you know." You could almost see the wheels turning in her head thinking about what Evan's departure from the competition would mean. I could tell she loved diminishing our aunt Pippa too. That did not sit well with either of us.

"Evan, just please wait," Jane pleaded, glaring at Lady Sarah. "Don't make any hasty decisions. We don't know what Francis will want to do either. He didn't want to pull out when his father died. Maybe he will want to stay in to pay tribute to Christopher. Please—"

"The police are doing everything possible to get to the bottom of this," Chief Inspector Marquot said to us. "I understand your concerns and fears. Lady Jane, I will need the details of the press and photographers attending your event today. I want to see all the photographs. I need you all to remain vigilant and take every precaution. I am going to dismiss you for now. I will need to speak with you later to continue discussions as we find out more. My men have finished with the other guests in the dining room as well. You're free to go. Lady Sarah, your phone, please."

Lady Sarah smiled and handed it to him. "There's nothing here. Did you erase it?" Chief Inspector Marquot asked incredulously.

"Oh, did I accidentally do that? So sorry."

"I'll take this with me. We can retrieve the data." Chief Inspector Marquot smiled. Lady Sarah shrugged her shoulders and walked out to the hallway.

"Bet she's going to call her royal godparents to get her out of this one," I whispered to Kyle.

"She's probably already texted them and countless papers by now. I told you she is shameless. Absolutely no class."

We walked out into the main hallway and met the other riders. Many were anxious to leave and fairly bolted out the door. Lucy Etheridge and Byron Brown walked over to us.

Lucy was holding her head. "Awful headache," she explained. Lady Sarah, Jane, and Althea joined us. "I'm so sorry," Lucy said to us all. "The estate competition has been so horrid. We were just told about Mr. Madden," she said squeamishly.

Byron jumped in. "Look, I know this has been terrible. I've talked with the production company. They ask that no hasty decisions be made," he said nervously, almost pleading to Evan and Jane.

"Evan wants to quit," Lady Sarah said. Byron passed her a harsh glance.

"Of course we'll remain in," Jane said, a little too hastily. Byron looked at Evan, who remained quiet.

"Sir?" he asked.

"Right now I cannot see us participating further," Evan said curtly. "I need some time. And I want to consult with Gemma and Kyle. I will let you know." He turned to Lady Sarah. "You can stop with any statements regarding our family. I won't tolerate it." Lady Sarah turned ashen.

As we waited for our car to be brought round, we saw Francis being carried down the stairway on a stretcher. Dr. Cooke told us, "I've sedated him for now. He wanted to go back to Shipley House. I've arranged for a private ambulance to take him there. I will stay with him tonight to make sure he is OK."

"Thank you, Doctor," Lord Paunchley said, walking to us from the library. "I'm sure that will be best."

Our car was pulled round to the front entrance, right behind Lady Sarah's. We said our good-byes and got into the car. Lady Sarah pulled off in front of us, squealing her tires.

Kyle drove us back. We were all in a state of shock riding back to Cherrywood. I called Ma-ma to let her know what had happened, and Evan called Aunt Margaret.

"I don't remember seeing Lord Paunchley and Althea in the hunt field. Did you?" I asked Evan and Kyle after our calls.

"They were standing close to Jane when we had our toast with port. I really didn't think they were going to ride, given Lord Paunchley's health," Evan replied.

"I'm afraid I wasn't focused on them." Kyle smiled over to me. "Lord Paunchley is a very experienced rider and has been for most of his life. He and Althea could have followed the hunt field on an alternate course, one without all the terrain challenges and jumps that we had with the hunt course. Longthorpe Manor has been his estate for many years. I'm sure he knows the terrain inside and out."

"What about the grass and mud stains on their riding pants? I'm sorry, but if Lord Paunchley fell, I doubt he would be able to get back on his horse and continue riding. It doesn't make sense."

"That sounded suspicious to me too," Evan said. "But why would they lie? Surely they can't be behind the shootings. Jane was begging me to stay in the competition. She said they would be ruined without it. Surely they would have to know that this shooting has put the competition in great jeopardy. The police may force Rosehill Productions to cease everything. Three of the competing estates have had murders associated with them, if you include the deaths of the Hemsworths. I'm with Chief Inspector Marquot on this one. I don't believe these are coincidences anymore."

"Our event is next," I said, "if there is a next event. The killer may have started initially to get people to drop out of the competition or stop it from happening. No one's dropped out except the Hemsworths. Francis was determined to stay in the competition, and Jane is too. Lady Sarah is adamant about it continuing as well, although it's obvious she does not have anything good to say about us. We didn't drop out after being run off the road and me being nearly pushed off the cliffs. Rosehill Productions has too much invested to stop this competition. It's like someone is playing cat and mouse with us to see whom they can crack. I don't like the danger, but I want to catch this killer before he or she strikes again. The best way we can catch the killer is to go on with our event. With the police, enhanced security, and all of us watching, we're more likely to catch whoever it is."

"We need to remember that murder is not a rational act," Kyle said. "Whoever is behind this is not rational. This far into the competition, we may still be targeted by this maniac. Gemma has a point, Evan. If we go on with the dinner gala with police participation and enhanced security, we are more likely to be able to catch the killer. He or she targets the competition events and wants the attention."

"Mother was crying when I told her what happened," Evan said. "It would devastate her if any of us were harmed or killed. I understand all your comments, but I just don't know."

"It's better to be on the offense against any further attack," Kyle said. "If we hold the dinner gala, we can control things much more than just dropping out and wondering if or when someone is going to attack. I say we continue. I want to catch this bastard."

"I agree," I said, looking back at Evan. "By the way, did anyone notice Lady Sarah's car when she pulled out in front of us today? It was a black coupe—a black sports coupe."

"I saw," Kyle said. "I was already planning to notify Chief Inspector Marquot."

Evan grimaced at this news. "Let's see what Rosehill Productions and the police want to do and if they even support going forward. I don't like it all, but this needs to stop."

The rest of the ride was quiet as we each contemplated what had happened. The snow of the morning had melted, and the landscape now looked very gray—just like our hearts and minds.

16

The Day Before the Gala

No rack of lamb, no lobsters, no Seascape china, no Irish crystal..."Ugh," I said, waking from my frantic dream, visions of missing food, china, and crystal swirling in my head. It was the day before our Two Princes of Kingwood dinner gala. I hadn't felt this much pressure since the final days of my PhD dissertation when I was worried about passing my orals and written requirements.

The Two Princes of Kingwood Dinner Gala was receiving tons of publicity, particularly with the tragedies that had occurred at the previous formal tea and hunt events. The famous British press was out in force. Lady Sarah had been adding to the publicity fire, giving "exclusive" interviews to several not-so-stellar tabloids (interviews that were most likely "funded"). She missed no opportunity, it seemed, to tell her story of the events.

Her royal godparents must have intervened again on her behalf. No charges were being pressed by the police for her deliberate leaks to the press. The pressure was on to make our dinner gala a first-class event, with no murders this time. Luckily our royal guests had not canceled on us. We still had a killer to catch and had been working closely with Chief Inspector Marquot's team to ensure that everyone would be safe.

The weekend before, Ma-ma and Aunt Margaret arrived at Cherrywood Hall to help us get ready for the big event. I was glad they had come, even though Ma-ma could sometimes be more a distraction than a help. I had shown them the dresses I pulled a few weeks before, so we could dress as the Lancaster Ladies for the dinner gala. They were both thrilled, with Ma-ma choosing a dramatic gold lamé evening gown and Aunt Margaret still deciding between a long rose-gold sequin dress and peach chiffon gown, both of which highlighted her elegant frame equally well.

"What a lovely idea, Gemma," Aunt Margaret said. "Your Aunt Pippa is going to be very proud of us in these beautiful gowns. I'm sure she'll be watching." She winked. Ma-ma looked a little confused. She didn't yet know about Pippa's ghost.

Cherrywood Hall was an estate in transformation. In addition to all the security requirements, police details, and equipment, Kyle had decided to have the front entrance enclosed under a tented walkway to protect the incoming guests. Every day now the chance of inclement weather increased as we transitioned into winter. All through the house, everyone could hear the hammering of the structure, the laying of the red carpet, and the decorating of the front entrance with fully grown cherry trees. Aunt Margaret had come up with the idea of the cherry tree decor, for that was how Cherrywood Hall had acquired its name.

Kyle scoured the countryside to find nurseries that could provide the trees for the event. He decided to get the Maidenford villagers involved in the decoration of the containers and invited the local school to bring over its students to paint the containers with whatever designs they fancied. Each day for the past week, children from the Maidenford elementary school came to paint a container. It was quite a production but charming to see the children paint in earnest. Their works were going to be seen by Prince Hadley and Prince Camdon and their wives, in addition to the other VIPs attending, so it was quite important for them to do a good job.

Aunt Margaret enjoyed this activity in particular and spent her time with the children each day, praising and encouraging them. Sally Prim, of the *Maidenford Banner,* came out after the final container was painted to take pictures of the children with the containers for the paper. We all enjoyed a luncheon in the dining room that Aunt Margaret had put together for all the children and teachers who had helped. Everyone got to sit at the table where the prince would soon be, and it was heartwarming to hear the laughter and excitement of the children.

Ma-ma was taken by the beauty of the decorations being put up in the dining room and had been following Bridges everywhere to see the crystal, china, and silverware to be used. She helped me put the old and reproduction photographs of guests attending the first Prince of Kingwood Gala into the silver frames.

"I can't believe you found these pictures, Gemma. What a great idea to feature them," she said, coming over to kiss my cheek.

"Charles and Sally found most of them at the *Banner* archives. It was a huge event back then, so there were lots of pictures taken. Here's a new one of Aunt Pippa. Wasn't she striking?"

"You do look a lot like her, you know," Ma-ma said. "She would be very proud of all your accomplishments. You've done the family very proud. Of course, with Evan and Kyle too!"

Evan had dropped his own surprise a few evenings before at dinner. "I'm very happy to announce that my girlfriend, Simone Alexander, will be joining us for the dinner gala. She was able to reschedule some events she had planned and is able to attend ours. I'll be picking her up from London the day before our event. Please make sure to make her feel welcome," he said, glancing over at his mother. Lady Margaret kept her head down, concentrating on her chocolate cake. I gave him a reassuring wink, although I didn't quite know what to think myself.

Evan was off to London to meet Simone at the airport and bring her back to Cherrywood Hall this evening. I had been able to talk with Evan and learn more about his secret love after his surprise announcement the other night. We had taken a walk on the sea path yesterday before breakfast. The fog had really socked in, but it was nice and brisk outside.

"Go ahead and ask, Gemma," Evan said, smiling. "I know exactly why you wanted to take a walk in this weather."

I punched him gently on the shoulder. "Why didn't you tell me about Simone? The only hint you gave when you picked me up from the London airport was saying you were seeing someone off and on in South Africa. I didn't pursue it because it sounded as if it wasn't a firm relationship. I've wondered about you the past few weeks. You've seemed pretty glum at times."

"Well, it's complicated," Evan began. "Simone is twenty years older than I am, and she's a black African. I'm afraid Mother isn't enthusiastic about our relationship, for many reasons."

"That's nothing, Evan. This kind of thing happens in Malibu all the time, although it usually is older men with younger women. But times have changed. Hey, it's a badge of honor to be a cougar." I laughed.

"Well, it's a bit more than that. We're not as liberally minded here as you are in California," he said anxiously.

I stopped and stood in front of him. "What is it, Evan? Is Simone OK? Surely in this day and age, it's not because she is black?" I asked, starting to worry for my cousin.

"Well, I cannot deny that her being of color is not received well by some in the aristocracy. And her being an older woman is an issue as well. You see, I'm supposed to produce an heir to inherit my title and estate. Simone quite adamantly wants no children. I'm afraid my title is a very big issue with her as well. You see, Simone is involved with some extreme groups in South Africa that are working for equality for all, given their history of apartheid. I'm afraid there are still many economic and social inequalities in their society. Much blame is given to the royals and aristocrats that come down to their country to relax and safari. They're—*we're*—being blamed for not doing enough to help on these issues. Her late father, Sir Jean Alexander, was actually knighted for his work tearing down the walls of inequality. He was one of the first self-made billionaires in South Africa, and he personally funded major reforms. Simone continues his work, but she also heads a very loud, very extreme social-media empire that heavily criticizes the inequities. She has been secretive about our relationship because I represent a lot of what they are fighting and protesting against. I love her so much, but it's very hard."

I now understood why Evan had been so secretive about Simone and why Aunt Margaret was upset. I had experienced some of the British aristocracy bias myself as the *American* working on the event. To many it didn't seem to matter what degree you had or how much money was in your family if you weren't a blue blood. I was sure that Simone, being of color and part of an antiaristocratic, antiroyal group, was going to be exposed to some of the same bias, if not more—no matter whether she was a billionaire. Evan looked at me anxiously for my reaction.

I looked at him lovingly as things soaked in for a moment but then laughed and gave him a big hug. "You goose! Why didn't you tell me? Do you have a picture of her? I can't wait to meet her. She sounds fascinating."

Evan was visibly relieved. "Yes, yes," he said, thumbing his phone for the picture. He handed me his phone so that I could see her. She was a lovely woman with black plaited hair that cascaded down her back. She had beautiful brown eyes and a warm smile.

"She's beautiful, Evan," I said, handing his phone back to him. "You make a striking couple. I'll put her to work! How tall is she?" I bombarded Evan.

"I'm sure she'd love to help." He laughed. "But why on earth do you need to know how tall she is?"

"Well, it's kind of a surprise," I teased, "just for us Lancaster Ladies. You see, Ma-ma, your mother, and I are all wearing gowns from the closet. Mine is the one that Pippa wore at her 1934 party. I picked out gowns for Aunt Margaret and Ma-ma. They loved them. I want to do the same for Simone. I'm sure Mrs. Smythe can handle any alterations. I can use Simone's help. She won't mind, will she?"

"Gemma, you are a gem. Put her to work. I know she'll love being included. She's certainly heard enough about all of this the past few months. Thank you for your thoughtfulness. It means a great deal to me, as I'm sure it will to Simone too," he said sincerely.

We headed back to Cherrywood Hall along the sea path. "Evan, I'll talk with Aunt Margaret if you'd like. Have you told Simone that our dinner gala is honoring the two Princes of Kingwood and that Prince Hadley and Prince Camdon will be attending with their wives?" I asked somewhat apprehensively.

"I think it would be good for you to talk with Mother. You can see she's having a tough time with it. But I thought if she could just meet Simone, she would feel differently. Simone knows who is attending our event and has promised to be on her best behavior with the royals. She can be a bit of a spitfire when she wants, but I think we'll be fine." He smiled.

"Does Kyle know about Simone? He hasn't mentioned her to me."

"He does. We've had many discussions about her. He wouldn't mention her. He's very discreet and a true gentleman, Gemma. I'm glad you two are becoming friends."

So here we were today, waiting for Simone's arrival. I decided to take Aunt Margaret to the newly renovated closet room with me to pick out dresses for Simone. The closet room was now gigantic, having combined four separate rooms into one. It had marvelous displays and lighting to house and showcase the beautiful Lancaster apparel items.

I could tell she was anxious, but I wanted to try to make her feel comfortable. I had a couple of ideas on dresses for Simone that I wanted Aunt Margaret's thoughts on, and it gave us a perfect opportunity to talk. She sat by the newly renovated gilded, three-panel mirror in the closet room while I hunted for the dresses. I found the ones I thought would work well with Simone's coloring and height and took them over to where Aunt Margaret was seated.

I took the first dress out of the garment bag to show her.

THE CROWN FOR CASTLEWOOD MANOR

"He does love her, you know," she said as she softly touched the first pick. It was a peach-colored tea-length dress with long, hanging sleeves made of gold silk brocade. It had a subtle shimmer that highlighted the richness of the fabrics.

"I believe he does, Aunt Margaret. But he loves you too and is so desperate for your approval. You mean the world to him," I said softly.

She looked up at me and smiled. "Times are different today; I know that. Believe it or not, I contribute to many of the causes Simone endorses. I cannot say that I agree with some of the things she's written and spoken out about with respect to the aristocracy and royals. One can't change hundreds of years of tradition, either good or bad, overnight. Not all of us are bad, you know, and it feels unfair to be grouped together when we're not all alike. It's just"—tears welled up—"I thought I would have grandchildren. I'm afraid now that I won't." I gave her a hug.

"Oh, Aunt Margaret, just talk with her. I understand that Evan is supposed to produce an heir, but I am not so sure they want children. But if that changes, there are so many ways that they could have children these days. They could have a surrogate mother—or adopt. I'm sure if they decide on children, they could find a way."

Aunt Margaret finally smiled. "I understand. It's just hard to think about this being our end. Evan has become enchanted with South Africa and the land there, with Simone by his side. I'm not even sure he wants the responsibility of Cherrywood Hall or his title anymore."

"Let's face that when the time comes, Aunt Margaret. Right now we have another member of our Lancaster Ladies to find a dress for," I said as I pulled my second pick from the garment bag. It was a bronze metallic-embossed black velvet gown, with cascading bell sleeves.

"Oh, Gemma, this is stunning!" Aunt Margaret said as she looked over the exquisite dress.

"I love this one, Aunt Margaret. I think it will fit Simone beautifully. Have you seen her picture?" I asked quietly.

Aunt Margaret smiled and nodded. "Yes, Evan did show me her picture. She's a stunning woman. I think this dress will be beautiful for her."

"Well, let's take these up to her room—I mean, Evan's room— so that she can decide. I do hope she picks this one. Mrs. Smythe can get them set up on the dress forms for her to see." I smiled.

Since I was sure Simone was going to stay with Evan in his suite, I thought I might as well help get that cleared up.

Aunt Margaret was a little more progressive than I gave cred- it for. "I think that is a smashing idea, Gemma." We gathered the two dresses and headed down to give them to Mrs. Smythe to put on display in Evan's suite.

At four o'clock, Ma-ma, Aunt Margaret, Kyle, and I wait- ed at the front entrance for Evan to pull up with Simone. He had called a few minutes ago to let us know they were on the estate grounds. I hadn't been able to see much of Kyle lately. We had all been consumed with the final days of preparation. He looked especially striking today in a green turtleneck and black riding pants tucked in his leather boots. I could see his tight chest muscles against the cashmere of his top. I was hav- ing a hard time not putting my hands on his chest and giving him a "proper" kissing.

We heard the crunch of the Balmore turning in the drive. Evan got out and went over to open the door for Simone. We were standing on the red-carpeted stairs under the newly constructed tent covering, waiting to see her. As she emerged from the Balmore, we were struck by her regal African beauty. She was around five feet four and had her long, black hair pulled back and tied with a silk scarf. She wore a stunning red-and-gold brocade full-length coat with black turtleneck and pants underneath to ward off the British chill. When she saw us at the stairs, she beamed a beautiful smile. Evan brought her to us, holding her arm. He was beaming himself.

"Mother, Aunt Jillian, Gemma, Kyle, please meet Miss Simone Alexander," he said, smiling with pride.

Aunt Margaret came down the stairs first to greet Simone, kissing both her cheeks and welcoming her with a warm handshake. "Welcome to Cherrywood Hall, dear. I'm so glad to finally meet you."

"Thank you, Lady Lancaster," Simone said softly. "I'm so glad to meet you as well."

Ma-ma came down next and warmly shook Simone's hand.

"Aunt Jillian is an actress and has a lead role on the *Castlewood* series," Evan explained to Simone.

"Oh, I'm a big fan of Jillian's," Simone said, laughing.

Ma-ma was enchanted, of course. I came down next with Kyle by my side.

"Hello, Simone," I said, opting to greet her with a big ole American hug.

"Evan's told me about you, Dr. Phillips." She laughed. "You've enchanted him. You're all he's talked about the past few months."

Kyle came over and air-kissed both of her cheeks.

"My, you are handsome," she said teasingly. "Evan didn't tell me how handsome." She laughed and kissed Evan on his cheek.

The footman came to unload her suitcases.

"Let's go in, everyone," Aunt Margaret said. "I've had Bridges set up tea in the conservatory for us. I'm sure we all need some nourishment."

She guided our group to the grand room. Bridges had set up a large round table in front of the waterfall.

"Oh, it's stunning," Simone said. "Evan's told me about it, but I never imagined it so beautiful."

"Kyle designed it," Aunt Margaret said proudly.

"No, actually I just enhanced the design." Kyle laughed and corrected her. "Pippa designed it originally."

"Oh yes, the famous Pippa, the American Lancaster." Simone laughed. "I've been told about her too."

We sat down and enjoyed a lovely afternoon tea complete with a wide selection of sandwiches and pastries. Tea and champagne were served to honor Simone's arrival. She told us of her estate on the coast of Johannesburg and the ranchland she and Evan spent time on. Her love of her country and her causes was evident. Evan beamed at her when she talked.

When we finished tea, Aunt Margaret and I walked with Simone and Evan up to their room. "I have a surprise for you," I said. "You don't have to participate if you don't want to." We went into Evan's suite. Mrs. Smythe had artfully displayed both gowns Aunt Margaret and I had picked for her. Simone walked slowly over to them as I explained why the dresses were there.

"We're wearing period dresses and thought you might join us as a Lancaster Lady," I said.

Simone looked at me, tears welling in her eyes. "Thank you, Gemma. I would love to be a Lancaster Lady." She smiled, looking lovingly at Evan.

"Then so you shall be, my dear," Aunt Margaret said. She went over and gave Simone a hug, which was returned. I was almost crying myself at the sight, and so was Evan. He beamed at the two women he loved most.

"Now," Aunt Margaret said, regaining her composure, "which one do you like? Pick one. Evan can take you to the vault to pick out matching jewels, of course."

"They are both beautiful, but I think the black velvet with bronze metallic designs is stunning. Thank you both so much for including me. It means more than you know." Simone smiled.

"Have Evan show you the secret buttons to get into my room if you'd like to talk or need to borrow anything. You'll be amazed at the secret lights to the passage this room has." I smiled.

That night, since they were decorating the dining room for the event the next day, Evan and Simone had a quiet dinner in Evan's suite with Aunt Margaret, so they could get to know one another. Ma-ma, Kyle, and I had sandwiches and soup served in the small sitting room adjacent to the dining room, enjoying the warmth of the fire.

"Margaret took me down to the vault room today. I couldn't believe my eyes! It was just like going into a fabulous jewelry showroom in New York or Paris!" Ma-ma smiled. "I picked out the most magnificent yellow and white diamond necklace and tiara to go with my dress. I'm going to look fabulous," she said, laughing.

"I'm sure you will, Ma-ma. What dress did Aunt Margaret choose?"

"The long rose-gold gown. She found a stunning tourma-line stone necklace and earring set in rose gold that matches perfectly. She's going to wear her own tiara, of course."

"Of course!" We laughed. As Americans, we were not quite used to the concept of having one's own tiara.

After our dinner, Ma-ma left us to say good night. "I won't be coming down again, but don't stay up too late, you two." She laughed as she kissed us good night.

Kyle and I snuggled on the love seat in the sitting room and looked at the fire. He reached over and parted my hair, putting his arm around my back. I looked up into his deep green eyes and smiled. He bent over to kiss me with sweet, gentle kisses.

"I have something for you," he whispered. He took a small ring box from his pocket and handed it to me. "I know you'll be wearing Pippa's jewels tomorrow night." He smiled. "I can't compete with those."

"Nobody can compete with those jewels." I laughed.

"This was my mother's ring. She designed it and had it commissioned. It would honor me if you wore it tomorrow night."

I lifted the blue velvet top of the ring box. In it was a stunning art deco ring, blue sapphire and diamond set in platinum, a design I had never seen before. It was crested in the middle, with a large round diamond on one side and a blue sapphire of the same size opposite it. On either side of the larger stones was a triangular setting of pave stones, sapphires for the diamond side and diamonds for the sapphire side. I put the gorgeous ring on my right ring finger. It fit perfectly and sparkled like nothing I had ever seen.

"Oh, Kyle." I put my arms around his neck. "Thank you. I will wear it with pride tomorrow. It's perfect," I whispered, kissing his lips.

A discreet knock came at the door between the sitting and dining room. We separated and said, "Come in." Bridges was at the door. He and his staff had been working all day getting the dining room decorated just as Pippa had it in 1934.

"Would you like to see the room, Miss Gemma? And Mr. Kyle?" he added. "I don't want to disturb you, but I thought you might want to see it now that we've almost finished."

"Of course, Bridges," I said, jumping from the love seat, Kyle by my side. "Thank you so much for thinking of me."

Bridges opened the door between the rooms to full width. The dining room table had been set with the Seascape china, Irish crystal, and gold flatware, just as in 1934. The candelabras had beautiful blue taper candles burning. All around the room were five hundred lighted tea candles, which sparkled next to the thousands of gold and silver beads. I had never seen anything so beautiful in my life.

"Bridges, it's magnificent," I said with tears in my eyes. I gave him a huge hug and kiss on his cheek. I knew he was not used to this American display of affection, but I could tell he appreciated it.

"Um, thank you, Miss Gemma," he said appreciatively. "It has been a pleasure to work on this. We haven't held an event of this magnitude in many, many years."

Kyle left to go to the sitting room and returned with three glasses of whiskey.

"To Bridges and the magnificent Cherrywood staff," he toasted, and we raised our glasses.

"To the Two Princes of Kingwood Dinner Gala," I said, raising our glasses again. "Hear, hear!"

Bridges walked us around the length of the table, pointing out the exquisite decor. The staff had been meticulous in making sure every detail was followed.

"I think Lady Pippa would approve, miss," Bridges said warmly.

"I'm sure she would approve, Bridges. In fact, I bet she shows up tomorrow evening. She wouldn't miss a party like this." I laughed. Kyle and Bridges laughed with me, until several of the candles blew out in the candelabra. Silent, we all looked at one another. We were certain that Pippa had just let us know it was time to retire. There was a major event tomorrow!

17

The Two Princes of Kingwood Dinner Gala

The day for our Two Princes of Kingwood Dinner Gala had arrived. We breakfasted in our rooms since it was pure pandemonium in the dining room and conservatory with last-minute preparations. I went down to the kitchen after I had eaten and dressed. Chef Karl was walking from station to station in the kitchen areas to ensure that everything was on track. Sous chefs and line cooks were busily chopping and cutting all the ingredients for tonight's grand dinner.

"Good morning, Chef Karl." I smiled. He came over to shake my hand and give me a tour. "It smells yummy down here. Do you have everything you need?"

"Everything is in place, Miss Gemma. It will be a fine meal." He smiled. "Your mother has been a tremendous help, making sure we're prepared."

"Oh, I am sorry." I grimaced. "I will try to keep her away from the kitchen today."

"No, you misunderstood." He laughed. "With all her experience at attending the awards dinners and benefits in America, she had some great ideas for us in terms of plating and service. I was quite enchanted by her knowledge and expertise. In fact, after this dinner, we are planning to spend some time together collaborating."

Ma-ma's charm had struck once again. "I see. I'm sure she will be glad to know she's contributed to our success. Call me if you need anything today, or a rescue." Chef Karl smiled at me and waved me off as he went on to deal with the preparations.

I grabbed a cookie and went upstairs to the dining room. Last evening Bridges had told me to come here this morning to see the final details. I walked in and was even more enchanted than I had been last night. Bouquets of fresh white roses and blue orchids—Pippa's favorite—in silver flower bowls were everywhere. The fragrance was wonderful.

"What do you think, Miss Gemma?" Bridges asked. I walked slowly around the huge table, admiring the precision of the placement of every fork, spoon, knife, glass, and plate sparkling against the gold and silver beads.

"It's magnificent, Bridges. I couldn't imagine it being more beautiful than it was last night, but it is. The flowers are absolutely stunning in the silver bowls. Well done. They're going to love it." Bridges smiled, clearly pleased with the compliment.

Evan and Simone walked into the dining room, amazed to see its transformation. "Oh, it's beautiful," Simone said, coming over to give me a hug and kiss my cheek.

"Well, it's been a team effort." I laughed. "Pippa's plans, Bridges's and the staff's magnificent work...Everything is finally in place!"

"I can't believe our day is here," Evan said, walking over to give me a hug. "Can you even imagine almost two months have passed? Gemma, I can't thank you enough for all you've done. You've been amazing, cousin."

"Let's go into the library. Charles and I have something to show you," I said.

Charles Linford had set up the computer screen to project onto a large-screen television we had brought into the room. Mama, Aunt Margaret, and Kyle had been summoned by Bridges earlier and were waiting for us in the library. I walked over to the desk next to Charles and began.

"This young man," I said, looking at Charles, "has put together the videos for the virtual tour of Cherrywood. We wanted to play it for you this morning. It's brilliant!" Charles beamed. "I have to acknowledge Kyle as well. Many of the images you're about to see are courtesy of his drones that are flying over the estate. Let's take a seat and get started." I pointed to the chairs that had been placed in front of the television screen.

For the next hour, we watched as the images of the Cherrywood exterior, including the sea path, follies, vineyard, and agricultural grounds, were shown as if we were walking or riding around ourselves. Going through the front entrance, we saw the magnificence of the grand hallway and were led into each of the downstairs rooms and terrace, highlighting the panoramic sea views. Charles had dubbed classical music in the background of the video.

"We'd like to have narration dubbed in for the sections that go up on the website," I said as we watched. "I thought that you could narrate, Ma-ma, since you're the actress of the family. Evan and Aunt Margaret could do placed interviews to go over the history of Cherrywood Hall. Kyle, I thought you could talk about the grounds, the changes that have occurred, and the new ventures planned."

"This is really brilliant," Evan said as we finished watching. "Fantastic job, you two. This will be of great benefit to Cherrywood Hall, no matter what happens with the competition."

"I thought you might want to give this to the selection committee, Evan, present it to them after the dinner tonight," I suggested. "I think it does a brilliant job of capturing the highlights of Cherrywood Hall and could refresh the committee members' memories after they leave the gala tonight. Some of them might have too much champagne and not remember all the details from this evening." I laughed, thinking of Lady Sarah.

"I think that is a magnificent idea, Gemma," Aunt Margaret piped in. "You all have invested so much time and effort; I want them to have Cherrywood Hall front and center in their memories. We want to win this!"

"Hear, hear!" everyone cheered, laughing at Aunt Margaret's enthusiasm.

"Ladies and gentlemen, if you would come with me, we're ready for you to see the dining room and conservatory," Bridges announced from the library doorway. Aunt Margaret and Ma-ma gave excited little claps of their hands as they rose to follow Bridges. Evan turned and stopped me and Charles before we joined the others.

"You two have really done a marvelous job. I've been so behind in getting this completed, and now here it is," Evan said. "I can't thank you enough." He smiled. Charles blushed at the compliment but was very pleased.

"Well, I'm glad we've got this much done. There's still a lot to finish up, but I know Charles can do it." I smiled. "Now let's join Bridges. He's done so much in the dining room and conservatory, and I know he wants to show us." We walked across the grand hallway to the dining room, where Bridges was showing off all the details of the decor.

Kyle grabbed my hand and pulled me over to a corner, out of sight of the others. "Nice work, Gemma." He smiled as he bent down to give me one of his delicious proper kisses. "I am becoming more and more impressed at your talents. Do you think after tonight is over that I can steal you away to expand your knowledge into the area of proper cuddling? I have a feeling you are going to like it, Dr. Phillips," he said, kissing me once again.

"I want to learn the art of proper cuddling, Mr. Williams. I think I'm ready," I whispered, looking into his eyes.

He lifted me up, hugging my body next to his. "You're an excellent pupil, Gemma. I look forward to our lessons. Now, I think we better rejoin the group before your ma-ma comes looking for us." He laughed, lowering me gently to the floor. We came around the corner just as Bridges was leading the group in to tour the conservatory.

Evan smiled at me as we rejoined the group. "Nice of you two to rejoin us. I thought I was going to have to send Bridges to find you," he teased.

"I was just showing your cousin some of the details she might have missed earlier, sir." Kyle grinned mischievously. "We want her to be fully knowledgeable before our honored guests arrive."

"Uh-huh, nice try, old man," Evan said, winking at us both.

Simone kissed his cheek. "You will have to show me some of these details, Evan." We all laughed and lined up next to Bridges.

"As you can see, we've moved some of the plantings around. I wanted to show you this detail, which will be unveiled tonight formally by the Prince of Kingwood," Bridges said, pointing over to a new little berm area that had been constructed in front of the waterfall. It was covered with a cloth detailed with the crest of the Prince of Kingwood. He pointed to Aunt Margaret. "Lady Lancaster, would you care to do the honors for this practice session?" He handed Aunt Margaret a gold cord to pull.

"I'd love to, Bridges. Thank you," Aunt Margaret said, taking the cord and giving it a tug.

We all gasped a collective breath. Underneath the cloth crest was a perfect depiction of the Prince of Kingwood crest made up of gold mums for the lions, red roses for the shield, white lilies for the lyre, and blue violets for the fields. It was stunning in detail. I was sure Prince Hadley would love it. Ma-ma came over to hug Aunt Margaret, both with tears in their eyes.

"Mr. Kyle came up with the idea," Bridges said, clearly proud of our reaction.

"I was scouring the countryside for the cherry trees for the entrance pavilion. I saw so many beautiful flowers at the nursery; it was easy to be inspired. I'm glad it worked out," Kyle said humbly. He was quickly surrounded by Ma-ma, Aunt Margaret, and Simone, who all gave him kisses on his cheek. Evan came up to him last and gave him a brotherly hug.

"Thank you. It's stunning, old man," he whispered.

Bridges was beaming with pride. "Well now, ladies and gentlemen, lord and ladies, you have a ball to get ready for. May I suggest you retire to your rooms to refresh yourselves? Tea will be sent up at the bottom of the hour. Please let me know if you require any assistance," he said, dismissing us.

Aunt Margaret and Ma-ma went upstairs to their suites. Evan, Simone, Kyle, and I walked Charles to the front door to see him off. "Go get yourself all dressed up," I said, and smiled. "Lots of people are going to want to meet you tonight."

"Thanks, Dr. Gemma. Thank you all." He grinned, almost skipping out to his car. We grinned at his enthusiasm.

"Shall we have one drink before the storm?" Evan asked. We went into the sitting room. Evan poured us a glass of the Cherrywood sparkling rose, and we sat in front of the fireplace. "Is everything set with Chief Inspector Marquot?" he asked Kyle.

"His team is working with ours as well as the Royal Protection Services. Several of them will be dressed as staff and guests for the evening event. Others are dispersed throughout the grounds and hall in camouflage. I don't think you will see them." He smiled. "We've also installed some new surveillance tools—discreetly, of course. There will be a lot of eyes and ears at tonight's event, Evan, more so than at any of the others."

"We weren't expecting murders at the other events. I don't want a recurrence tonight," Evan said. "I hope we've made the right decision to continue. The thought of anything happening makes me ill. By the way, Francis called earlier. He will not be joining us tonight. He's still very distraught. I feel so sorry for him." We all lowered our eyes in remembrance of Christopher.

Simone gently squeezed Evan's leg. "It will be all right, darling. I'm sure Kyle has everything under control. I'll be glad to help subdue anyone who gets out of line. You had to report me, remember?"

"Report you? Why?" I asked.

"Simone has a black belt, Gemma." Kyle smiled. "It's technically classified as a lethal weapon. We had to report all the weapons we have at Cherrywood Hall to the police and protection services, so they know what to look for."

"Simone, I am so impressed. I'll be standing close to you tonight." I laughed.

Evan rose from his seat and raised his glass. "To all of you, please be careful tonight." We raised our glasses in silence and drank the remainder of our wine. We walked out to the grand hallway to say our good-byes to Kyle. Evan and Simone left us to go up to their suite.

Kyle lifted me up once more and gave me one last proper kiss before leaving. "Until our next lesson, Dr. Phillips," he said, lowering me down slowly, "I will take your leave, for now. I can't wait to see you, Gemma." He kissed my hand as he left. I turned and floated up the staircase to my suite.

The production company sent over a squadron of hairdressers and makeup artists to help Ma-ma, Aunt Margaret, Simone, and me to prepare ourselves for this evening. Mrs. Smythe and the staff she had for the evening showed them to our suites, and the dressing began.

We all relished getting pampered and readied for the big event. Our nails were manicured, our toes were pedicured, and our hair and makeup were styled to complement the necklines and colorings of our dresses. We gathered in Aunt Margaret's suite to take a late-afternoon tea together in our robes before we left to change and make final preparations for the evening. Kyle and Evan had been banished from seeing us until we walked down the Cherrywood staircase arm in arm tonight. We wanted to surprise them before the guests arrived and had arranged to meet them at seven.

Aunt Margaret, Simone, Ma-ma, and I met in the hallway outside our rooms to make our way down to the grand staircase.

We gasped as we saw one another in full dress, sparkling and shimmering in our gowns and jewels. Each dress complemented the figure and coloring of its wearer to perfection. Aunt Margaret in the rose-gold ensemble, Simone in the bronze metallic and velvet creation, and Ma-ma shimmering in the gold lamé dress looked magnificent.

I think I did Pippa proud as well. My hair was styled up, and I wore the Lancaster blue sapphire and diamond tiara, necklace, and earrings that matched my blue sequined Parisian gown as if they had been made for each other. I wore elbow-length gloves and slipped Kyle's mother's ring over them as the sole ornament on my hand. Its radiance complemented the other jewels well.

We joined hands and made our way to the top of the staircase leading down to the grand hall. Kyle and Evan stood at the bottom of the stairs and looked up at us, beaming. "May I present the Lancaster Ladies," I announced as we walked down the stairs to join them.

Kyle and Evan made their way to each of us and kissed our cheeks. "I can't believe how beautiful you are," Evan said to us.

"The dresses are magnificent, ladies." Kyle smiled.

"Gemma did this," Aunt Margaret said. "She pulled the dresses that she thought would be right for each of us." She nodded to Simone and Ma-ma.

"Thank you, Gemma," Simone said, and they all clapped softly in appreciation.

"And look at you, Gemma," Evan gushed as he twirled me around. "You look just like Pippa must have all those years ago. It's amazing." He smiled.

We went into the sitting room to have a glass of champagne before the guests arrived. Kyle poured and handed us each a glass.

"A toast," he started, looking at everyone with loving eyes, "to all of us and to Cherrywood Hall. No matter what the outcome of the competition, Cherrywood Hall will always be the best estate in the world. Our family and friends are the best."

"To Cherrywood Hall and our British family and friends," I added. "Thank you from your American cousins." We laughed and drank our champagne. In just a few minutes, the festivities of this long-awaited night would begin.

Aunt Margaret, Ma-ma, and Simone went to the conservatory, ready to mingle with the guests and make sure everyone received cocktails and hors d'oeuvres when they were shown to the room. The starlight lasers beamed around the room and set off the magical setting. Their jewels sparkled radiantly in the lights.

Kyle, Evan, and I made our way to the entrance staircase to greet the arriving guests as they drove up. Lucy Etheridge and Byron Brown joined us, representing the production company executives. Dame Agnes, Sir James, and Lady Sarah arrived next and went to join Aunt Margaret, Ma-ma, and Simone to greet the incoming guests and take notes for their judging. I noticed several men and women whom I had not recognized, all in formal attire, standing inside the hallway and outside. I assumed these were members of the police and the Royal Protective Service Kyle had mentioned. I crossed my fingers and wished that nothing would happen tonight.

Fairy lights coupled with colored spotlights gave an elegant look to the tented entrance. It had started to rain, so the tent covering for the entrance was well worth it. Kyle had set spotlights highlighting each of the painted containers holding the cherry trees lining the walkway. The artwork of the children was charming, making the setting more meaningful for Cherrywood Hall.

Promptly at eight o'clock, the stream of limousines made their way up the estate road and stopped in front of our lighted entryway. Actors and villagers arrived dressed in full splendor. A magnificent Royale limo pulled up, and the Prince of Kingwood and his wife, Princess Alyce, exited the car and made their way up to us. Photographers snapped pictures of their arrival.

"Good evening, Your Royal Highnesses." Evan bowed. "May I present my cousin, Dr. Gemma Phillips, and my business partner, Mr. Kyle Williams. They have been instrumental in helping me with the estate competition." Evan smiled.

"Yes, we've heard," Prince Hadley said. "Please don't dish up any murders tonight, Evan. The protective service members are a bit nervous."

"No murders tonight, Your Highness," Evan replied, trying to smile.

Prince Hadley addressed me. "I want to thank you for the inspiration of the Two Princes of Kingwood Dinner Gala, Dr. Phillips. It was nice to know that cousin Joey once stood on these very steps so long ago. The queen compliments you on a very thoughtful plan," he said, smiling.

"Thank you very much, sir, ma'am." I nodded to Prince Hadley and Princess Alyce, beaming. "It was a wonderful party in 1934, and I am sure tonight will be just as memorable."

"Kyle, very nice to see you. We saw the polo field being constructed out front. Can't wait to play there," said Prince Hadley.

"Thank you, sir. You'll be sure to get an invite as soon as it's completed."

As they made their way up the stairs to greet the others, Kyle warmly squeezed my hand. "The queen," he whispered. "Very impressive, Dr. Phillips."

"Your polo field got royal notice too. Not bad yourself."

"I think Mother told the queen about your plans, Gemma, so that she knew this was being done from a family perspective," Evan explained. "Family means a lot to her. You passed. You both did." He smiled.

Another royal limousine arrived at the entrance, and Prince Camdon and his wife, Duchess Priscilla, emerged. I marveled at how lovely Priscilla was in person and so tiny. She and Prince Camdon beamed their wonderful smiles to Evan and Kyle, whom they knew, and greeted the two men warmly. Evan introduced me to the young royals, and they happily shook my hand. Once again the photographers went wild.

"We loved visiting America." Prince Camdon smiled. "Priscilla cannot wait to go back with the children. She wants them to know your country."

"I'm sure tonight will be grand," the duchess added. "Good luck with the competition. We're very excited to see the new *Castlewood Manor* series."

The final limousines drove up, dropping off their finely dressed passengers. Lord Paunchley, Lady Jane, and Althea were among the last to arrive.

"Well, I hope your event doesn't have the same curse that ours did," Jane said with a sneer. Lord Paunchley rolled his eyes at her comment and slowly made his way up the stairs. Althea brought up the rear and nervously shook our hands. She looked different tonight, having worn a lighter color gown and applied some makeup to her normally colorless face.

"You look lovely, Althea," I said.

"Thank you, Gemma," she said graciously.

Charles was our final guest. He was a little breathless, having parked his car down by the stables, he explained.

We made our way into the hall and started walking to the conservatory, where the chatter and laughter of the group was in full swing. Kyle pulled me back for just a minute to give me a proper kiss.

"Shine tonight, Gemma. Pippa's watching." He smiled and led me into the conservatory.

The guests looked marvelous, shining in the blue and green starlight. They were making their way around the paths of the conservatory, enjoying looking at the pictures of the 1934 party and guests. Champagne and drinks flowed. Evan beamed with Simone by his side. I was happy for him. Aunt Margaret played lady of the manor and basked in the compliments offered for her lovely home. Ma-ma was magnificent. Even though she had to share the lead roles for the *Castlewood Manor* series with Dame Agnes and Sir James, tonight she played the star and highlighted her American connection to Cherrywood Hall. Kyle was taking question after question on the design of the waterfall and room and loved showing his work. I looked over and smiled, seeing Charles talking with the shy Althea. Lady Sarah walked over to them and started whispering to them in an animated fashion. What is she up to? I thought.

I turned the corner and saw Chief Inspector Marquot discreetly standing by the wall. He was dressed in a tuxedo but not as a guest. He was carefully watching the guests and every now and then speaking into what I thought had to be a microphone. I wondered how many "eyes" there were on us tonight. But I was thankful for the surveillance. I didn't want a tragedy on our hands tonight.

Bridges, in grand fashion, brought the room to a hush as the Prince of Kingwood and Princess Alyce were walked over to the

VERONICA CLINE BARTON

covered berm area in front of the waterfalls by Evan and Aunt Margaret. Kyle and I followed behind.

"Sir," Evan said, handing Prince Hadley the gold cord attached to the crest cover, "If you would be so kind to start us off on our Dinner Gala." Prince Hadley pulled the golden cord, and everyone saw the beautiful floral-depicted Prince of Kingwood crest appear. The whole room oohed and aahed in appreciation and clapped.

"It's lovely." Princess Alyce smiled, beaming at her husband, who was also moved by the beautiful tribute.

The dinner gong sounded promptly at nine, and we made our way into the dining room. Bridges and his staff guided the guests to their seats. The room glowed with the tea candles and gold and silver beads. The flowers were lovely and graced the room with their perfume. We took our seats, and a selection of Cherrywood wine was poured. Evan stood to make a toast before dinner began.

"Your Royal Highnesses, lords, ladies, and gentlemen, thank you for coming to support our event here at Cherrywood Hall tonight. You grace us with your presence, and we hope that you enjoy our lovely estate. To Cherrywood Hall."

"To Cherrywood Hall," everyone said in unison.

Like precision clockwork, Bridge's staff brought the carefully prepared food to the table. Course after course was served, just as it had been in 1934. The food was absolutely delicious. Chef Karl and his staff had truly set the bar high tonight. I looked down the table and smiled.

Pippa would be so proud tonight, I thought. Kyle was seated a few seats down from me, but I caught his glance and raised my glass to him. He nodded and looked at me intently with his deep green eyes. Dame Agnes, Sir James, and Lady Sarah were seated close to the royals and were basking in the questions being asked of them regarding the judging and production. Lady Sarah tried and tried to insert herself in every conversation, but I was glad to see the rigorous royal training on how to hold conversations was in full force tonight. The royals knew how to quiet someone not following conversation protocol.

The production company executives, selection committee members, and the actors seemed to be at ease as the dinner progressed and no tragedies occurred. After the past two events, I'm sure this was a welcome reprieve. I thought about Francis and the tragic deaths of his father and Christopher. Christopher would have loved this dinner, I thought sadly.

The locals, including Mayor Brown, Vicar Hawthorne, and Sally Prim, were seated close to Ma-ma. She was delighted to be relaying the current news on the production front for *Castlewood Manor*. The vicar looked like he was in seventh heaven. Ma-ma had a new best friend in him after this evening.

I was asked and answered many questions about my research on the American and British family reunifications. I was proud that my work of the past few years was of interest without the American bias or comments I had been subjected to in previous encounters.

After the last course had been served, Evan stood. "I hope you have enjoyed the lovely meal tonight. We have one more surprise for you this evening. If you would please join us and come to the terrace, I think you will be pleased."

I looked at Evan and Kyle and mouthed, "What's going on?" I hadn't known about this twist. We made our way to the terrace that overlooked the sea. It was eleven thirty, and the clouds and rain that had plagued us earlier had dried up, leaving a clear sky with magnificent starlight. Kyle came up to me and placed his arm around my shoulder.

"What have you two been up to?" I asked him and Evan and Simone, who had joined us.

"We wanted one more icing on the cake for our event," Evan said, smiling. "Kyle has planned the grand finale of all grand finales. Turn around, Gemma."

I turned as directed and soon was treated to a spectacular fireworks display. The fireworks sailed high in the air and exploded, their trailing remnants falling into the sea. Everyone was oohing and aahing, including the royals, the villagers, the actors, Ma-ma, and Aunt Margaret. Evan held Simone close in his arms. She was beaming at the beautiful display.

The sounds of the explosions shook the house and terrace. We marveled at one magnificent explosion after the other. The grand finale finally came and enchanted us with its grandeur. I smiled at Kyle, who still had his arm around my shoulder. He kissed the top of my head.

With the last explosion, everyone gasped and started to clap. I had raised my hands but suddenly fell to the ground, knocked out of Kyle's arms. I lay on the cold marble tiles that covered the terrace. My forehead, chest, and shoulder were covered in blood, quickly dulling the shine of my blue sequined dress. I had been shot.

The last thing I remember was the starlight shining in the dark sky and the frantic screaming of the guests. Kyle was bent over me, cradling my head and whispering, "Hang in there, Gemma. Help is on the way, darling. Please, hang in there." And then, silence.

18

Frantic Fear

"Hold on, Gemma. Hold on." It was her.

Pippa, is it you? I can't go with you. Not yet, I thought in my gray zone of consciousness, searching for the owner of that voice.

"Hold on, Gemma," the soft voice commanded.

I drifted in and out of my fog. Kyle had lifted me off the terrace floor and brought me to the library, where I was now lying on the leather couch. Dr. Moore from the village had been called and was on the way. My wounds included gunshot wounds that had grazed my forehead and some shot pellets into my shoulder. Luckily for me, they caused more bleeding than harm. Whoever had taken the kill shot had missed.

I opened my eyes and tried to focus. Kyle was kneeling on the floor by my side. Evan was standing with Ma-ma in his arms, both looking at me with concern. Simone was comforting Aunt Margaret, who was seated in a chair across the room. Chief Inspector Marquot stood at the library door standing guard and talking into his cell phone.

"What happened?" I whispered.

"Gemma, oh thank God," Ma-ma cried and knelt down by my side next to Kyle. Everyone looked very concerned and shaken. I started to sit up, but the pain was too immense. I sank back down into the leather couch.

"Don't move, darling," Kyle said. "You've been shot—well, shot at, anyway. The bloody fool missed, hitting your tiara instead of your head. The shot ricocheted, though, unfortunately, hitting your forehead and shoulder."

I put my left hand to my head, feeling a blood-soaked cloth that had been placed there, and then felt my right shoulder, which had also been covered. I reached for the tiara I had been wearing. It was gone.

"Kyle, the tiara is gone!" I cried, fearing I had lost it.

"The tiara saved your life, Gemma," he explained again. I couldn't seem to remember anything. "We have it. Don't worry. The bullet hit the frame of the tiara and ricocheted off. You were hit, but it could have been so much worse," he said, tears welling in his eyes.

Chief Inspector Marquot got off his phone and walked over to me. "You're very lucky, Dr. Phillips. We're on lockdown right now, looking for the shooter." A knock came at the door. It was Dr. Moore from the village. He came over to the couch where I lay and got some things out of his doctor's bag. He turned to the others.

"It would be good to give us some privacy, please."

"I should see about the guests," Aunt Margaret said, wiping her eyes.

"We'll go with you, Mother," Evan said, taking Simone's arm. He looked back to me. "Gemma, you're going to be OK, and we're going to catch this bastard. We'll be back in a bit to see how you are. I love you, Gemma," he added, his voice quivering.

"I love you too, cousin. Go on now and check on your guests." I tried to smile.

Kyle, Ma-ma, and Chief Inspector Marquot stayed in the room as Dr. Moore looked at my wounds. "You're very lucky, Miss Gemma," Dr. Moore muttered as he peeled back the blood-soaked cloths and looked at my wounds. I squinted as he probed a little too close to my head wound.

"There, there," he said softly, "just let me clean this a little more." Ma-ma cringed and turned into Kyle's shoulder.

"My poor baby," she cried, the stress getting to her.

"Can you give her something, Doctor? This has been too much for her, I'm afraid," I said, looking up at Ma-ma.

"In time, dear. Right now I want to examine the wounds to see what needs to be done and give you some injections. You need to keep calm now, Miss Gemma. When was your last tetanus shot? I'd like to take you to your room so that you can get undressed and be made more comfortable. I can clean and bandage the wounds and administer the injections more easily." He smiled. "Can you have a stretcher brought up by any chance?" he asked, looking over to Kyle.

"Of course, let me call down to the staff," he said, picking up the receiver for the house intercom.

"Now, let me see to you while we're waiting," Dr. Moore said to Ma-ma, leading her over to a chair.

"I'm all right," she said tearfully. "Is Gemma OK?"

"She's going to be fine, Ms. Phillips. Here, take one of these," he said, handing her a pill and a glass of water. "She'll be better knowing you are well. We don't want our patient worrying any more than she has to, do we?" Ma-ma dutifully shook her head and swallowed the pill.

Chief Inspector Marquot pulled up a chair next to me on the sofa. Kyle had gone downstairs to help the staff locate the stretcher and bring it up to me.

"Have you caught anyone yet?" I whispered.

"Not yet, Dr. Phillips. The secret alarms along the property were triggered when you were shot at, so we know the general area of the perpetrator," he answered. "Or perpetrators. Several sets of footprints have been found."

"What about the royals? Are they OK? They will never attend another event I'm afraid," I said, trying to smile.

Chief Inspector Marquot smiled at me. "They've been safely taken away. They were more concerned about you, Dr. Phillips. The British royals are very solid, you know. Been around for thousands of years. They aren't going anywhere." I grinned at the chief inspector's attempt to cheer me.

Kyle came through the door with Bridges, carrying the stretcher. A policeman was there as well, summoning Chief Inspector Marquot, who rose to go speak with him. Dr. Moore left Ma-ma's side and came over, instructing Kyle and Bridges on where to hold me to lift me to the stretcher.

"One, two, three," he counted. Kyle and Bridges lifted me gently from the sofa to the stretcher. I grimaced a little but was glad to be going up to my room. Ma-ma came to my side and held my hand.

The policeman left, and Chief Inspector Marquot came over to us. "They are starting to release the guests to go home. Two guests are missing," he said with concern.

"Who?" Kyle and I asked in unison.

"Charles Linford and Lady Sarah Effington."

"Charles and Lady Sarah?" Kyle said incredulously. "Well, they must be here somewhere. Certainly they aren't the ones? They didn't even know each other until this evening." His voice drifted off.

"We've asked Lord Paunchley, Althea Jones, and Lady Jane to stay here at Cherrywood tonight, for their safety," Chief Inspector Marquot said. "This attack is obviously connected to the competition. I've sent a detail over to Shipley House to check on Lord Francis as well. We've located a rappelling rope at the base of the cliffside next to the terrace. That's where the footprints were found. We're also checking the security videos for that area."

"I saw them talking earlier this evening: Althea, Charles, and Lady Sarah," I started to mumble. "I thought they were meeting for the first time, but Lady Sarah was acting as if she already knew them. She does know Althea, of course, but not Charles. She was acting as if she was upset."

"Why would she be upset with them?" the chief inspector asked. "I don't believe Mr. Linford was a guest at either the Shipley House or Longthorpe Manor events."

"He wasn't there," Kyle said firmly. "He was only at the event tonight because of the work he had been doing for the Cherrywood Hall virtual tour and archive project."

"The Cherrywood Hall virtual tour?" Chief Inspector Marquot asked.

"Charles had been working with me to get videos of the grounds and rooms here at the hall for the website and our archive project," I started to explain.

"I'll show you later, Chief Inspector," Kyle said, shaking his head for the chief inspector not to quiz me more.

"Of course."

"Let's get you up to your room," Dr. Moore said as Kyle and Bridges lifted me in the stretcher. They thought it would be faster to carry me up the grand staircase instead of going around to the elevator in the back of the house. As we made our way into the grand hall, I saw Evan, Simone, and Aunt Margaret at the entrance of the sitting room. Jane, Althea, and Lord Paunchley were standing with them.

"Gemma," Jane called, starting to walk over to my stretcher.

Lord Paunchley jerked her arm to pull her back. "Let her be, Jane," he said, his eyes looking at me. Althea cowered next to him.

Why, he's quite strong, I thought as we made our way past and started up the stairs.

Slowly but surely, Bridges and Kyle took one stair at a time as we progressed up the staircase. Ma-ma and Dr. Moore stood by my side just in case I started to slip. We finally reached the top of the stairs, and they swiftly took me down the hallway to my room. Mrs. Smythe was waiting there with another maid to get me undressed and into my nightgown. She had set the fire in the fireplace to get the room nice and toasty for me.

Ma-ma went to her room to change. Dr. Moore waited with Kyle outside in the hall.

"Let me get the poor girl undressed, please," Mrs. Smythe said, shooing them out of the room. Bridges left to take the stretcher back down to the storage area.

Mrs. Smythe and the maid carefully rolled me to my left side as they unzipped my gown and carefully took it off me. They laid it on the side of the bed and put a soft cotton nightgown over my head. It had an elastic neckline that Mrs. Smythe stretched and put under my right underarm to keep my shoulder clear. As she adjusted the gown, I looked at the beautiful blue dress, now stained with dried blood.

"I've ruined Pippa's dress." I started to cry.

"Don't you worry about that dress at all, miss," Mrs. Smythe said sternly, motioning for the other maid to take it out of my sight. "We'll get it back to new. Just you see. The most important thing is that you're OK." She started to sniff. "You poor girl... You're so good, and these terrible things have happened to you here. It's not right," she said indignantly. She took off my earrings and brushed back my hair, carefully avoiding my wounds. I still had my long gloves on. She rolled them off one by one.

On my right hand, I still had Kyle's mother's ring on. She handed it to me as she took off the glove. I put the ring back on my finger. I wanted it close to me—at least for tonight.

"There, that's much better, miss." She wiped her eyes and went to let Dr. Moore in, still keeping Kyle out. "Not just yet," she warned him, yet gently squeezing his arm. It seemed our blooming romance was now known in the servants' hall.

Dr. Moore walked quietly into my room. "Now that's better," he said, eyeing my nightgown. He wiped out my wounds with alcohol and antiseptic. I winced as he took out a bit more of the shot in my shoulder. He placed bandages over the cleaned wounds. "Can you roll over to your left side once more so that I can give you these injections? I'm giving you a tetanus shot, just in case."

I did as he asked as he lifted my gown and gave me two quick shots in my rear. He pulled down the gown and helped me get straightened upright in my bed, adjusting my pillows.

"You'll be asleep soon," he whispered. "Your shoulder and arm are going to be very sore for a while. The scrapes on your forehead should heal well. You may want to get a little plastic

surgery just to make sure there's no scarring of that pretty face."
He gave me a soft pat on my head and let Kyle into my room.

Kyle came and sat on the bed next to me. His tuxedo shirt was
unbuttoned, showing his beautiful hairy chest. He bent down
and properly kissed my lips.

Dr. Moore cleared his throat. "She's going to be asleep soon.
Watch that shoulder." He smiled to Kyle.

Ma-ma, now changed into a velour jogging suit, entered the
room. She sat on the other side of my bed and kissed my hand.
"I'm staying with her," she announced.

"Me too," added Kyle.

"Well, that's fine. Just remember she needs rest after all this,"
Dr. Moore said. He looked at Ma-ma. "You will be asleep soon too,"
he said, reminding her of the pill he had given her in the library.

"I don't care. I'm staying with her. I'll sit there," she said,
pointing to the chair by the fireplace.

"Fine." He smiled. He looked at Kyle. "If she wakes up, see
if you can get her to eat some broth," he instructed. "She's had a
shock to her body."

"I'll take care of her," Kyle said as Dr. Moore left.

I was already getting drowsy. "Where are Evan and Simone?
And Aunt Margaret," I asked sleepily.

"They're in their rooms, dear," Ma-ma said, tenderly holding my left hand. "I saw them when I went to change. They had
just gotten Jane, Althea, and Lord Paunchley settled in the guest
rooms. Everyone is pretty worn out. It's almost two in the morning." I looked up at Kyle, who was still sitting carefully next to
me on my right side.

"What is Chief Inspector Marquot doing?" I asked.

"Don't worry, Gemma darling. He and his men are still here.
They're looking for Charles and Lady Sarah and also checking

on Francis to make sure he's OK. Don't think about them. You're safe now," he said softly.

I drifted off to sleep. The last thing I saw was Pippa's portrait glimmering in the firelight, her steady gaze watching over me. Ma-ma let go of my hand and kissed me once she saw that I was asleep. She went around to the other side and kissed Kyle's cheek as well.

"Thank you for taking care of my daughter," she whispered, wiping a tear from her cheek. "She's all I have." Kyle softly got up from my bedside and led Ma-ma over to the chair by the fire. He sat her down and pulled the ottoman over to set her feet on. He covered her with a blanket. "Please sit with me," she asked. He pulled the other chair closer and sat down, holding her hand. They looked at the fire, and soon Ma-ma was asleep. He sat there, nodding off himself.

At four in the morning, I woke up, having to use the bathroom desperately. Kyle heard me stir and came to my bed. "Hi," I said, trying to smile. "I have to wee." He laughed at my predicament.

"Let me help you, darling, my damsel in distress." He laughed, helping me carefully out of the bed and leading me to the WC in my bathroom.

"I can manage," I said, trying to go in the WC myself.

"No, milady," Kyle said gently but sternly, "I'm not taking the chance of you hitting a marble floor again tonight. Your throne, milady," he said, pulling up my nightgown and sitting my bum on the toilet. He stood discreetly, back to the door, as I took my wee. He helped me back to my bed when I was finished and washed up.

He plumped my pillows to make me comfortable. "Are you hungry, Gemma?" he asked. "Dr. Moore wanted you to have some broth if you woke. And perhaps some tea?"

"I'd love some, but I'm sure no one is up yet," I said.

"I'll go down and bring up a tray. I'm pretty handy in the kitchen, you know." He smiled, kissing my lips.

"I want to see your cuddling skills. You owe me lessons, you know."

"You will, darling. I promise," he said, kissing me once again. "But for now, some food for milady." He smiled. He checked my room over before he left.

I looked over at Ma-ma, still slumbering, gently nestled up in the chair. The fire crackled as a log fell, stirring up some sparks. I looked at Pippa's gaze in her portrait and started as I heard a movement from the other side of my room. I squinted to see in the darkness. Slowly, like a dark ghost moving silently across the floor, I saw a hooded figure dressed in black, slowly making its way over to me. A cleaver glistened in the firelight.

"Who are you?" I said, trying to see who the figure was. "What are you doing? Why do you want to hurt me?"

The figure said nothing, creeping closer to my bed. Ma-ma was still out cold, slumbering from the sleeping pill Dr. Moore had given to her.

I tried to move in my bed, but the nightgown was caught under me, making it very hard for me to move. The figure was coming closer, the cleaver looming overhead.

"Stop it," I yelled, throwing a pillow at the figure.

"That won't help you," it growled. "I'm killing you myself. You're going to die," it said evilly.

"Who are you?" I screamed, frantically trying to push the secret buttons on my bedside table that Evan had shown to me. I prayed that he would see the lights and come in through the secret panel door. The figure made its way around the end of my bed, coming straight for me. "Help!" I screamed when the figure had nearly reached the bed.

I heard the panel door being slammed open. Someone rushed to the back of the figure, giving a lethal chop to the back of its neck. The hooded figure stopped and crashed down to the floor, totally knocked out. Ma-ma screamed as she woke up with the commotion. Evan and Kyle both ran into my room through the hallway door.

Evan switched on the light as Kyle dropped the tray he was carrying and ran over to me, stepping over the figure lying on the ground. I looked up as he put his arms around me, still trembling. I looked up at my hero. It was Simone. She had karate chopped my attacker, saving my life. Evan came to her side and held her.

"Now I know where I've seen you," Ma-ma said, looking at Simone. "You're the world title karate champion from 2000," she gushed. "I was such a fan!"

"Secret is out," Simone said, smiling.

"Yes, yes, of course," Ma-ma said, trying to recover herself. "Well, thank God you were here. You saved Gemma's life." She pointed to the dark hooded figure lying on the floor, now starting to moan.

"Who is that?" she cried. We all jumped when we heard another person crashing through the French doors in my room. Kyle ran and knocked down the second intruder. It was Althea.

"What in the world are you doing?" Kyle said, angrily grabbing Althea and standing her up.

"I came to try to stop him," she said, pointing to the downed first intruder. "He's insane."

Kyle let Althea go and went over to Evan. They bent down and lifted the moaning figure to its feet. Simone picked up the cleaver

and took it across the room, where it could not be grabbed. They
sat it down and lifted the dark hoody from its head. Wiry, small,
not frail, Lord Paunchley had been unmasked. Our mouths fell
open upon seeing him. His face was stretched in an unnatural
look, his eyes bulging. He started to get up and attack, but Evan
and Kyle held him down. He began to scream and talk wildly.
Foam dripped from his mouth.

"You bastard," Ma-ma screamed, starting to run over and
hit him. Simone gently grabbed her by the waist.

"He's not worth it," she soothed, keeping Ma-ma at bay.

Chief Inspector Marquot ran into my room with two more
policemen. "We've caught them," he said. He and his men
stopped dead when they saw Lord Paunchley and Althea in
my room. "What in the world has happened? Why are you all
here?"

"Lord Paunchley climbed up the side of the hall into my
room. He was going to kill me," I said, pointing to the cleaver
Simone had placed across the room. "Kyle had gone downstairs to get me some broth. He checked the room before he
left. Ma-ma was asleep from the sleeping pill. He just kept
coming toward me, no words, nothing, just the glint of the
cleaver. I remembered the buttons Evan told me about for the
panel door adjoining our rooms. Thank goodness Simone
saw the lights in their suite. She busted through the door
and knocked Lord Paunchley out cold. She's a black belt, you
know," I said, beaming over to her. "And then Althea came
through the French doors after. She must have climbed up
the side too."

"I did," Althea said, crying. "As I said, he's insane. I heard
him leave his room and saw him crawling up the side of the hall
to get to Gemma's room. I'm afraid he's killed before. I couldn't

let him kill Gemma too. No more..." Althea was sobbing now, clearly in distress.

Lord Paunchley sneered, "They're idiots. Couldn't do anything right. You were supposed to be dead!"

Chief Inspector Marquot's men had been called in for reinforcements. "Handcuff Lord Paunchley and take him in. Be careful. The chap's mad," he directed. "Miss Jones, you are going to have to come to the station as well." Althea nodded and was escorted out. Her head hung very low.

"Who did you catch?" Evan asked, going back to Simone's side and hugging her. Kyle and Ma-ma got me straightened out in bed and sat down beside me.

Chief Inspector Marquot moved to stand in front of the fireplace, trying to gather his thoughts with all this new commotion. He turned slowly to our group and smiled. "I came up to tell you we caught Charles Linford and Lady Sarah. Charles was an easy catch. He was hiding behind some haystacks in the barn. We heard the horses whinnying and went to investigate. He started to cry as soon as he saw us."

"Did he and Lady Sarah try to shoot me? Why? Where did you find her?"

"No, Miss Gemma, Charles did not shoot at you. Lady Sarah did, with her accomplice."

"Her accomplice? Who was helping her?" Kyle asked.

"Francis Hampton helped her with the shooting. We caught them, trying to hide in the tunnel leading from the winery to the hall. They had the shotgun they used with them. Part of the tunnel wall collapsed where they were hiding. They were covered in dirt and bricks. Couldn't move."

"How did the wall collapse? I just had them reinforced," Kyle said.

A log in the fire fell and sent up sparks. We all looked over, hearing the noise. The extra sparks made Pippa's portrait above the fireplace glisten. She seemed to be smiling down at us all.

"Pippa!" we said in unison.

19

Wrapping Up Loose Ends

The morning after the attack, Lord Francis Hampton, Lady Sarah Effington, Lord Frederick Paunchley, Althea Jones, and Charles Linford were arrested and charged with their crimes. The charges were not released to the public immediately due to the ongoing investigations. Chief Inspector Marquot told us we would be the first to know in a few weeks, once the complete set of charges was ready to be released to the public. The police were taking great care due to the seriousness of the charges and the impact all of this was going to have on the estate selection for the *Castlewood Manor* series. The utmost of discretion was being deployed. This time, the chief inspector made sure that even Lady Sarah could not squeeze out a leak.

Life went on at Cherrywood Hall, and everyone was busy with the upcoming holiday and events. Kyle had the immense task of making sure the Cherrywood winery met their Christmas and New Year holiday order commitments. The notoriety from the estate competition had given the winery much publicity, and orders had skyrocketed, which deeply excited the distributors. He had also lined up his construction team to begin repair to the fallen tunnel wall where Francis and Sarah had been caught. He was determined to find the cause of the wall collapse, but no matter what he found, I was sure Aunt Pippa had given some ghostly help to catch the criminals.

Evan and Simone were going to focus on getting Cherrywood Hall ready for the upcoming Christmas events. Given all the tragedy of the past few months, Evan wanted to make this holiday season extra special for the village and community guests who would be coming to the hall. He and Simone were working a calendar of events with Mayor Brown and Vicar Hawthorne so as not to conflict with any preplanned village or church functions. Sally Prim had promised to publish the calendar of events in the *Maidenford Banner*. Evan and Simone knew there was going to be a good turnout. Everyone wanted to come and see the scene of the crime. Bridges, Chef Karl, and Mrs. Smythe had full authority to bring in whatever help they needed to prepare for the expected large crowds.

Since I had been shot, everyone determined I needed to focus on getting well. I spent the next few weeks in London with Ma-ma and Aunt Margaret at the Belgravia house. The shot fragments that had grazed my forehead and shoulder had left some scarring, as Dr. Moore predicted. Ma-ma insisted that I get them taken care of immediately and of course engaged the best (in other words, most expensive) plastic surgeon in London. I was able to do most of the surgeries as an outpatient and only stayed one night in the hospital. Kyle, Evan, and Simone did manage to come down once to see me, even in the midst of their hectic schedules. Kyle had been traveling back and forth between Cherrywood Hall and Oxford, where most of the distributors were located. It was good to have him hold me and give me proper kisses again. I was missing them.

Evan held several meetings at Rosehill Productions with his solicitor, Mr. Gowen. The murders and associated crimes were not the only events being investigated. Lady Sarah Effington had been found to be in collusion with the late Lord James Hampton, now Lord Francis Hampton, and the late Mr. Christopher Madden to throw the results of the estate competition to Shipley House. This scandal ripped through the production company, and all public relations resources were being used to make clear to the public and investors that Rosehill Communications and the other *Castlewood Manor* selection committee judges had had absolutely no knowledge of their efforts. The path forward for the series competition was in twenty-four-seven negotiations. Evan was under oath to not disclose any details. We were going to have to wait to see what the outcome would be once negotiations were completed.

Luckily my wounds were almost completely healed now. I was leaving the Belgravia house to travel back to Cherrywood Hall the day after tomorrow.

"I need to see some Christmas lights in here." I smiled, sitting in the sun-room with Aunt Margaret and Ma-ma. "It's just what the doctor ordered to make my recovery complete. Evan and Simone are decorating Cherrywood Hall with Mrs. Smythe and Bridges. It will be done before I get there, most likely. Please, Aunt Margaret, can we decorate? It won't seem like Christmas..."

Ma-ma and Aunt Margaret looked at each other and rolled their eyes at my dramatic request and then laughed. "Nice job,

Daughter." Ma-ma giggled. "You may have some theatrical blood in you yet."

"I'm glad you asked, Gemma. Jillian and I were already talking about decorating. I have some lovely mercury glass ornaments that haven't been put out for a long time. Now that I have family with me, it's time to showcase them once more. James has found a place for us to get a Christmas tree near Kensington Palace. I'll have him send out for one immediately to be delivered this afternoon—with garland for the stairway banister, of course." Ma-ma and I clapped our hands in anticipation. We were all excited to begin decorating.

Aunt Margaret, Ma-ma, and I went up to the attic, where the decorations were stored. I was amazed at how neat and orderly everything was.

"Ah, here they are," Aunt Margaret said, pulling out a container with her mercury glass ornaments. She unwrapped one to show us. It was an angel, and it shined radiantly with its mercury glass finish.

"Look here," Ma-ma said, pulling out a large wood crèche and crystal figurines of Mary, Joseph, and the Christ child. "Margaret, these are stunning. Are they Irish crystal?"

"Yes, they are. They're Pippa's, actually. She had them commissioned before the war. She loved the sparkle they have with the Christmas lights. I haven't put the crèche scene out in many years. We'll put it out on the round table in the entry in honor of our American cousins." She smiled. "You girls are a very brave lot."

That afternoon an eleven-foot-high tree and garland for the banisters were delivered. The twinkling lights, smell of evergreen, and the beautiful ornaments made my spirits soar. We set up the tree in the sitting room and, with help from the staff, had the tree and banisters decorated by evening.

"It's beautiful," I said, sitting on an ottoman by the fire. Aunt Margaret had turned off all the lights except those on the tree and mantel. The room was stunning.

"It's so nice having people here with me," Aunt Margaret said. "I haven't done much entertaining these past few years."

"Well, we will change that, Margaret," Ma-ma chirped, getting up to pour us a refill of our wine. "I'm staying with you for the foreseeable future. I'm sure the cast of *Castlewood Manor* would love to have dinner parties at your beautiful home. You know how actors are. Chef Karl and I are planning some collaboration too. Maybe he has a friend."

"Oh, Jillian, really." Aunt Margaret smiled. "What have I signed up for?"

"I think you two ladies are going to have serious fun with the start of the *Castlewood Manor* production. You'll be the talk of London." It was good to see Ma-ma and Aunt Margaret's friendship revived. I knew Ma-ma would definitely keep things interesting at the Belgravia house.

I did my Christmas shopping my last day before leaving London. I combed the stalls on Portobello Road in Notting Hill for unique gifts for my family and newfound friends. For Ma-ma, some lovely Victorian garnet drop earrings; for Simone, a beaded choker of cabochon-set sapphires; and for Aunt Margaret, a Victorian set of mercury glass ornaments and crystal garlands to go into her collection. I bought Evan gold cufflinks shaped as an elephant's head to remind him of his beloved Africa. For Kyle, I had found an elegant gold watch. I had the back engraved with a drawing of Cherrywood Hall. I knew how much he adored

Cherrywood, and he was always there for me, in good times and bad.

I left for Cherrywood Hall the next morning. Aunt Margaret had her driver take me there. She and Ma-ma would be coming up to join us in a few days. My wounds had healed nicely, and the plastic surgeries ensured that minimal damage would show. The countryside was beautiful in the crisp December air. I hugged my maxi-length faux fox vest close to keep me warm. I loved being able to comfortably wear my faux furs and boots. I had looked and saw that Malibu was hitting ninety degrees this week—difficult for faux fur in those temperatures.

I missed my cozy beach cottage in Malibu at times, especially the sounds of the waves hitting the shore at night. This would be my first Christmas without Michael. I hadn't thought of him much these past few months. He had tried calling and texting me at first but soon stopped when I didn't answer. His betrayal still stung but had been replaced by the love and comradery of the people here at Cherrywood. I was blessed to have my family with me this Christmas and looked forward to the relationship that was growing between Kyle and me.

The limousine pulled in front of the Cherrywood entry. Kyle, Evan, Simone, Bridges, Mrs. Smythe, and Chef Karl were standing at the entry, waiting to greet me. I gave them hugs, a non-English thing to do, but it was Christmas, and I wanted to hug the people who had taken such good care of me.

"Wow, I can't believe you all are here. I missed you so much," I gushed.

"We missed you too. Cherrywood Hall wasn't the same without you. Here, let me see you in the light," Evan said, pulling back my hair and looking at my forehead. "Wow, fantastic. Gemma, I can't even tell where you were hit." My welcoming contingent all took a look at my forehead and were pleased that I had not been permanently scarred.

"Ma-ma had only the best plastic surgeons for me." I laughed. "I have to admit they did a stunning job. I didn't want any trace of that horrible night."

Kyle hugged my waist and led me inside the hall. "No one will hurt you gain," he whispered.

I couldn't believe the transformation I found in the grand hallway. I breathed in the crisp smell of newly cut evergreen that pervaded the air. Fairy lights had been placed around the garlands and mantles, making everything I looked at twinkle and sparkle. I felt like a princess walking into a Christmas castle.

"You guys, this is stunning. Look at all the work you've done. And this tree—it's magnificent." A twenty-foot pine stood at the end of the hallway, glistening with lights and sparkling ornaments. A large gold gilded chair sat beside the tree, a perfect place for Father Christmas to hand out gifts.

"It is beautiful, isn't it? Bridges and Mrs. Smythe and their staff did most of the heavy lifting. I was amazed to see how quickly they can get things done. Evan and I just did as they directed." Simone laughed.

Tea was set up in the conservatory for us. Kyle had added more laser lights, and as we drank our tea and ate our yummies, we sparkled with the colors of Christmas. Ornaments hung from the larger plants and trees, giving the room more seasonal whimsy.

"So what is planned for this wonderful week?" I asked.

"Well, the main events are on Christmas Eve," Evan said. "Mother and Aunt Jillian will be here the day before. We host a luncheon on Christmas Eve for all the workers and their families here at Cherrywood and many of the villagers we worked with in

Maidenford for the competition. They'll have a chance to see all the decorations and trees in the grand hallway and conservatory, and a gourmet lunch will be held in the dining room. Kyle has even agreed to be Father Christmas for us and hand out gifts to the children." He laughed.

"Ho, ho, ho," Kyle deadpanned. "Better have a few more of these scones," he said, reaching for another one from the silver tiered tray on our table. "We're hoping for a major snowfall that day," he said in-between bites. "I've had the horse sleighs taken out of storage and made ready. If we're lucky, we can give the folks sleigh rides in the afternoon and hopefully ride them into town for the church service on Christmas Eve. We're supposed to have blizzard conditions early Christmas morning."

"Oh, that sounds wonderful," I gushed. "Please, please, please let it snow." I made a wish. Everyone laughed at my child-like enthusiasm, but deep down I knew they wanted the snow too.

"On Christmas Day, we'll open gifts and relax. Kyle has scheduled a top-secret reveal with the family that we are all eagerly awaiting on the twenty-sixth, Boxing Day. Of course, our big day is New Year's Eve," Evan finished quietly.

"The competition is still on?" I gasped.

"Yes, I've just heard from the solicitors. Rosehill Productions is continuing the estate competition with just Cherrywood Hall and Longthorpe Manor still in consideration. Believe it or not, Dame Agnes is supposedly pushing for Cherrywood Hall to be selected, and Sir James is pushing for Longthorpe Manor. Shipley House was eliminated, of course, once the scandal with Sarah Effington and the Hampton crowd was discovered."

"Jane is staying in, even with her father's illness and charges?" I asked. Simone, Evan, and Kyle looked at one another with sadness and then turned to me.

"Well, I'm afraid there is news," Evan began, "and it's not good. Lord Paunchley hanged himself two nights ago. He left a note, according to Chief Inspector Marquot. He apologized to his daughter, Jane, for bringing this shame to the family. And he apologized to you, Gemma, for all the harm done to you. I understand his death will be announced publicly tomorrow afternoon. Chief Inspector Marquot has requested a meeting with us tomorrow morning if you are up to it. He will brief us on the charges to be made against everyone. This information will be released publicly tomorrow afternoon as well."

"I'm so sorry all this happened. What a tragedy," I said, tears welling up.

"Let's show Gemma the rest of the decorations," Simone said, trying to lift our moods. "You should see the terrace, Gemma. It's so lush and beautiful."

We got up and made our way to the terrace to see the decorations. We sat by the huge Christmas tree in the grand hallway that evening and had a light dinner of sandwiches and soup. It was to be an early evening. We were having murder debriefs in the morning.

Bright and early, Chief Inspector Marquot joined us for breakfast in the dining room. A full English breakfast was being served this morning, and everyone seemed to be ravenous from the anticipation of learning what had happened. Even Chief Inspector Marquot was tucking into the delicious food this morning. I thought I saw him crack an unforced smile, something I had not seen him do in the past weeks. When we finished eating, the dishes were cleared. We refilled our coffee and teacups as Chief Inspector Marquot stood and began to tell us what they had learned from the suspects and investigations.

"I wanted to tell you what we know at this time. As you know, Lord Paunchley has committed suicide. He confessed to the murder of Lord Hampton and Christopher Madden in his written note. Althea Jones was his accomplice. He promised her a great deal of money if she would assist him. Being a poor relation, she took what she thought was her only opportunity out of poverty. Originally, he had only planned the death of Lord Hampton. He couldn't stand the thought of that man and his estate being compared with Longthorpe Manor. His grievance against Lord Hampton and the rumored relationship between his wife and her subsequent suicide festered for many years."

"Aunt Margaret said there was a dramatic change once Lady Paunchley died. Why did he kill Christopher, though?" I asked.

"Lady Jane Paunchley made the decision to enter the estate competition without Lord Paunchley's knowledge. She had secretly entered because she had incurred much debt. Lady Jane unfortunately has gambled away most of the Longthorpe Manor estate assets. Winning the competition and infusing the estate with millions of pounds of cash was her only way to get out of the debt. Lord Paunchley reluctantly agreed to her plan. They brought in Althea Jones to assist with the effort. He saw that she could easily be influenced to help him carry out his devious plan.

"Lord Paunchley thought Lord Hampton's death would deal Francis such a great blow that he would remove Shipley House from the competition. He also thought you would be scared out of the competition, Lord Evan. He didn't anticipate the collusion between Lady Sarah and the Hampton crowd to throw the competition off course. After Lord Hampton's death, Francis did not withdraw, as we know. Mr. Madden's flamboyant behavior and dress infuriated Lord Paunchley the day of the hunt, especially in front of Prince Andres. This was their event, and he thought the Hamptons were purposely trying to sabotage it. He went out at the last minute and first shot pellets at Miss Gemma's horse as a distraction. He then shot Christopher Madden. He and Althea had grass stains because they were posturing for a shot in the wet snow and mud. He had to kill the horse Christopher was riding after it fell in the snow. I think that pushed his mental collapse as well.

"He was sure in his insane mind that Francis would withdraw from the competition with Christopher's death. He also once more counted on your withdrawal. When neither of those occurred, he went certifiably insane."

"When did he poison Lord Hampton?" I asked.

"At the tea and garden tour, Lord Paunchley, with Althea Jones's help, put strychnine into the whiskey flask next to the decanter in Lord Hampton's library. He had obtained the poison from an old shed that was on the Longthorpe Manor estate. You saw them go into Shipley House, Dr. Phillips, under the guise of Lord Paunchley not feeling well. They knew that Lord Hampton had been drinking whiskey all day. They put the poison in his flask. They were sure Lord Hampton would fill it and take it into the tea event. Althea and Lord Paunchley encouraged some of Francis's friends to go into Lord Hampton's library, knowing that when Lord Hampton found them, he would explode, drink more whiskey, and fight with Lord Francis. Lord Paunchley tried to make it look like Lord Francis was the key suspect in his father's death. You heard Francis say he hated his father."

"So if Francis had dropped out of the competition after Lord Hampton's death, Christopher would be alive today. How did the Hamptons and Christopher get in cahoots with Lady Sarah?" I asked.

"Unfortunately, Mr. Madden pressed Lord Francis to stay in the competition, sure that they would win with Lady Sarah's help. You see, they had invested a considerable amount of money in Lady Sarah's stock fund that she managed, which failed due to her embezzling her client's funds. She needs money and lots of it to survive in her rich lifestyle. You'll read of that news later this week. Lord Francis was enraged when he found out the stock fund was ruined, but Lady Sarah tried to convince him that she could help sway the estate competition to Shipley House, making them millions. She used Christopher's love of glitz and glamour to persuade Lord Francis to remain in the competition and help her eliminate the other estates. She first targeted the Hemsworths. She and Lord Francis cut the brake line of the Hemsworths' car, causing them to crash."

"What a horrible woman," Kyle said. "I knew of her reputation for years. She caused one of my college friends to commit suicide after publicly humiliating him. She used her royal godparentage to keep the press coverage down on that one. All she does is use people." I put my hand on his shoulder and gave him a squeeze.

"So was it Sarah and Francis who tried to run us off the road? Did they try to push Gemma off the cliffside as well? How did they know where we were and when Gemma would be out walking?" Evan asked. "Gemma just arrived in this country. What possible motive would they have for harming or killing her?"

"They needed you to pull out of the competition too, Lord Evan, after the Hemsworths' deaths. They knew your fondness for Dr. Phillips. They enlisted Charles Linford's assistance in getting them information about the estate and where you all would be. Charles, with his knowledge of your computer and security systems, gave them the information in exchange for some hefty payments. Lady Sarah tried to run you off the road in her coupe. She spoke to Charles Linford right after your first luncheon with him in Maidenford. She and Lord Francis also attacked Dr. Phillips on the cliffside at Cherrywood Hall. In both cases, Charles told them where you'd be. They were counting on you being a gentleman and wanting to protect your cousin. They did not count on Miss Gemma's American spunk and desire to continue." He smiled. "Lord Hampton's death was a gift to them. Lord Francis suspected it was Lord Paunchley who had killed his father. He knew of the years of pent-up rage. His father's death didn't mean anything to him. Christopher's death did, however. He and Sarah planned to kill you the night of the Two Princes of Kingwood Dinner Gala, Dr. Phillips, to get Lord Evan to pull out of the competition once and for all. Charles Linford planted the gun on the hillside by the terrace for them to shoot at you. They took the shot at you, Dr. Phillips, during the fireworks. Everyone was looking up at the sky, not at the surrounding hills. Lord Francis was not expected at your gala, so he would not be missed. Lady Sarah left as soon as it got crowded on the terrace, going to join Lord Francis to make the shot. They were going to try to blame everything on Lord Paunchley."

"Their plan might have worked had Simone not knocked Lord Paunchley out in Gemma's room and had Althea not come to her senses and confessed. Unbelievable," Kyle said, shaking his head.

"I'm so disappointed with Charles. He seemed like a nice young man—a bit shy perhaps, but very talented technically," I said.

"They needed him for access to you and the computer and security systems here at Cherrywood Hall," Chief Inspector Marquot explained. "Lady Sarah did her research. She found some postings Charles had made on social media, explaining the work he was doing at Cherrywood Hall and the winery. She managed to meet up with him and use her feminine wiles and payments to sway him. Don't feel too sorry for Mr. Linford or Miss Jones. They committed criminal acts in return for financial gain. People were killed because of their actions and assistance."

"So Charles was driven out of hiding by the horses, and Sarah and Francis were caught because of the tunnel wall collapse. We had two sets of maniacs trying to kill everyone. Thank goodness Kyle had installed all the security systems, so we could find out where these maniacs were. We are all incredibly lucky," Evan said. Simone hugged his waist.

"Or we were protected by the Cherrywood Hall ghosts," I said and laughed, thinking of Pippa. I was beginning to believe this. Kyle rolled his eyes at me and smiled. I think he was beginning to believe it too.

"I have to admit that this set of murders is one for the history books: two sets of killers, unbeknownst to each other, killing off each of their competitors. Throw in the production company, the *Castlewood Manor* series, the royals, four sets of aristocrats, perhaps with their ghosts—I have to say again, this is one for the history books. We'll be using this case as a training tool for years." Chief Inspector Marquot smiled. "In the end, though, it boiled down to greed, hatred, and revenge, some of the oldest motives in history that lead to murder."

"I still don't see how Jane is going to continue with the competition, even if Sir James's vote is in her court," I said, looking at Evan. "Her father just killed himself after murdering two people and trying for a third. Her estate is broke with no assets." Evan scrunched his shoulders and lifted his hands as if questioning her viability as well.

"Lady Jane Paunchley is a rather insensitive woman. I don't think she will be mourning the loss of her father for long," Chief Inspector Marquot said. "She is also an incredibly lucky woman. You see, apparently Lord Hampton wasn't a complete cad. It turns out he had loved Jane's mother when they'd had their affair and was quite upset when she committed suicide. He suspected Jane might be his daughter. He rewrote the entailment for his title and estate. In the event of his death, and the deaths or incapacitation of his heirs, the total estate comprising Shipley House was to go to Jane Paunchley. With Francis's arrest and the likelihood he will be in prison the remainder of his life, he has been deemed incapacitated. Lady Jane gets everything. She no longer has a financial problem, at least for now. As I said earlier, this is one for the history books. I must say, I cannot wait to hear who the winner of the estate competition is on New Year's Eve. I can tell you this. The Marquot household will be rooting for Cherrywood Hall. I have become quite a fan of your Lady Pippa."

20

Treasures Found, and the Crown Goes to...

"Have you heard from your mother and Ma-ma?" I asked. Evan, Simone, Kyle, and I were tucking into a lovely pre-Christmas breakfast Chef Karl had prepared for us in the dining room. Pumpkin spice waffles with heavy cream and walnuts, quiche lorraine tartlets, sausages, and assorted pastries tempted our appetites and senses. It was a late breakfast for us. We'd stayed up late playing charades the night before, imbibing quite a bit of Christmas brandy after Chief Inspector Marquot left us and we'd had a chance to absorb all he told us. We were admittedly shell-shocked with all his revelations. It was hard to believe what greed and revenge could do to people.

"Yes, they rang a half hour ago and should be here anytime. There's considerable snow on the roads, so Bates is taking his time," Evan answered. "Everything is all set for the luncheon party tomorrow and Christmas Eve service. Are you up to strength, Father Christmas? You have a lot of presents to hand out," Evan teased Kyle.

"I'll be ready," Kyle said, smiling. "I'll have my elf here to help." He smiled at me and winked. "I've also got some of my crew to help with the sleigh rides tomorrow. They've been working on grooming some paths this morning to take the guests on. I don't think they were planning on having this much snow, however."

"I love it," I gushed, taking a bite of waffle. "I went out earlier this morning. There's already a foot of snow. If the blizzard they predict comes in tomorrow night, we'll be snowbound for weeks."

"Well, this is certainly a change for me from the weather in South Africa," Simone said. "I love it, though. Evan and I are going to try cross-country skiing this afternoon. Would you like to join us?"

"Sounds great to me," I said, looking over to Kyle.

"I'd like that. In fact, we can pull double duty by cross-country skiing along the groomed path we'll use for the sleigh rides tomorrow. I wanted to check them anyway to make sure they're safe. I do not want any more mishaps at Cherrywood Hall—certainly not until after the winner of the estate competition is announced."

"Amen to that. I don't think I could stand any more surprises—especially the violent kind," Evan said.

We heard the front doors being opened by some fast-moving footmen. Ma-ma and Aunt Margaret had arrived, shivering in the cold and amazed they had made it here safely, given all the snow. We rose from the table and went to the grand hallway to greet them.

"Gemma darling, can you believe this snow? I love it. I had to have snow trucked into the yard last year for my Christmas Eve party in Malibu," she said, going to everyone for air kisses and hugs.

"Well, we don't have that issue this year," Aunt Margaret said, taking off her coat and handing it to Bridges. "We need fires lit, Bridges. It's much too cold in here," she said, looking at the grand hallway fireplace. She turned and stopped when she saw the magnificent Christmas tree that stood at the end of the hallway. "Oh my," she whispered, walking over to the stately tree. "This is wonderful. You have done a truly great job."

Evan walked over to her and gave her a hug.

"Just like old times, isn't it, Mother?" Evan said. "This year is the best Christmas in a long time here at Cherrywood Hall. We have friends and family here to share it with—and incredible holiday weather."

"It is perfect," Aunt Margaret said, dabbing at her eyes. "I'm so glad we could all be together this year. It's wonderful to be with you—all of you."

Ma-ma and Aunt Margaret decided to have tea up in their rooms and get unpacked from their trip. Evan, Kyle, Simone, and I bundled up and walked down to the barn to get our cross-country skis on. Kyle's crew was just returning on the tractors they used to groom the sleigh paths. It was snowing lightly now. Our skis cut into the newly groomed path, and we were soon gliding across the pastures and hills of the estate. It was stunning to see everything covered in icy white. The path prepared was over a mile in length. The children were going to enjoy a great sleigh ride tomorrow.

That evening Bridges had set up a dining table in the grand hallway in front of the stately Christmas tree so that we could have dinner in the glow of its lights. Chef Karl prepared an elegantly trimmed pork crown roast with all the trimmings. Stuffing, poached apples and pears, and pumpkin and mince pies filled out the menu tonight. We laughed and joked through the evening, comparing American and British Christmas traditions.

The next morning, Christmas Eve arrived in pure, white, snowy splendor. It had snowed a few more inches during the night, making this a record for the county. We had an early breakfast that morning and went up to dress for the Christmas luncheon and gift presentation that would occur before lunch with the children. I chose one of my favorite holiday ensembles, a bright red silk maxi-length skirt, black turtleneck, and blue watch plaid scarf thrown over my shoulders. I wore some emerald stud earrings and the emerald bracelet Ma-ma had given me for graduation. I finished my outfit with some black suede ankle boots. This elf was ready to have the party begin!

As I went downstairs to the grand hallway, I heard the voices of choir singers who had been bused in for the luncheon from the village. I listened as their angelic voices rang through the hallway. The Christmas tree, garland, lights, and music had transformed the hallway into a magical setting. The gold gilded chair tufted in red velvet had been set out in front of the tree, surrounded by red poinsettias on either side. I ran my hands over the soft velvet, smiling at the wonderful scene this was. I heard the entrance door open and a loud "Ho, ho, ho!" echoed down the hall.

Kyle, now Father Christmas, came down the hallway in full Christmas splendor, greeting everyone who came to shake his hand. I saw him smile beneath his beard as he came up to me. He bent close and whispered, "Have you been naughty or nice, young lady? Naughty isn't all bad, you know."

"Well, you'll just have to see later, won't you, Santa," I teased back at him.

"That's Father Christmas, young lady. You're in Britain now. You, my dear elf, better be prepared. The children should be arriving very soon."

Aunt Margaret, Ma-ma, Simone, and Evan joined us. We heard a loud knock at the entry door, and soon the children of the estate workers and villagers ran down the hallway to see Father Christmas. Parents and special guests were served glasses of champagne as they watched the children get their presents. I was the dutiful elf for Father Christmas and read each child's name to him as he handed a specific gift to each child. The children ripped into their presents with squeals of joy once all the gifts had been handed out. We headed into the dining room, which had been decorated with shiny red and green ornaments for the holiday. Silver bowls were filled again with fresh white roses and blue orchids in a holiday tribute to Aunt Pippa.

The luncheon was a magnificent feast of beef Wellington, Welsh rarebit, roasted root vegetables, and breads. For dessert, individual plum puddings were served, each shimmering in the firelight as it was served. Eggnog and coffee were served as Father Christmas led the children and their parents into the conservatory, where it glowed with Christmas cheer. The choir's music rang through the house.

"Who's ready for a sleigh ride?" Father Christmas boomed.

"We are, pleasssseeee," the children yelled, running to get their coats and Wellies on. Father Christmas led the crowd of children and adults down to the sleighs to begin the rides. The sleighs were filled with riders, and those of us waiting were treated to hot mulled wine and Christmas cookies in the barn. Heaters were roaring to ward off the cold air. Aunt Margaret loved being with the children, and she was introducing Ma-ma to the estate workers and villagers. Everyone enjoyed the festive afternoon. I even saw Bridges crack a smile once or twice, breaking his formal reserve.

Late afternoon the sleigh rides came to an end. The children were exhausted from the excitement and fun of the day. We said good-bye to everyone and gifted boxes of cookies and treats to be taken home by our guests. We decided to rest the remainder of the afternoon once the last guest had left. Kyle joined me in my suite. We lay down on my bed, holding each other close. We did exchange a proper kiss, but the exhaustion and food and mulled wine soon had us snoring at each other.

At six o'clock, Mrs. Smythe lightly knocked on my door. "Time to get dressed, miss," she said quietly. She waited in the hallway. Kyle got up from my bed and pulled on his shoes.

"It was relaxing to lie next to you," he said, pinching my chin softly. "I still have to give you proper cuddling lessons, you know."

"I've already asked Father Christmas to bring me that. I know he won't let me down," I teased. "You better go change. Your Father Christmas overalls are looking a bit rumpled."

"I've got a change of clothes in one of the guest rooms. Don't worry. I won't embarrass you."

"I'm never embarrassed with you, Kyle. I love our time together," I said, reaching over to him for one last proper kiss. Mrs. Smythe coughed gently as a reminder to us we needed to get ready.

"Go, you. I'll see you downstairs," I said, pushing Kyle away. Mrs. Smythe came in to help me dress. I had picked out a red velvet pantsuit with a sparkling silver turtleneck to wear this evening. It was going to be a cold evening, so I put on some layering garments as well to make sure I stayed warm. I was soon ready and went downstairs to join the others in the dining room.

A cold buffet had been laid out for us to enjoy before we headed over to church. I was the last one down. Evan, Simone, Aunt Margaret, and Ma-ma were standing, having a glass of champagne. Kyle was over at the bar, pouring a glass for me and him. He brought it over, and we made a toast.

"Happy Christmas!" we cheered. We sat our glasses down and loaded our plates with the yummy sandwiches and salads Chef Karl had prepared.

Promptly at eight o'clock, we loaded ourselves into the sleighs, which had been adorned with bells, ribbons, and battery-powered twinkle lights. Evan steered one sleigh with Simone and Aunt Margaret snuggled in fur blankets, and Kyle steered our sleigh with Ma-ma and me snuggled the same. The snow had finally stopped, and it was a clear, cold night. The horses plowed through the light snow on the estate road and whisked us through the two-mile drive on the main road leading to the village. We pulled in front of Saint Mary's Church and exited the sleighs. Aunt Margaret, Ma-ma, Simone, and I headed into the church to our seats while Evan and Kyle blanketed the horses and gave them some water and feed before joining us.

The choir angelically sang the Christmas music through the service. Vicar Hawthorne gave a charming sermon and was beaming from ear to ear at seeing Ma-ma in his audience. We held lighted candles during the service, which served as the only light in the church. It was one of the most magical Christmas Eves I had ever experienced, with the flickering candlelight. Next to the people I loved most, I was in a church that had stood for centuries.

On the way back to Cherrywood, we took turns singing Christmas songs at the top of our lungs, each of us trying to outsing the other sleigh. We laughed and giggled the whole way home. Chef Karl had tucked in some thermoses filled with hot mulled wine for our journey back from church. As we pulled up to the front entrance in the sleighs, groomsmen were waiting to help us unload and take the horses and sleighs back to the barn. We were blinded by glaring lights as we made our way up the stairs to go inside. A black sedan pulled up and stopped. We squinted to see who it was that was joining us. A tall man exited the car and came toward us.

"Surprise, Gemma! Merry Christmas!"

It was Michael West, my former boyfriend from California, now wishing me a Merry Christmas at Cherrywood Hall! Michael, standing in front of Cherrywood, acted like nothing was wrong. It took me five seconds to walk down the stairs and go straight to him.

"Merry Christmas," I said as I swung my hand back and forcefully sucker punched him in his nose. The force and surprise of my punch caused him to slip in the snow and fall. His shocked face soon turned to an angry snarl.

"Why, you—" Michael started to say when a large block of snow from the roof fell directly on him, stopping an ugly tirade that was moments from exiting his mouth.

"I think Dr. Phillips has asked you to leave," Kyle said as he walked down and pulled Michael up to his feet. He was covered in snow and blood from my punch. He started to lunge forward at me, but Kyle moved and stood in between us.

"A word of advice? Don't," Kyle said.

"I second that," Simone added, coming down to stand by me. I think Michael finally understood he was not wanted here.

"You'll be sorry, Gemma. I was the best thing that happened to you."

This time Ma-ma now made a lunge toward him, but he was quicker on his feet this time. He backed up and got in his car. The tires squealed, and the car fishtailed as he tried to get away as fast as he could. Ma-ma picked up some snow and threw a snowball at his car.

"Bastard. I hope he gets a lump of coal tonight from Santa," Ma-ma said, brushing the snow from her hands.

Kyle put his arm around me and Ma-ma and walked us up the stairs into the grand hallway. "Never would have guessed you for a sucker-punch girl." He laughed, breaking the tension. "I'm quite impressed." I kiddingly punched him on his shoulder and then turned to give Simone a kiss on her cheek.

"I knew I was safe as soon as Simone came to my side. Michael should be glad he didn't try anything else."

"She hits my shoulder all the time. I hope Father Christmas has taken note." Evan laughed. "Are you OK, Gemma, really?"

"Evan, I feel better than ever. I was so surprised at seeing him; I just acted out what I've been feeling all this time. I hope Father Christmas gives me a pass." I smiled.

We stood in the hallway and finished taking off our coats. The Michael drama had temporarily made us forget how cold it was standing outside. We went into the sitting room and warmed ourselves by the fire. Bridges had set up a table with a soup tureen filled with lobster bisque and tiny mince pies for us to enjoy. We drank hot mugs of the bisque and enjoyed the savory-sweet flavors of the mince pies. At midnight, the chimes of the Cherrywood Hall clocks struck twelve o'clock in unison. It was midnight, and Christmas had arrived.

We toasted each other with a glass of port. "Happy Christmas!" we cheered.

I crawled into bed early at around three o'clock. The fireplace was blazing, making the room toasty warm. I lay in bed and looked up at Pippa's picture. I had grown to love this aunt so much in the past months. The truth was I had loved everything about coming here to England. I had found myself, found a new man, had wonderful family. Cherrywood Hall had become my home. I was enchanted, just as Pippa had been so many years before me.

"So what happens if we aren't selected for the series?" I whispered, looking at Pippa's portrait. "What will I do?" No answer came, just the drowsiness of sleep. I was going to have to wait until New Year's Eve to find out what the future held.

I was truly a blessed girl. Christmas morning as we opened presents, I was presented with the blue sequined gown and tiara that had once been Pippa's. "I can't believe it," I cried as I marveled at the beautiful dress I thought I had ruined. The dress had been impeccably cleaned and brought back to its former glory, sparkling all over. Aunt Margaret had handed me the second box, which contained the diamond and sapphire tiara.

"All girls need a tiara, Gemma." She smiled sweetly. "And there are not many girls who can literally say a tiara saved their life. I feel certain the Lancaster ladies would want you to have it." I was truly overwhelmed with their generous gifts and knew I would always take care of them.

"I love it, Aunt Margaret," I said as tears welled in my eyes. "It's too much, really."

"We couldn't have done the competition without you, Gemma. You deserve a grand prize for all the lovely work you did for us." Evan smiled.

Kyle and I had decided to exchange our presents privately that night. We had gone into the grotto in the conservatory. Kyle opened a bottle of champagne and poured a glass for each of us. He handed me a beautiful red box with a green satin bow.

"Happy Christmas," he whispered, the reflection from the water and lights bouncing off his face. I opened the box and saw a hammered gold choker with a twisted gold infinity loop artistically placed in the center of the choker. It was a stunning, one-of-a-kind piece. I had never seen anything like it. Kyle helped me put it on. It fit perfectly around my neck.

"It was a piece that my mother created," he said.

I scooted next to him and put my arms around his neck. "Thank you so much," I whispered, kissing his lips.

I gave Kyle his present, which I had wrapped in a blue box with white ribbon, Pippa's favorite colors. The gold etched watch was stunning and looked elegant on Kyle's wrist with its gold links. He loved the Cherrywood engraving on the back of the watch.

"I know how much you love Cherrywood Hall, and I appreciate everything you have done to make sure the estate is pristine. You've saved me time after time too. No matter what happens, I want you to know how much I appreciate what you have done for me, for all time." Then Father Christmas granted me my wish. I had my first proper cuddling lesson that night.

Boxing Day started once more with another grand breakfast in the dining room. "I have a surprise for you," Kyle announced. "The tunnel between the winery and hall is completed. I guarantee you there won't be any cave-ins—unless, of course, Pippa intervenes." He laughed. He turned to Aunt Margaret. "I think you will be very pleased about what has been found."

We plied him with questions all during breakfast, but he would not give us a clue. We couldn't wait to eat and grab our coats. We walked down to the winery to enter the tunnel from the ground floor and follow it back to Cherrywood. Kyle led our group through the stone and packed-mud tunnel. He had lights installed to keep us out of the darkness. It was a bit eerie as we made our way down the long tunnel.

"Where does this lead?" Aunt Margaret asked.

"Almost there, ma'am." Kyle smiled. "You're going into a room you've never seen at Cherrywood Hall."

"You've found a hidden room?" Evan asked. "Where is it, old man?"

We reached the end of the tunnel. Kyle turned to answer our questions. "During the renovation of the closet rooms, I scoped behind the walls to see if I could find any hidden rooms up there. I didn't find a room, but I did find a staircase. I walked down the stairs and found myself in a very secure room. It's located a few feet away from where we have the vault now. I can't believe we didn't find it before. The room is behind this door. Are you ready?"

"Yes," we yelled as Kyle opened the door, and we went in.

Our mouths opened in amazement. The surrounding walls were literally lined in silver and gold—bars, that is. I could not believe my eyes.

"Kyle, this is amazing," Evan said. "There must be hundreds of bars of silver and gold worth millions."

"Several million I would guess, old man. I haven't counted all the bars yet. I wanted to have you see them, as they've been standing here for almost seventy years. Lady Margaret, I wanted to show you this." He led us over to some trunks on the floor.

He opened them, and we saw more beautiful gowns and jewelry, carefully packed away.

"The old Lancaster garments—you've found them," Aunt Margaret exclaimed.

"I found this as well," he said, handing me a leather folder with a handwritten letter inside. "It was written by Pippa."

I opened the diary and read the passage, recognizing Pippa's handwriting.

> Hello to the future heir who is reading this. I'm sorry for the mystery, but I decided one day to have this secret room built. My friend Queen Regent Eugenie suggested and encouraged it. We're in the depression, you see, and times are very unsettled. Another war is approaching as well, I'm afraid. There's even been talk of Cherrywood Hall being bombed. I've hidden quite a bit of our fortune in these rooms for safekeeping. I could not resist putting away some of the earlier Lancaster ladies' gowns in this secure room. They are hundreds of years old and quite delicate. I'd like to know they will survive should anything dire occur. I don't know when this room will be found, but when it is, I hope it brings joy for all who see its contents. It's never in poor taste to put something away for a rainy day. Enjoy, my dear family. Your loving Pippa.

We all had tears in our eyes and could not believe the fortune that had been found. We spent the rest of the day going through the trunks of dresses and jewels. Evan and Kyle started counting the bars of silver and gold. It was an amazing Boxing Day.

On New Year's Eve, Evan had planned a large gala that included many of the villagers and county supporters who had worked on the events for the estate competition. Everyone was to arrive at eight o'clock. The announcement for the selected estate was set to be broadcast on British Network at eleven thirty. The grand hallway was bustling with production technicians, who were bringing in large-screen televisions and cameras for the live-feed event broadcast. The Christmas tree and garlands had been left up, giving the hallway a glamorous, festive look.

The dining room was configured for a buffet dinner, with small round tables set round the room. Chef Karl was presenting surf-and-turf hors d'oeuvres and entrees for our feast tonight, with stations for each positioned around the room. Guests would be able to eat when they wanted to keep a relaxed atmosphere.

Tonight I was wearing a black taffeta maxi skirt with a black turtleneck. The gold infinity necklace Kyle had given me for Christmas looked stunning against the black background. Mama had given me a hammered-gold cuff bracelet with a gothic skull ornament, which I wore. It was a perfect finishing touch to my edgy, elegant ensemble, from people whom I cherished the most.

Television, Internet, and press crews were setting up downstairs to cover the event live. This was also being done at Longthorpe Manor with Jane. The winning estate would be broadcast live. Neither one of us knew if ours was to be the estate featured live or not. Dame Agnes had come to Cherrywood Hall, as her vote was cast for us. Sir James was at Longthorpe Manor with Jane.

At eight o'clock, Evan, Kyle, and I stood at the front entrance to greet and thank our guests as they came in. Everyone was dressed beautifully for the evening and the ringing in of the New Year. A quartet band played in the hallway as cocktails and champagne were served. Ma-ma, Aunt Margaret, and Simone mingled with the guests. Several of the actors from the *Castlewood Manor* series were here at Cherrywood Hall, which delighted Mama as she showed them around the ground-floor rooms.

Electricity was in the air as it rolled round to eleven thirty. We stood in hushed silence as the televisions were tuned to the British Network broadcast. The broadcast and journalist crews were ready to pounce, no matter what the news.

Evan, Kyle, and I held hands as Lucy Etheridge walked onto a small stage that was set up in front of the Christmas tree. Byron Brown was at Longthorpe Manor with Jane. Both of the estates were congratulated on the hard work that had been put into the competition.

We held our breath as they announced, "Three, two, one... the winner is...Cherrywood Hall!" We screamed in excitement and hugged one another in pure joy and amazement. Our guests gathered round and joined our glorious glee. The cameras rolled as we celebrated the win.

"Can you believe it?" I said as I hugged Evan and Kyle. Evan lifted me and twirled me around.

"I am beyond words. What a magnificent win," Evan said, putting me down and giving Simone a hug.

Kyle drew me close and kissed my lips. "Well done, Gemma."

Ma-ma came up to us and hugged our waists. "You see, Gemma, I knew this was where you were supposed to be. Well done, daughter. I couldn't be prouder," she said, tears welling in her eyes. "I love you."

"I love you too, Ma-ma. Thank you for always being there for me."

"Everyone, hurry; come out to the terrace. We have one last surprise," Lucy announced from the stage. As the clock struck midnight, fireworks lit up the sky, welcoming the New Year and the selection of Cherrywood Hall for the series. The sounds were deafening, but no one seemed to care as we partied on the terrace.

Kyle gave me another proper kiss. "I have to ask. You are staying, aren't you, Gemma? I couldn't bear it if you left us now."

"I'm staying, Kyle. I wouldn't miss this for the world. I'm so happy we won. I have my place for now." I kissed Kyle once more.

I was staying on at Cherrywood Hall to help with the series and work with Kyle and Evan on the new business ventures that had been planned. I felt a peace and contentment as well as a new purpose for my life. And just for a second, as the party roared on, I heard a voice whispering in my ear, "Welcome to Cherrywood Hall, Gemma."

I smiled, for I knew that Pippa was by my side—my American almost-royal cousin.

About the Author

Veronica Cline Barton earned graduate degrees in both engineering and business and has had successful careers in the software and technology industries. Her lifelong love affair with British murder mysteries inspired her to embark on a literary career. *The Crown for Castlewood Manor* is the first in what she calls her My American Almost Royal Cousin Series. When not traveling and spinning mystery yarns, she lives in California with her husband, Bruce, and her two cats, Daisy and Ebbie.

Printed in Great
Britain
by Amazon